PRAISE FOR RADIO UNDERGROUN

"Radio Underground tells a thrilling story of family and loyalty in the face of oppression. Its richly evoked historical setting took me back to the Cold War era, while its warm-blooded characters stole my heart. A propulsive read and a timely reminder that maintaining our humanity requires courage as much as love."

Kim van Alkemade, *New York Times* best-selling author
of *Orphan #8* and *Bachelor Girl*

"When I discovered Alison Littman's Radio Underground I was stunned by its ambition and scope. What an undertaking! But could Littman pull off setting such a tumultuous scene vividly and accurately, plus share an emotional family drama? The answer is a resounding yes! Littman's debut novel is a delectable blend of history and heartstrings, sure to please the palates of literature lovers everywhere."

Selene Castrovilla, award-winning
author of *Melt* and *Luna Rising*

"Set during the Hungarian Revolution of 1956 and its heartbreaking aftermath, this vivid and compelling novel is a story of courage, family and the importance of 'breaking the silence.'"

m Class

"Alison Littman writes with unusual clarity...The author thrusts readers right into the inner worlds of the characters — tense, tumultuous, and reeling with varying emotions... Radio Underground reads like a movie; it is a story with powerful historical references, a strong plot, and characters that force readers to follow them. A revolutionary tale written with style."

Readers' Favorite

ALISON LITTMAN

Radio
Underground

Last Syllable Books

Last Syllable Books Edition, November 2018

ISBN 978-0-9964306-2-3

Book design by Damonza
www.lastsyllablebooks.com

Printed in the United States

For my grandma

ESZTER TURJÁN
Budapest, Hungary—October 23, 1956—Midnight

THE CUTS IN my hand opened wide. The blood dispersed in thin, chaotic lines across my palm. I held my breath as the pain peaked and relented in nauseating pulses. Plucking all the tiny flecks of glass from my hand would take hours, and I didn't have hours. Burying the broken wine glass in the trash, I tried to hide the evidence of my recklessness. I ran my hand beneath the faucet, hoping that would dislodge the stubborn shards.

I leaned closer to the radio as Radio Free Europe began its midnight broadcast. It always came on at the right time, when I could barely endure living without myself anymore. I had been who the government, who my family, wanted me to be all day. Now, I could finally reconvene with my real self.

According to reports, thousands of students had compiled a list of demands, mandating Soviet troops leave the country and that we elect a new leader in free elections. The reporter, a Hungarian émigré, commended the students for their courage. But I knew better. These kids, too young to know failure, didn't understand their passion was no match for a government trained in killing hope. And those harboring it. The part of me that knew what I had to do to protect these students felt numb and ready to click into autopilot. The other part of me—the part that clung to the same hope they did—was just as terrified as they probably were in the brief moments they caught their mothers looking at them with concern. They too would break, like the wine glass hidden in my kitchen garbage.

This Radio Free Europe broadcast missed too many key points. The information I spent my day secretly gathering would not appear on its airwaves for hours, at best. Would it be too late? Regardless, I would do my job. And it was time.

I could hear my husband and teenage daughter snoring in their rooms, reassuring me of the isolation I sought, and needed. I wrapped my hand in gauze and tiptoed toward the door. Yielding in tiny whines, the floorboards lamented their years of abuse, of children's toys crashing, of parents stomping off livid. With every step, I verified my family continued on in their perfect oblivion. Step. Snore. Step. Snore. Until, with shaky hands, I found the doorknob. A turn, and I slid into the night.

My hand throbbed, reminding me to be careful, even though I needed to hurry. I only had twenty minutes to reach Antal. I was bringing him information that would change this restless city entirely. We had been quiet for far too long. We taught ourselves how to make plans in whispers. We knew how to hide in routine. We turned down Radio Free

Europe or the BBC so our neighbors couldn't hear us listening to the banned Western broadcasts and report us to the secret police. The information I carried with me would break the silence—if I could just reach Antal in time.

Passing the music academy and a row of darkened offices, I crept onto Lenin Avenue and began making my way north. A bitter breeze blew past me, as if exhaled by the dank, rat-filled alleys in my wake. Flickering lamps hung on wires suspended over the streets. I stuck close to the buildings, where the light could hardly reach, and prayed no one could see me.

A black Zis-110 idled ahead of me, the car's curtains drawn on its passenger windows. I shivered at the sight of the secret police's hallmark car, thinking of all the friends who had disappeared for no reason, taken away by henchmen in the middle of the night, never to return. It was no coincidence the Zis looked just like a hearse. I scurried onto a side street, dodging the car and the poor captives I assumed sat, trembling, inside of it.

I tiptoed past the Ministry of Interior, where red geraniums lined the building's windows. In the secret prisons below, police tortured people with whips, limb crushers, nail presses, and scalding and freezing baths. Or else they just executed them. But the geraniums were always fresh.

I slid my fingers across the building's dusty exteriors, imagining I could somehow transfer my nerves onto the cold, unfeeling brick. I had snuck through the streets after curfew for years, but tonight was different. I could feel the regime sensing our newfound courage, like a dog pushing its nose high into the air, catching the subtle perfume of a rabbit nearby.

After walking several blocks, I spied smoke unfurling in the path before me, like a languid snake expanding as it digests a fresh kill. Following it, I found Antal, his eyes closed, relishing in a cigarette.

"Antal, it's me," I said, coughing on the smoke now choking me.

Antal smiled and opened his eyes, his cataracts reflecting the glow of the street lamps. "Eszter, it's good to see you."

"It's good to see you too." I kissed Antal on both cheeks, feeling his dry skin against mine and wondering how long he'd been outside waiting for me in the cold.

"Tell me, what information do you have for me today?"

"It will happen tomorrow," I said. "Today, technically."

It was already past midnight.

"So it's here, isn't it?" Antal said.

"Yes," I said. "I went to their meeting. The students decided they're going to march. I heard them talking about gathering arms."

"How many people are participating in this … this march?" Antal asked as he stamped his cigarette into the ground and lit another one.

"Hundreds, thousands, maybe. I can't be certain."

"It doesn't take a genius to predict how Gerő will react."

"Gerő will slaughter them," I said, feeling dizzy as I said aloud what we both knew. Hungary's leader, Erno Gerő, was a Soviet puppet with an arsenal at the ready. "Without enough people hearing about it and organizing, it will just be a bloodbath."

Antal fell back against the brick wall, suddenly losing his breath. He was always so levelheaded, so much so it often drove me to even greater heights of anxiety as I tried to compensate for his indifference. His fingers, still clutching the cigarette, quivered as his eyes searched the space behind me.

"The state radio will probably ignore this and just keep spewing out its propaganda," he said.

"Exactly. We're going to print with this too. But *Realitás* won't reach enough people in time. An announcement on Radio Free Europe is the students' only hope." I held on to Antal's shoulders to steady him. "It has to happen first thing in the morning, so people will have time to plan."

The closest Radio Free Europe outpost was in Vienna. If Antal left now, he would get there by four in the morning.

"I already have meetings scheduled in Vienna for today," he said. "I'll visit our Radio Free Europe contacts as soon as I get there and cancel my other meetings to get back in time for the march. Gerő will think I cut short a routine visit to be by his side."

Our lives by day were lies—Antal's more than most. He served as the regime's Deputy Interior Minister. After being forced to coordinate the executions of his friends—communists who threatened the power structure when they became too popular—he resolved to undermine the regime in any way possible. He began relaying intelligence to the American-run Radio Free Europe. With the freedom to travel at will and deep knowledge of the government's inner workings, he also became an asset to *Realitás*, the underground newspaper I ran.

"It's already one in the morning," I said. "What will you do when they ask you why you're crossing the border so late?"

"This is normal for me. I go to Vienna at all times of the day and night, just to keep them guessing. Just in case I run into a situation like this."

"Smart. Well, you better leave now before Gerő tries to get in touch."

We both knew Antal's phone could have been ringing right then. I wondered what it would cost him—or his children and grandchildren—if he wasn't there to answer it.

"I'll be back," Antal said, coughing into his hands, still shaking from what I knew was the fear we all shared.

"Wait." I pulled out a tattered piece of paper, wincing as the cuts in my hand protested the sudden movement. "Take this with you. A student gave it to me yesterday. It's a coded list of meeting points and times for the march. You have to get this on air too."

Antal nodded as I slid the paper into his coat pocket, making sure to secure the meticulously crafted plans of the brave, hopeful students. They probably didn't even realize that at this moment, Soviet troops were almost certainly readying their tanks at a base nearby.

DORA TURJÁN
Budapest, Hungary—January 16, 1965

ESZTER.

Her mom's name stared at Dora in dizzying multitudes, splayed across the walls of the alley hundreds of times. It dripped over knots of curse words and lewd sketches. It zigzagged across faded propaganda that told Freedom Fighters they'd better tremble in their sleep. It bore down on Dora with a crushing might as she tried to walk faster, frustrated she took this shortcut in the first place. She reminded herself there was no way these names referred to her mom. Some kid named Eszter—or maybe the girl's boyfriend—had defaced the alley.

Ever since her mom was taken away nine years ago, Dora had trained her mind to think about anything but Eszter. Anytime someone called out her mom's name, Dora plodded on, refusing to look up. At work, when she spotted *Eszter* on a letter, she read all the words around it before filing the paper away. At home, her dad, Ivan, wouldn't dare mention his wife's name.

As she walked through the alley though, the sheer number of *Eszter*s laid siege to Dora's defenses. Lifting her head just a little, she saw a version of her mom's name that looked familiar. It had the same style as how she'd drawn as a kid, the "E" capped with big dots, the "z" larger than its neighboring letters. Dora was always so proud of those drawings. When she brought one home from school, she'd clutch it high over her waist and study the ground, intent on avoiding any puddles. When she presented it to her mom, Eszter would act surprised and say thank you in the voice she typically reserved for babies. Later, Dora would find the drawing in her mom's bathroom, spotted with eyeshadow and powder, its edges curling up from the water Eszter had just used to wash her face.

Dora stepped closer to the graffiti. She slipped off her gloves one finger at a time, reluctant to expose her skin to the biting cold but unable to stop the predetermined trajectory of her hand. She traced the gritty edges of her mom's name, her fingers lingering on the "z" as she savored its dramatic angles.

Dora knew she shouldn't indulge in memories of Eszter. She shouldn't think about that one time Ivan was held up at work, and Eszter found a bar of chocolate as big as Dora's head in one of their kitchen cabinets, too awkwardly shaped to hold anything but things meant to be forgotten. After Dora and Eszter ate the whole chocolate bar, they got into their pajamas and jumped on Eszter's bed. Dora remembered feeling so delighted that she asked her mom if they could do it again next weekend. Eszter just got that far-off look in her eyes, the one where she seemed to slip into some alternate reality where she wasn't Dora's mom.

For a long time, Dora remembered her childhood as marked by a persistent melancholy. She realized as an adult, though, it wasn't sadness that characterized her past, but a constant sense of waiting. Dora thought the day would come when Eszter would want to spend time with her. Dora just had to grow up more. She would be patient. Except, sometimes she would go out looking for Eszter, who would leave unannounced for hours on end. Dora pretended she was just playing hide-and-seek, searching in neighborhood parks, abandoned factories, and train stations for Eszter. Dora never once found Eszter, who would usually come back long after Dora had given up and fallen asleep. If Dora convinced herself she had only lost another round of the game, she could get up and live another day to try again.

Dora heard children playing on the far side of the alley, rousing her from her stupor. Her fingers began to ache, a sign they would soon go numb in winter's grip. There was no need to stay there, or ever come back. An alley full of graffiti would never give her the mom she had always wanted. Dora burrowed her chin into her coat and walked to the restaurant.

*

"You made it," Ivan said, wiping his clammy forehead with his napkin. Her dad sweated constantly, a relic of his formerly plump self. He had lost more than eighty pounds since the revolution.

"Sorry, I got caught up in something." Dora smoothed out her hair, its thin brown strands succumbing to the static of her winter cap.

The restaurant, its tablecloths as white as her dad's pale forehead, boasted a clientele of middle-aged bureaucrats who, hunched over their plates in near-silence, seemed resigned to the bland sauces and overcooked chicken before them.

"Are you okay?" Ivan scanned Dora's face.

"What do you mean?"

"I can tell you look … shook up."

"Oh, it's just the cold. The walk was longer than I expected." Dora tried not to give herself away. Sometimes her expressions lagged far behind, loitering in the past. She was frustrated she paid any attention to Eszter this afternoon, a small relapse that would linger for days, maybe weeks.

"Look, I know it's easy to get … well, distracted, by things." Ivan alluded to what they would never discuss. "Just remember that you're doing great."

"Thank you." Dora shifted the conversation to something they could easily talk about. "Work is going well."

"How many letters did you get through today?"

"One hundred already."

At twenty-six, Dora had a secure job with the government, monitoring and censoring people's mail.

"That's enormous." Ivan smiled, a rare occurrence.

"What about you? Any new policies I need to know about?"

Ivan leaned across the table toward his daughter. "Actually, that's why I asked you here today. I have some exciting news for you."

Dora raised her eyebrows, inviting him to continue, as the waiter delivered two plates of *paprikás csirke*—apparently Ivan had ordered for her, like she was a little girl. She wished he would stop that.

"Your department is about to get a very important assignment," Ivan began, but paused to watch Dora.

She examined her chicken, now settled under shiny pockets of fat. Ever since the revolution, eating felt like a chore. Dora found herself fighting nausea before she took her first bite of food, though she managed to finish most of her meals. Ivan had developed the habit of staring at her in the moments when she was mustering the strength to eat.

Ivan waited until Dora lifted the first piece of chicken to her mouth. "This assignment requires us to make some changes. And they have to do with you."

Dora's stomach lurched. She hated change and how it toyed with her, like a cat pawing at a perfectly wound ball of yarn. It always seemed like a fun game at first, until, string by string, she became unraveled.

But before Ivan could continue, a barrage of radio static interrupted him. It pierced through the restaurant, surrounding them in a strident din. The shrill static churned Dora's thoughts, thwarting their usual, linear pattern.

She turned around to the window behind her. Outside, on top of the windowsill, sat three radios. A group of boys, probably university students, huddled over them. They prodded at the knobs, oblivious to the people sitting behind the glass.

"Someone has to tell them to move. This is awful." Dora began massaging her temples.

Ivan leaned back in his chair and bent his arms behind his back.

"I actually like it."

"What? You do?"

"Yes. It's sending a good message."

"Oh, that's right. Of course."

Dora remembered herself, and who sat across from her. Obviously, Ivan preferred the static. This was better than the alternative.

"Kids should know that they can't just listen to rock 'n' roll whenever they want," Ivan said. "It's just capitalist propaganda."

"Well, at least you stopped them this time," Dora said.

As part of Ivan's work at the Ministry of Cultural Affairs, he orchestrated a massive operation that blocked Radio Free Europe's broadcasts and replaced them with a jarring racket.

"This isn't my doing," Ivan said.

"What do you mean? You didn't jam the radio today?" Dora asked.

"Nope. We've shifted our priorities elsewhere, at least temporarily. I'll tell you about it when this ends." Ivan nodded toward the window. "Anyway, it doesn't even look like we need to jam. Look at them; they can't find the station."

Dora smiled meekly at him. She could feel a migraine coming on. She pressed her fingers into her ears. Closing her eyes, she thought about something that would make her happy.

The image of Boldiszar inched into her mind, as it often did. She thought about his black hair and how his curls overtook his dark eyes. She remembered the smile that pulled his entire face into it, like the eye of a hurricane. She remembered how, every birthday, she wished she could be old enough to date Boldiszar instead of being his first and longest babysitting job. When Dora's thoughts inevitably collided with the terrible thing that happened to Boldiszar, she opened her eyes and ears, preferring the static over her wandering memories. But, it soon gave way to something much smoother. For a split second the noise tickled Dora, producing a lightness at the bottom of her stomach.

Surrounding them were the undeniable notes of The Beatles' "She Loves You." The boys belted, "She loves you, yeah, yeah, yeah …" as they teetered back and forth like penguins, trying to dance in their stiff winter coats.

After only a minute, the song faded, and a honeyed voice took over.

"Our countdown continues on Radio Free Europe. We're playing the top hits of 1964 for you today." It was Laszlo Cseke, or Uncle Lanci, the Hungarian disc jokey who fled to Munich and became a Radio Free Europe icon.

"We've finally reached the top, so without further ado," Uncle Lanci continued, "here's the number one song of 1964, 'I Want to Hold Your Hand.'"

Forgetting herself, Dora wiped away the condensation accumulating on the window so she could see the boys better. Turning up the radio and shedding their coats, the boys belted out The Beatles lyrics, even trying to hold the hands of passersby, who shuffled to the other side of the sidewalk as if avoiding a massive sinkhole.

Ivan sat there frowning and puckering his lips as if a lemon slice was wedged between his teeth. He summoned their server with a flick of his hand. "Excuse me, what is your name?"

"Lajos."

"Lajos what?"

They all knew why Ivan was asking. Ivan would hold this Lajos accountable for whatever he was about to ask him to do.

"Adler."

"Do you like this music?"

"No, not in the slightest." Lajos vigorously shook his head.

"Good, because Radio Free Europe is just trying to brainwash you. They think if you like The Beatles, you'll like capitalism."

"I understand, sir."

"Good. Then can you please tell those men to go elsewhere, Lajos Adler?"

"Yes, right away, sir."

As he confronted the boys outside, Lajos pointed inside at Dora and Ivan. In unison, they craned their necks toward the window. They zeroed in on Dora, their eyes scaling her high cheekbones before descending to her lips, where they lingered far too long. She looked down, finally getting the motivation she needed to focus on eating her chicken.

Dora heard a muted version of Ivan's name percolate

through the glass. They had recognized him. Soon the words "I want to ..." met their end. By the time she looked up again, they had disappeared.

"It's actually good we just witnessed that," Ivan said.

"Oh, really? How come?"

"Uncle Lanci, Radio Free Europe, The Beatles ... they are all connected to these changes I was talking about." Ivan smiled and lifted his coffee mug, the veins in his arms jutting out, abandoned long ago by their fatty cushions. "You see, we're picking up some intelligence .... We've heard that some counterrevolutionaries are making plans."

Following protocol, Ivan referred to the Freedom Fighters who battled against the regime in the 1956 revolution not as revolutionaries, but as counterrevolutionaries.

"What kind of plans?" Dora asked.

"It looks like some of them are talking about leaving Hungary ... illegally."

"But I thought people could go abroad now?"

"Some people can, but others can't. Especially counterrevolutionaries. We've installed extra security at the border, but we need to catch them before they get there."

Now Dora understood where this conversation was going.

"That's where you come in, Dora. I thought you could be extra vigilant with the Uncle Lanci letters."

Dora censored mail for a living, focusing specifically on letters written to Uncle Lanci. Using code names, his fans wrote to him to request their favorite rock 'n' roll songs and to relay messages over the air. But these requests weren't as benign as they seemed. In their letters, young people attacked communism, recounted abuse by the state police, and now, apparently, discussed plans to illegally leave the country. The regime hired people like Dora to monitor the letters and black out any subversive content. They didn't just throw out the letters altogether because they had to give people some freedom—and provide them with enough small victories— so they didn't agitate for another deadly uprising.

"Uncle Lanci has a huge influence over these young people, especially the counterrevolutionaries. We think they'll use Uncle Lanci to escape," Ivan continued.

"And that's why you don't want to jam the radio ...." Dora was figuring it out. If they completely jammed Radio Free Europe, people would stop writing to Uncle Lanci. Any discussion of travel plans would be funneled elsewhere.

"Exactly. Now they'll write to him and ask for help, I'm sure. And we will be there to catch them."

"What will happen to them?"

"That's for the police to decide," Ivan said. "They might be put in jail or sent to a work camp."

"I'll pay special attention to the letters." Dora held her breath, hoping that was all her dad wanted. She didn't tell Ivan that one of her favorite letter writers might have been a counterrevolutionary. He used a pseudonym, as so many letter writers did, calling himself Mike a Korvinközből. The name referred to a famous movie theater-turned rebel stronghold in the 1956 revolution. Mike may have fought there, but he never discussed it in his letters. Writing in English, or "the tongue of The Beatles," as he called it, Mike described a love life that far surpassed anything Dora ever experienced. His broken English made him seem sincere and innocent, despite his womanizing tendencies. Mike reminded Dora of Boldiszar, in a way. They both had an easy sweetness about them, one that didn't demand reciprocity and instead existed solely as an inherent, inescapable part of their personalities.

"There is something else," Ivan started in that self-important tone, the one Dora knew her dad expected her to mirror. "We want you to work exclusively on these letters, as Joszef's second in command."

"Joszef?"

"Yes. This is a huge opportunity for you."

Dora resisted the urge to immediately decline the opportunity. Though she would finally get the recognition she deserved, the thought of sending Mike, or others, to jail tainted the moment. She believed in the party, and its goals, but she didn't want to actually go after her letter writers.

"That's such a big role, and I would want to do it right. But, I already have so much to do. What about Tamás?"

"We thought about that, but it wouldn't work."

"Why not?"

"There are some English letters in this collection. And no one knows the language like you."

Ivan was right. Dora was the resident expert on English. She had studied the language in her free time in hopes of getting a promotion. She never thought she'd be terrified of it when the time finally came.

"Here, you can take a peek at what you'd be dealing with." Ivan slid over a tan envelope, heavy with papers inside.

"Thank you. I'm looking forward to it." Dora's shoulders fell, though she tried to give Ivan a thin smile, hoping he would interpret her apprehension as nerves more than anything else.

"I know you'll give it your serious consideration, *angyalkám*."

Dora cringed when she heard the endearing namesake, *my angel*. Ivan used to call her that, and other love names, when she was little. He had stopped when she'd sprouted breasts and grew as tall as her mom. But, when Eszter was taken away after the revolution, Ivan began using the pet names again. They were like porcelain dolls yanked out of a dusty attic. Though brought back into the light, they seemed forever relegated to the dingy, lonely space from which they came.

"I better get back to work." Ivan kissed Dora on the forehead. "Good luck with these. We're counting on you."

Before Dora could say goodbye, Ivan hurried out of the restaurant.

She hadn't seen her dad that eager in awhile. He usually exuded a stern confidence, supported by the conviction that people would do as he said. The last time she saw Ivan that persistent was a year before the revolution, when he was pleading with Eszter to stay loyal to the party.

*

Dora had come home early from school that day, expecting to be alone, when she noticed the walls faintly emitting her parents' voices, which rose and fell at varying decibels. At age sixteen, Dora could detect a fight in an instant, even if it sounded like a mere whisper. She crept through the hallway, toward the voices. As she approached her parents' bedroom, the voices grew louder. Dora knew if her mom and dad had retreated to their room, this was a bad fight. She pressed her ear against their door, convincing herself she was ready for whatever she might hear.

Her dad said, "You can't do this, Eszter. Writing a secret newspaper? I can't believe it."

Eszter shot back, "I don't care. I have to. I can't be silent anymore. The conditions at the factory are insufferable."

"You don't understand. If they find out, they will arrest you. And me."

"No one is ever going to find out. I'm being careful."

"Careful? It won't take long for them to figure out who wrote this. This isn't being careful. They're killing people for this kind of stuff."

"I'm fighting for something bigger than myself."

"This isn't just about you or your movement anymore," Ivan said. "Apparently, she's not even a consideration for you. If we're gone, Dora could be sent to an orphanage. Or … worse."

"Dora will be fine. You know she always is."

Eszter's tone changed, flattening until it sounded almost casual. It made Dora want to cry. She wanted to hear some concern—or would even settle for anger—in Eszter's voice.

"Dora would not be fine," Ivan barked, with all the anger and fire Eszter lacked. "Stop pretending it would be okay."

"You're the one who's pretending. You're living in a

fantasy world supporting this party. You're going to pay for that one day."

"You've gone too far, Eszter. You're the one who is going to regret it."

Dora knew she should run to her room, but she still held out hope she could detect one, even minuscule, hint of love from her mom.

"Just promise me one thing," Ivan said.

"What?"

"You will stop involving Boldiszar in your schemes. You know he's only twenty-one. He's too young, and he'll get caught up in this lethal crap."

Boldiszar? Did Dora hear that correctly? What was he doing with Eszter? She wanted to stay, but knew her parents' fighting patterns all too well. Once her dad started bargaining, Eszter would see the opening and agree to his terms, though she rarely kept her word. Before Dora got caught eavesdropping, she tiptoed swiftly to her room.

Dora curled up in her bed, clutching her knees to her chest, and cried. Her mom loved herself more than anyone else, and the constant reminders of that sickened Dora. She wanted Eszter to get caught. She deserved it. Someone needed to punish her for the pain she caused them. But Boldiszar didn't deserve to be punished. Dora couldn't afford to lose someone who actually loved her. Couldn't her mom recognize that? Eszter should have never started messing with Boldiszar or even with this dissident stuff in the first place. There were real consequences, yet somehow she didn't see them, or maybe she just didn't care.

Dora wanted to fix it all, but she didn't know how. The best she could do was promise herself one thing: She would never be like *her*, like Eszter. She would care about other people. She would practice caution. She would follow the rules.

*

As Dora got up from the table, she remembered that long-ago promise. The new position Ivan offered her would be one more way for Dora to become anything other than Eszter.

Back at her office, Dora opened the envelope her dad gave her. She sifted through the letters, which clung together as if protesting the unrightful disturbance. Some were hand-written and others were typed. She came upon one, scribbled in a messy collage of sentences. It was Mike's. She dislodged it, took a deep breath, and began to read.

MIKE A KORVINKÖZBŐL
Budapest, Hungary—January 14, 1965

Dear Uncle Lanci,

It was so glorious when you played "Surfin' Bird" for me the night previous. So sweet, I am resigned to even put it into words here. I will try with my groovy English dictionary to convey all the meaning to you. You envision, when I heard "Surfin Bird," it was better than even losing my virginity. Let me explain.

It all commenced yesterday, when I had a great surprise from a beautiful woman entering my shop. This woman, you envision, is the most pristine woman imaginable. When she asked to get her radiator worked on, I said we should work on a bit more than that. Okay, okay, I refrained though. I interpreted she would not have minded so much. Anyway, I played Mr. Nice Man and started to fix her car.

But, something disturbed me as I labored. Her radio was turned down. The height of its volume could reach but a wee whisper. I amended that problem right up front as best I could (they are shit speakers), and guess what came out? Radio Budapest! Just the name makes me grow bumps on my arm. Does it do that to you? I just couldn't stand the government's radio blaring from those minimal speakers, and if her maximal breasts listened to this, it would just make me mad.

I transformed the radio to your station and inquired after her name.

"Hedvig," she said.

My heart mostly desired to vomit. Her name was the same exact one as my mom. Her attractiveness dispersed. I turned up your program loud now. So here I am, fixing her radiator, and what song appears at that very moment? "Surfin' Bird." I berated myself with laughter. I mean, sincerely, it's like you were sending me a sign with those lyrics, "bird, bird, bird, bird is the word." I should be staring at unique regions on the woman before me, instead of being so sullen over her name.

How do you know me so well, Uncle Lanci? Let me just say, with her, bird became one hundred percent the thing present in my forethoughts. It's as if I could fit anything I wanted, but mostly all that I have lived through, under one major umbrella of music. It's like *The Blob*, eating and overcoming all that I love.

Swiftly, it all did not manifest as so serious anymore. I laughed and greeted her with my name too. (Which, of course, I will refrain from writing here!) I know Hedvig desired my attention by the way she eyed my caresses over her radio. She did pardon herself from my presence momentarily—it's hard for women to be around me too long without touching me.

I persevered to fix her car like a truthful repairman, and what do you know, but three hours later it was in tip-top form. But not before I did a little something to it …. I nullified every individual station on her radio settings and switched them all to Radio Free Europe.

When she returned to her car, I turned up the volume to maximum height and "Love Me Do" came out of it. I could tell her innards jived to the music. That's when it struck me that she could be my pristine Hedvig.

She could be my Hedvig in real life, not the one in the past tense life, as is my mom. I could belch her name from the streets. Imagine me fixing myself at Nyugati Station with a guitar and singing "Hedvig," "Hedvig," "Hedvig!"

I thought you would be proud of me. I speculate you are wondering what happened admist Hedvig and I. Perhaps I could inflate you with some pride. Well, I received her numbers and I called her but a short number of hours following.

We convened later that night at a secret concert. My friend Andras has a fake band that plays all the songs from your radio program. If the police find our concerts, they always break them up, so I had to practice cautions. I told Hedvig to meet me somewhere special, but didn't tell her what we were doing. When she immersed herself in the venue, I could tell she was pleased.

We commenced our date with talking and drinking when the most miraculous occurrence happened. There we were, Uncle Lanci, suckling our alcohol, when the band commenced playing "Surfin' Bird." The entirety of the audience initiated singing. So we spurted upward and danced, caressing hands. Well, I thought, the forecast looks supreme for the rest of the evening, so I asked her if she would like to return to my home. She said, "Yes." And it's all because of you, Uncle Lanci! If it wasn't for that song, I would be a lone man.

For the rest of the night, we retreated to my apartment. I showed Hedvig a photo of John Lennon I bought on the black market. She couldn't halt herself from staring at it, so I had to intervene. I placed my hand atop of her shoulder and queried if she would like to see my room. She instantly affirmed my congenial offer.

Our kisses initiated slow, like when you truly think this is it, the excellence of this moment could surpass no other. Naturally, other parts of my body had more to say about the situation. I tenderously took off her shirt and was behold by the most tender but stable breasts I have ever faced off with. They were like petite moons settling and rising as I maneuvered them. They went for an arduous ride, and after about three minutes, I concluded I should give them a break.

Hedvig asked me if I cared to explore more, ever so piously. I am a gentleman and heeded her gratuitous request, so I commenced to take off her clothes. Wow, her underwear was the type that deconstructs brains to shards. I knew that Hedvig donned it especially for yours truly—it came directly from Africa, she confessed. It was composed of velvet with the skin of a cheetah. I commenced to rub my cheek against this pleasurable offering, forgetting almost completely I had other work to complete.

By this point, I was raging with pleasure, in all parts of my body, but I harnessed focus on the task at my fingertips. I peeled forth her underwear. Oh, how happy I am I did that. I have never spied anything of this nature in all my twenty-seven years.

Hedvig, it turns around, had the most illustrious design sketched onto her nether region. Instead of the normal fluff, which I must profess, I do sincerely enjoy partaking in, Hedvig's hair forged a peace sign!

I will confess, I feared deconstructing the marvelous design Hedvig adorned. My potential animal nature would make me peruse her in absolute force, and who could guess what could possibly take place, what parts of her beautiful design could falter?

We moved on to the momentary act, for a

plethora of gluttonous moments. (I said momentary, Uncle Lanci, because that's the length of time females last in my presence, if you grasp my meaning. Let me say something to you, though, this is one hundred percent normal.) After I ensured she was cared about, I braced myself against her, until I bowed down to pleasure. After, we dropped into a very serious sleep, gripping each other's torsos with utmost affection.

Tonight, I cannot grace Hedvig with my presence since I will be laboring away at my night job cleansing the Ministry of Interior. That is my second job next to being a car technician. I don't receive much pleasure from this and dream of being a dentist. I applied for college, but they turned me down on account of my middle-class origins. They punish me because my family has too much (even though we don't), so now I am a worker. As you sit cozy in the West, conducting your loose radio programs, it seems so impossible to achieve becoming as glorious as you.

So, I request you elevate me out of that desponded building on Adrássy út, because I'll be there all week, as you like to say. Please don "Surfin' Bird" on your radio. And when you do, say that it is from Mike a Korvinközből to Hedvig.

Sincerely,
Mike a Korvinközből
Desire is fueled by all, but fulfillment. —Ernő Osvát

ESZTER TURJÁN
October 23, 1956—Morning

I barely slept, except for a few hours in the morning. When I woke up, I discovered Ivan and Dora were both still home. They should have been at work and school. I should have been at the factory.

I wandered, half-asleep, toward Ivan's study, the only room in the house he spent time in. He slept there most nights unless he suspected I had snuck out. Then he waited for me in our bed, ready to question me and test my proficiency at lying.

"What's going on?" I leaned against the doorframe to steady my fatigued legs.

"Demonstration." Ivan sat next to the radio. We never moved it out of the kitchen, but now it sat on his desk, in silence. He had it turned off, knowing I would want to hear the news today.

"Is it a big one?"

"Not yet. But, I don't trust it. I think it will get out of hand."

I reached for the radio, but Ivan moved it beyond my reach.

"We're also not listening to this today. Best to just keep a low profile."

I really had no idea what had happened since I'd fallen asleep, though I'm not sure why I expected Ivan to engage me in a conversation about it or let me use the radio. The fact that he was scared meant the students had made some sort of impact on party members. I wouldn't, however, put it past Ivan to stay home just so he could make sure I didn't do anything that would threaten his career ambitions.

Dora sat next to Ivan on a tufted leather chair, pretending to read. When I rolled my eyes at Ivan, Dora caught me in the act and mouthed, "Listen to him."

If she only knew the horror her dad's party inflicted on people like me. I didn't want to punish her for siding with Ivan, nor did I want to tell her the truth: that one day, if things didn't change, her friends and—God forbid—Dora herself would be the ones targeted by her dad's government. It would be their phone calls, remarks, habits, and routines the secret police would be monitoring. It would be them who would be tortured with whips, limb crushers, and nail presses. I wasn't sure Dora would be able to handle it, with Ivan's constant sheltering and brainwashing.

I never thought our family would turn out to be so divided. I always knew Ivan and I were different. I fell in love with him because he was different. He came from the country, smelling like earth and with eyes the color of the Danube. I came from the city, wearing sparkly necklaces and knowing the names of different cheeses. Ivan didn't flood the conversation with words. He allowed me to talk about whatever I wanted, and he never missed one thing I said. He always responded with his own interpretation of my experiences, adding depth and color to my life.

Every time Ivan saw me, he brought me a different colored rose. I didn't even know purple roses existed until Ivan slid one into the empty vase on my parents' table one night, got down on one knee, and proposed to me. The first time we made love, Dora was conceived, and for a few years we enjoyed the illusion of family life.

When World War II happened, Ivan fled the country, to the Soviet Union, with other government officials, and I moved in with my family. When he returned, he wouldn't stop talking about communism. I found it endearing at first, clearly not understanding what it would mean for my family.

My parents had been part of the nobility, reaching their peak at a time when only a small number of families owned a disproportionately greater amount of property compared to everyone else. Under the post-war Communist dictatorship, my parents were deemed *kulaks* and considered "enemies" of "socialist construction." The government decided to liquidate them, sending families like mine to isolated villages or simply executing them altogether. Ivan, who was working for the regime at the time, participated in initiatives surrounding this extreme injustice. Because of my status as Ivan's wife, I was protected, but my parents disappeared one afternoon, before I could even say goodbye.

Ivan tried to explain that he couldn't stop their

deportation, but I wouldn't listen to him. I'm sure he could have done something. It would have cost him his job. But he could have. Others did.

Only a year after they were sent away, I learned both my parents died, alone, in a village I had never even heard of. After that, the only thing I cared about was reversing the damage Ivan's government inflicted upon my family.

As Ivan sat in his chair, his back to me, I reflected on the fact that nearly a decade after my parents' death, I was finally making headway on dismantling this repressive and abusive regime.

I walked over to Dora and slid her book out of her hands. "Come on; let's eat." Maybe if I lured Dora away from the study, Ivan would emerge and I could access our radio he had on lockdown. Dora started scooting herself off the chair, when Ivan handed her a different book and asked her to read him something out of it. Dora readily obeyed.

Giving up, I retreated to the kitchen and pried open the window, expecting to hear some commotion outside in the streets. I heard instead the fading murmur of a car puttering down the road.

"Why do you look more tired than normal, Eszter?" Ivan bore his eyes into my profile as he followed me into the kitchen, trying to hold my attention.

He knows, I thought. *He knows what I've done.*

Then again, he always knew. But why did he insist on testing me? I thought he had found some comfort in pretending that I had renounced my allegiance to the underground. I promised Ivan a year ago that I would, after I realized how desperate he was to move on from the whole matter. He had gotten to the point where he accepted my excuses and lies—they were better than fighting me. I continued writing for *Realitás*. Ivan went on burying himself in his work. And so it went, we spent our days creating worlds bent on undoing one another.

The phone rang, and Ivan's eyes followed my hands as they brought the receiver to my ear.

"Hello," I answered it.

"Eszter, this is Laszlo."

At the sound of his name, I stopped breathing. Laszlo never called me at home.

Gripping the phone so tight that my knuckles turned white, I watched Ivan's eyes snake their way up my arms to where my hands betrayed my anxiety. Ivan looked away and flipped open the newspaper, but I knew he was listening to me. I pretended it was my supervisor at the factory. Laszlo understood, but continued talking.

"Something has happened, Eszter. We need you to come down to the office immediately. It has to do with your meeting with Antal last night."

"Oh, so it just stopped functioning? Without warning?" My voice trembled in rhythm with my legs, so shaky I had to sit.

"I can't say much over the phone, just that your work needs you so come as soon as you can."

"Well, listen. I can't really be of much help over the phone, so let me come down there."

He hung up.

"A machine stalled," I stammered to Ivan, who scrutinized not my eyes, but my breasts and my arms, as if he could pull the truth out of my flesh. "I have to go to the factory right now. That was my boss. I am sorry, no breakfast today."

"Eszter, please, don't go out there."

"Why?" I thought maybe I could glean some information from him about the demonstration, to know what I might face outside.

"You know why," he snarled.

"*Hmm*, I really don't."

Ivan placed his palm on my shoulder, an act of self-righteousness, I assumed, to prove he could remain kind and loving, even when faced with my deviousness.

"Look, as I said earlier, it's not safe out today. There might be a march. No, there will be one, and we don't know how it will turn out."

"Well, all the more reason for me to be at the factory. I'll need to secure the machines."

Grabbing my keys before Ivan could respond, I said, "I'll be back soon, don't worry!"

Dora chimed goodbye without the slightest degree of suspicion, but Ivan remained silent. It didn't matter much to me anyway.

It could have been any morning, I convinced myself, except the streets were practically empty. Budapest still wore its fine necklace of dust and dog poop, but without the people and creatures responsible for the sidewalk's usual adornments, the city just looked dirty and ordinary.

When I finally reached the *Realitás* office—and Laszlo—
he seemed more shook up than I expected. Barreling toward
me, he slammed the door shut so hard the ceiling trembled.

"Sorry," Laszlo whispered. He studied my face. He
touched my eyebrow, tracing his finger along my forehead
until he got to my hair, which he pushed behind my ear. I
leaned into him, hoping he'd let our foreheads meet, at the
very least, but he pulled away immediately.

"Thank you for coming," he said.

"What's going on?" I pretended like we didn't just have
that moment, as I had done so many times before.

He fixed his eyes on the window and then backed slowly
toward his chair, pointing me to the one next to his.

He turned on the radio and pressed his fingers to my
lips. "Listen."

"We are announcing that a demonstration will happen
today," a reporter began. "Students are gathering across
the city to join a powerful march. We estimate thousands
will participate. Please, join the thousands and stand up to
Soviet repression. Send the Russians home!"

The reporter began reading the list of meeting points,
just as I had laid them out in my note to Antal.

A web of chills spread across my back. We did it. Radio
Free Europe reached almost every household in Budapest.
And if people weren't listening to that, they would be lis-
tening to the BBC, which surely would repeat Radio Free
Europe's message.

"Thank God, Antal made it." At the mention of Antal's

name, Laszlo leaned back in his chair and delivered a swift snort.

"So I assumed correctly, then. They got this information from you? Last night?" Laszlo's thick eyebrows converged on his forehead in a frown.

Laszlo had no qualms about expressing his disdain for working with Antal. He thought that by lending Radio Free Europe information, we were part of America's political agenda to persuade Hungary to become just like the West. Laszlo didn't want to be wrapped up in someone else's ploy.

The radio repeated the message.

"Yes, I visited Antal." I checked on our printer as I tried to hide the redness creeping into my cheeks. "I was worried, and of course I wanted us to print this in our paper too, but …."

"But what?" Laszlo demanded, his voice teetering, ready to fall sharply toward anger.

"I knew we couldn't afford to print every day and that the paper wouldn't go out for another week. I thought that the people should know what's happening."

"Why do you make these decisions without me? We made this thing together."

"Why do you not trust me?"

Laszlo did not answer. He waited a full minute. Then he made his case that we weren't just a newspaper, we were leaders, and had we verified that thousands were really participating in the demonstration? Was our estimate actually correct? If it wasn't, we would be responsible for instilling false hope in these kids, encouraging them to face off with a nasty and heartless regime.

Of course, Laszlo made a valid point. I hadn't verified my information with multiple sources by any means. But I saw those students talking last night, their determination fueled by an optimism far stronger than one Laszlo and I would ever feel at our age. If I hadn't given Antal that intelligence, they would have gone through with it anyway. At least this way, maybe they would find some safety in numbers.

That's when Antal burst into our office, wearing a scarf, gloves, glasses, and a heavy coat. He peeled off his disguise, his skin glowing beneath a veneer of sweat. I hugged him as Laszlo looked away.

"It's not good," Antal said. "Gerő's going to take action. He's planning an offensive."

"But they're letting the demonstration take place," I said. At this point, even the government's radio station had announced the march.

"Exactly," Antal sighed. "So they can get all the rebels in the same place, and …." None of us wanted Antal to finish that sentence.

"As if you didn't expect rhat." Laszlo slammed his hand on the desk.

Antal ignored him. He explained that when he got back to Budapest, he went directly to Gerő's office, knowing he had already probably missed multiple calls from him. When he arrived, Gerő handed him a whiskey, straight, and asked Antal to sit down. Antal tried convincing Gerő to let the students march rather than fighting them. That would only escalate the protest and embarrass the regime, perhaps on the world stage. "We can't," Gerő had said—intelligence indicated the students were far more powerful than they let on. They had connections to Imre Nagy, the ousted former prime minister and the only one who stood a chance at opposing Gerő.

Nagy had spent the last few months tiptoeing away from the political arena, terrified of anyone noticing his withdrawal. We all wanted him to put his heels down, turn around, and march back into the spotlight. Of course, it all made sense now, why wouldn't he do that? The students started mobilizing because someone had tipped off their leadership that Imre Nagy wanted to return. Plus, if Imre Nagy was behind this, then there would certainly be force behind him. I congratulated myself for spreading news of a demonstration that, yes, actually did have a chance.

"Do we really want Nagy to be in power? Is he going to be any better than Gerő?" Laszlo faced me and Antal.

"He fell out of favor with the Soviets, which means he could want something different," Antal said.

"But he is an old guard communist," Laszlo snarled. "Even if we are victorious, what kind of government would he put in place? And how do we know he wouldn't run right back to the Soviets?"

"It's not about that," I interrupted. "This is the intelligence we have, so we should report it."

"Eszter," Laszlo started, "How many times do I have to tell you we aren't real journalists? We have a bias, an agenda, to bring down this regime. You already decided our fate should lie in this student march. Now we have to decide if Nagy is the right person to lead this movement before we print anything."

"He already stood up to them once. He can do it again." Antal stood between us.

"But he lost," Laszlo said. "They ran him out of office."

"We are stronger now." Antal got closer to Laszlo and looked him straight in the eyes.

Antal certainly didn't look stronger. I placed a hand on each of their shoulders, hoping it would calm them down to feel my steady, unflinching hands. "Nagy is our only chance," I said. "And, maybe, even someone else will rise up through the ranks. There are only opportunities if we can unite people behind him, at least at first."

"Yes, Eszter is right," Antal bit his nails, something I had never seen him do before. He must have been excited. "And we can't waste any time."

I looked out the window and saw students walking together as the demonstration mounted. I imagined families bent over their radios, parents growing nervous, teenagers fidgeting in their fear, then excitement, then fear. And us? Like ventriloquists, we carefully threaded our hands through the strings that would lift the disparate parts of this move-ment into action. We felt invisible and invincible.

Antal began scribbling on a piece of paper, taking notes as he talked us through his plan. We would contact Radio Free Europe and tell them Nagy was ready to lead the student movement. We would also say Nagy was at home, waiting for the students to gather so he could appear and make his first speech as their leader.

"Radio Free Europe got us into this mess." Laszlo scooped up Antal's notes. "But *Realitás* will be the one that gets us out of it. If this is the demonstration's only hope, then we will be the ones to deliver the news. It's up to us now."

Antal lowered his face into his chapped hands and sighed. "I am too tired to fight you on this one," he said. "But just know that you better get this to everyone."

"We know," Laszlo said.

A brown, emaciated cat wound its way through our office, having hidden in the shadows since Antal came in. It rubbed its back against Antal's legs, meowing until Antal picked it up. As he pet the crook of its neck, Antal closed his eyes and his breathing slowed to the pace of the sleepy cat.

"Why don't you take a nap?" I made a move to grab the cat, but Antal held on tight to it.

"I should."

"You can sleep over there." I pointed to the orange couch, where newspapers and crushed cans sunk into weathered cushions. "With the cat."

"Here is fine." Antal lowered himself to the carpet and, balancing the cat on his chest, lay down. I would have insisted he move, but before I could even get up to clear off the couch, he had fallen asleep.

Once Antal began snoring, Laszlo searched Antal's pockets and beneath the layers of his sweaters and coats.

"I don't trust him."

"Don't wake him up."

"He'll be lucky if he wakes up."

"What, for God's sake, did he ever do to you, Laszlo?"

"He reeks of the party."

"Obviously, he is a spy. That's what they do."

"A spy whose children and grandchildren live in the party villas."

"So? It would look suspicious if he moved them out."

"He could find a reason." Laszlo finished searching Antal, finding nothing more than a few cigarettes and some tissue.

"Can we just focus on what we're going to do now?"

Laszlo moved closer to me and took my hand. He pressed his lips to my ears. "Are you ready for this?"

"Yes." I felt my body bend toward Laszlo, craving what he kept withholding. We had been together before, but it had been years. I fantasized about him constantly. I equated his gruffness with an irresistible masculinity, and it triggered in me a longing both carnal and mindless.

He grabbed my arm and led me into the closet. In the darkness, I couldn't see a thing. We were so close I could smell his scent, a combination of fresh coffee and rain. His warm breath crept along my cheeks.

"Then," Laszlo whispered into my ear, "Nagy it is."

Our lips slowly made their way toward each other. He kissed me, the warmth of his mouth barely detectible through his chapped and hardened lips. He pressed his body into mine and I capitulated, leading us to the floor.

"Please," I whispered to him. "Let it happen this time."

Laszlo ran his tongue across mine, delicately unlocking my trepidation. He tugged at the bottom of my lip with his teeth and pressed himself into me. He dove into my breasts, kissing and massaging them with the aggression of someone who hadn't loved in far too long. As he peeled back my pants, I could feel, against my thigh, Laszlo growing harder and harder.

Wishing he could erase, in this single moment, every time Ivan ever touched me, I raised my hips, beckoning him in. We collided, the years of holding back released from his body into mine, and mine into his. At that moment, writing and sex combined in one aphrodisiacal wonder. Writing had elevated us—we were responsible for shaping the world around us. Sex leveled us—we were human again, pawns to forces we couldn't control. And then, for a few glorious minutes, we were nothing. Free.

Afterward, Laszlo said nothing. I pressed my nose into the small of his back, allowing him to warm me up. His breathing slowed as he fell asleep. There would be no grand statements or confessions. There would be no talk of "us" or a next time. Laszlo's love was driven by physical desire, and once that left his body, it disappeared into the past and, I hoped, the future. I tried to hide my disappointment, diving into my work and leaving Laszlo to his dreams.

I focused on Nagy, creating a spectacular narrative on his ascent to leadership. I wrote on where to collect arms and how to organize militias. When Laszlo woke up, he began writing too. Antal was still asleep, his snoring long abandoned in the thick entrails of sleep. We worked in complete silence, putting to words something far bigger than us, which seemed much simpler than putting to words the complexity of our lovemaking. We printed a small pamphlet with Nagy splayed across the cover and a headline that read "Nagy to Lead Opposition."

We planned to deliver *Realitás* to the workers close to the arms factories. They would need to start stockpiling weapons as soon as possible. We would also give the paper to our courier service to distribute to the towns outside of Budapest. They promised to deliver *Realitás* to the Kilian Barracks, a major army post. I had no idea how our words would impact those soldiers, but we had to try every avenue.

Laszlo placed a stack of *Realitás* in my arms and quietly opened the front door. I would go straight to the factories in hopes that some workers had reported in today. If not, hopefully I could catch some of them on the streets nearby. I left a note for Antal and a copy of *Realitás* next to him, for when he woke up.

I had an hour before the march began.

DORA TURJÁN
January 17, 1965

DORA SAT ON a bench, surrounded by headstones that shot up from the ground like crooked teeth. Below them, weeds tormented the earth, uprooting the reluctant dirt, cracked and ugly. Webs of moss clung to the headstones, making it impossible to read the names of the deceased. It was in this graveyard that Dora allowed her mind a few seconds of freedom—to feel the pain she spent her days denying. She thought about Boldiszar and imagined him buried in the ground, beneath the jumbled mess of stone and green. As far as Dora knew, his body was still missing. He could be beneath the rubble of an abandoned building or in an unmarked grave in the countryside, in the tiny flecks of ash accumulating on a windowsill or in the crevices of the sidewalk.

At first, and for many weeks after, no one spoke of how it happened or where. Boldiszar died in the revolution, somewhere. Ivan told Dora the news with the mechanics of a trained bureaucrat. When she begged him for details, he said

Boldiszar was a Freedom Fighter who had been in the wrong place, at the wrong time. Dora yelled at Ivan, demanding answers, but he only shook his head and walked away. Dora couldn't believe this was the same dad who treated Boldiszar like his son.

Dora had known Boldiszar her whole life. When she was five, Boldiszar's mom came to Ivan and Eszter, begging them to help her with her son. Ever since his dad died, Boldiszar refused to eat dinner, play with his friends, or even leave the apartment, save for going to school. Ivan decided to give Boldiszar a distraction—he would be Dora's babysitter. At ten, the boy was barely old enough for the job. Still, without fail, he collected Dora every day after school. Dora would be the first to line up to leave, just so she could have the first glimpse of Boldiszar. On their way home, Boldiszar always asked Dora for every minute detail of her day. Lifting her up on his shoulders, he took Dora to the park and pushed her so high on the swings she had to beg him to stop. On hot days, he bought Dora ice cream, getting her two scoops instead of one. And it was clear Boldiszar could sense Dora's disappointment when, every day, Eszter failed to show up in time to see Dora before she went to bed. Many nights, Boldiszar stayed behind to play with Dora, trying to keep her up late enough to see her mom. Most of the time, Dora fell asleep, and Boldiszar did too.

A few years after his death, Dora tried to find Boldiszar's body. She visited the Bureau of Missing Persons and anonymously filed a body location request. Ivan, with his expansive bureaucratic tendrils, found out immediately about Dora's efforts. Waiting for her outside the office, he chided her for associating with a Freedom Fighter in such an obvious and public fashion. As if Ivan had planned it, he pulled from his pocket a tattered photo. Wincing as he lowered it to Dora, he showed her a picture of a bloodied heap of flesh. Dora could make out the black fluff of curly hair on the dead man's forehead.

"This," Ivan said, "was Boldiszar only a few hours after he died."

Dora's stomach disappeared. A weightlessness overtook her, like she was falling down and up at the same time.

"No," she whispered.

"Yes, Dora. It's hard for me too," Ivan said.

"Where is he?"

"We really don't know, Dora."

The certainty of Ivan's words suffocated the small, breathing creature of hope inside of her.

"Here." Ivan handed Dora the picture. "Let this be a reminder to you."

"I don't want this reminder." Dora started crying.

"I carried it with me for years. I've made us safe. That's always been my priority. You have to make yourself safe too, Dora."

Dora grabbed the picture and looked at it closer. It was undeniably Boldiszar. She could see the scar on his right hand, which was bent up by his head, as if he was about to go to sleep. She couldn't believe her dad had shown her this. She wouldn't take it with her everywhere like he did. It didn't make her feel safe. It made her feel that, at any moment, whatever love she had left in her life could be savagely killed.

After Ivan so brutally informed Dora of Boldiszar's death, she started sneaking off to cemeteries to mourn for him whenever she could, the process giving her some relief—at least she was doing something to honor Boldiszar's memory.

Dora grabbed a rock and placed it on a nearby grave, a mourning tradition she saw others do at the cemetery, when she heard the thud of clumsy footsteps behind her. Clad in a chunky sweater with neon green stripes emblazoned across it, Marta stood above her with a goofy smirk. Marta was Dora's childhood friend and colleague, a frumpy sidekick with protruding teeth and bangs that, by the end of the day, strayed in opposite directions. She sat down next to Dora and brushed her hair out of her eyes.

"I thought you'd be here."

"Yeah, I needed it today."

"Me too. I got another suicide."

"From who?" Dora feigned interest, wishing her friend could allow her a few more moments of quiet. But subtlety was not one of Marta's strong points, and her emotions typically required immediate attention.

"A woman in Szeged. She said she'd kill herself tonight."

"That sounds depressing," Dora said, though they received letters like that every day. This was just a normal work conversation, but Dora knew Marta needed these discussions for her own sanity.

"Who was the letter for?"

"Her son. He lives in Budapest," Marta said. Tears began

accumulating on the edges of her eyes, but she held them in. "She told him that she was sorry she couldn't make it to his graduation from university. She was sorry, too, that she bought him the wrong Christmas gift and that she tried to pretend that he wasn't in love with their neighbor, Maksim. She understood him more now than she ever would and that when she closed her eyes for the final time tonight, the whole picture of him, and who he is, will be in her mind."

With some research and a phone call, they could have alerted the son of his mom's crisis. No one would be shocked that someone read her letter. Most people harbored suspicions of the government's censoring practices, and it was normal for these suspicions to be confirmed at times.

Instead, suicide threats accumulated on their desks like frothy dishwater festering above a clogged drain. And Marta would, like they all did, simply record the author's lists of laments into a chart, redact any "subversive" information, and send it off on its way. Dora consoled Marta by telling her that it wasn't their role to alter this woman's life and that, while painful, being a bystander was the best thing a censor could do for the people. No one wanted their letters intercepted, and the more they could remain hands-off, the better.

"Dora, I'm just glad we're in this together." Marta put her head on Dora's shoulder.

"Me too." Dora patted Marta's head. "Although apparently things are changing for me here."

Dora told Marta about Ivan's new censoring initiative, producing Mike's most recent letter.

"It didn't say anything serious, did it?" Marta adjusted her sweater, which, to Dora's bewilderment, always seemed to reveal some part of her bra, even in the middle of winter.

"Just more fantasies for his beloved Uncle Lanci. It looks like he is still our Romeo."

"Well, Dora, if that's enough for him to qualify as your Romeo, then I know some men I can introduce you to. Although I'm not sure their English would be as... entertaining."

Offering her friend a tightly bound smile, Dora explained, for the third time that week, she had no plans to meet someone. Though Dora attracted men on a regular basis, she never gave them a chance. When suitors approached her, she would cross her arms, as if binding the layers of her personality to herself. Sometimes she felt like she was saving her love, though she didn't know what for. She felt it moving inside of her, pushing her toward extreme emotions—sharp pains of sadness when a song touched her or intense joy when the sun hit her face. In those private moments, she felt the promise of love and decided that was better than knowing real, human-attached love, with all its fragility and unwieldiness. Marta sometimes could push Dora to be more social, but Dora rarely made new friends and never a boyfriend.

"So what sort of wisdom did Mike grace us with anyway?" Marta tousled Dora's hair. "Who has he slept with this week? What song is he requesting today?"

Dora divulged the details of Mike's letter, concluding he wouldn't be considered a threat under Ivan's new initiative.

As she said it, a slight tightness gripped her chest—a barely discernable sign that she was lying. She sensed a subtle change in Mike, one that would go unnoticed by any other letter-reader. He had mentioned something that Dora long suspected could eventually lead him into trouble—his lost mom, which he brought up for the third time in a month. She worried Mike might make plans to find her.

The surviving Freedom Fighters were safe, as long as they stayed in Budapest. In case the thought to search for his mom ever crossed his mind, and Mike was indeed a Freedom Fighter, he may be denied a visa. Dora knew he wouldn't quit looking for his mom because some stuffy bureaucrat decided he couldn't travel. He would make "plans," as Ivan called it. After that, it wouldn't take long for them to find him.

"If this stuff is benign …," Marta snatched Mike's letter out of Dora's hand. "Why not just submit it to Joszef so that you can prove we have nothing to worry about? You could probably take Mike off the list of potentially subversive candidates."

Dora considered Marta's suggestion—it wasn't a bad idea. She had never thought to classify Mike in any way. Over the course of the years, he had become a fictional character over whom Dora had no bearing. She wasn't the author of his life, just a thirsty subscriber.

"Or," Marta continued, "maybe you can report him for luring women away from their communist morals because they'll have to viciously compete with each other for his attention?"

"That would be one list he wouldn't ever be able to get off of."

"And one that he could brag about."

"He'd love that."

Deciding to follow Marta's plan to submit the letter to Joszef, Dora spent the rest of the day filling out the necessary paperwork.

After work, she accompanied Marta to a KISZ rally where they were slated to speak about their jobs with the postal agency. KISZ was the Hungarian Young Communist League for children under the age of eighteen. Marta was not a staunch communist, by any means. She liked one of the chaperones, so insisted on going to the meetings and dragging Dora along too. Dora rarely saw the advantages of arguing with Marta, whose loyalty knew no obstacles. Once Marta pledged herself to an idea, a plan, or a person, there was no moving her.

On the way to the rally, Marta asked if she could drop something off to her cousin at the Ministry of Interior. Dora conceded, though it was her least favorite place in the entire city. Something seemed so unnatural about the building. Dora always felt a subtle terror next to it, but couldn't quite figure out why. She never knew when Ivan would pop out of its doors either, and she typically tried to avoid him in public, unless he summoned her. She had to endure his constant scrutiny enough at home.

Dora decided to wander over to the alley next to the building. She leaned against the wall, enjoying the cover it gave her. She heard a soft tapping. It came from beneath her, from the top of a small, barred window at her feet. Dora squatted down to inspect the window—maybe it was cracking from the cold. She could only see the top of it, the bottom half sunk below the ground, into the ministry's basement.

Steam clung to the glass, and Dora realized she must be peering into some sort of locker room or laundry facility. As she looked closer, she could make out a shape—a white circle, a dimly lit light fixture, surely. It must have been hanging next to an air vent, which caused it to hit the glass. She squinted, focusing her eyes on the circle, until its dimensions began to materialize.

It wasn't a light. It was a face, with eyes. Sunken in and murky gray, the eyes floated in space. They didn't register Dora. They stared back vacantly, as if they were watching a boring movie. Dora froze. She didn't breathe as she looked into them, like someone looking at a terrible accident. She was waiting. But for what? The eyes didn't blink; they didn't look away. The body—if there was one—was lost in the heavy steam of the room. Dora heard Marta calling her name from far away.

She wanted to go toward her friend's voice, but her legs refused to budge. She tried to take a step backward, but fell instead. She managed to scoot herself away from the window, the pebbles of asphalt digging into her hands. The eyes continued gazing out at her, with the same bleak expression. She felt a familiar sense of panic grip her body, halting her breath altogether. Sweat sprung onto her forehead and underneath her arms. Without warning, the eyes disappeared as if they were never there, the steam completely overcoming the window. Dora shot up and fled the alley, practically colliding with Marta on her way out.

"What is it, Dora?" Marta's smile instantly dropped the second she saw her friend.

"What?"

"Your face, it's the color of the sidewalk," Marta said.

"I'm just thirsty," Dora said, determined to forget what just happened. "I just need some water."

"Come on, you don't look well. I'll take you inside for some water." Marta grabbed Dora's hand, but only managed to reach her fingers, causing Dora to nearly fall over.

"No, thank you. I'll get some at the rally." The thought of entering the ministry terrified her.

"Okay … are you sure you want to go though?"

"Yes!" Dora needed a distraction as soon as possible.

Peering at her friend for only a few seconds, Marta shrugged. "Okay, let's go then, but I'm going to keep my arm around you."

As they walked, Dora fixed her gaze straight ahead, high above ground level. She resolved to never inquire about the ministry's basement where those eyes lived or—Dora shuddered at the realization—died.

MIKE A KORVINKÖZBŐL
January 22, 1965

Dear Uncle Lanci,

Sometimes I think a more than sparse number of women walk through the streets all day with heinous perceptions about themselves. They are incompatible with who they want to be. They walk along on Nagymező or Erzsébet út, and who they so desire to become walks by them. She's kilos lighter or monstrously breasted. How do I know this? Because I think Hedvig is one of them, and I know that I successfully combated it with just a mere compliment.

We were just meandering through the streets (the endless nights in my bedroom begged us to venture outward) when Hedvig suddenly looked at me like she was preparing shits and, elongating her arm toward another woman says, "She's so attractive. Isn't she so attractive?" First up, her question forced me to peel my eyes away from her, which no one particularly takes pleasure in. I couldn't ignore her question, Uncle Lanci, since then I would be an insensitive bratwurst.

Well, I said a big no to the urge to say, "Yes! She is one sexy specimen!"

This urge resonated immensely due to my rebellious persona. But I don't have the brain of a monkey. I am aware of what a remark would do to Hedvig. In plus, Hedvig is wonderfully beautiful. So, I told her so and said this woman was not as pretty.

The rest of the night we continued gleeful. She even said to me, "Mike, I know you switched the radio in my car. You are a clever genius."

Okay, I'm not real here. She refrained from using those precise words, but that's what I imagined she meant when she said, "Mike, have you heard of Radio Free Europe? I frequently listen to it in my car after I discovered it a few days proceeding."

I put on the most maximum smile possible and asked her if she liked it. She said yes one million times strong. I informed her how your station is the sole one to play The Beatles and The Rolling Stones so she could withstand how important your station is. She brought forth politics into the situation, saying that your station talks too much about it. I agree one hundred percent. Now how does *that* make you feel, Uncle Lanci? Anyway, I stored the information away that I was the one who put your station on Hedvig's radio. I would rather not be the robber to her feelings of discovery.

After I departed from Hedvig, I decided to pass time with my petite sister Adrienne. I accompanied her to her KISZ meeting, the communist youth group our father—who we simultaneous love and hate—forces us to attend.

There, Adrienne performed a feat that made me so proud to call her my sister. At the initiation of the meeting, they dispelled a video about, you wouldn't believe, *your* very radio show. A narrator with a much less pleasurable voice than yours began telling those moldable children that your programming would eventually place them in jail! Listening to your program would cause them to initiate an armed uprising that would be crucified, it said. These statements could not be placed any further away from reality! It's quite evident not one Hungarian possesses enough faith to try another revolution after 1956 was found faced up on its back. What a heap of dog shit.

Next, a boy, eight or nine years old, stood before us on the screen. He looked like a giant. He read a poem about what Hungarian children can achieve if they listen to their mom. Anyone who follows his mom can be viewed as a good person. Just like we listen to our moms, we listen to our mom government, additionally. This smelled of prime bullshit. I almost scrunched my face into a complete ball of absolute wincing. Adrienne spied me next to her with a monstrous wince on my face. We stood in the back, rest certain. Suddenly, Adrienne, who I honestly had no idea she even had such courageous tendons, galloped to the front most portion of the room, grabbed a radio out of her coat pocket, and began putting on your station!

Only God could plan such perfection, because the song that came upon the radio was "Twist and Shout!" All the children began laughing and dancing. How joyous it felt to be present in their petite rebellion. Adrienne screamed about grooviness as she sprinted throughout the bunches of these miniscule grown-ups.

I expect these meetings will not take place for a while now. The bureaucrats will have to recover from their embarrassment. They failed to even flinch as this took place. They just sat cold and absorbed. I wonder, with regards to them. Do they lack any passion with regards to their work? Are they frightened? Or, I speculate, they are feeling smudges of agreement with even people like Adrienne, and that's just enough to shut their mouths from spouting upward. That would be enough for me. It is enough for me. Does it not wow you when someone with so few years does something one hundred percent profound? More profound than you could do? Adrienne stood before three hundred people and unleashed the subject the regime considered despicable.

Following her performance, I praised her until she turned the pigment of a peach. If I could just achieve the same bravery as she. She begged me that I deny telling our father the story of her great feat. Why does she insist on destroying my heart with these petite requests? Did she sincerely believe that I, her most loyal follower, would report her misdeeds to our father? It doesn't take a genius to know he would collapse into worry the instant he heard his sweet child decided to challenge what he himself could not. I informed her I would never commit such a crime.

She looked like Hedvig did when I presumed she was about to have little shits. Adrienne's face became like a scrunched up orange and she requested I accompany her to the kitchen tonight to discourse something with Father. She possessed an announcement. I speculated that she would discuss her plans to leave KISZ, forage into the world on her own, just like I did when I was her age (that's twelve).

Instead she inquired from both of us, at the same time, where her mom went. She looked so old then. I wanted to halt her from talking so I could never view her wearing the pain of an older person. She pointed to her breasts, which closely invoked vomit in me, and demanded who would be there to explain them to her. Is it possible Adrienne could ravage my heart times two? My father delivered the answer he discoursed with us *ad nauseam*: She moved away when Adrienne was three. Things altered, Father told her.

Adrienne insisted he inform her where our mom

was placed. I interpreted my father at that juncture as so guilty for failing Adrienne on this monumental level. He would never be able to bestow upon her the love a mom could. Neither of us would be able to accomplish that.

At times, I discover Adrienne conversing with herself in a mirror. She carries on a complete conversation with her reflection. To say that I am not tempted to eavesdrop for even a short period of time would be an understatement. I spy on her. Usually she perches on the counter of the bathroom and stares at her reflection. She touches her mirror self's eyes, and bangs, and lips. That's all while she is conversing, of course. She says a line, then says a response. It's a back and forth exchange, with someone on the other end telling her masses of very loving things.

One time, I remember, she offered to herself a story about how she felt when she received an outstanding score on a test. For this mirror story, the teacher had paraded examples from Adrienne's writing across the class. When she peered sideways, she spied the boy she liked grimacing. But, only two days later, he proposed they meet behind the bathroom. When she followed his proposition, he kissed her. After, they both departed in the opposite direction. She never spoke to him again. She's twelve, so this disgusts me a little, but I keep listening. They never met again, but she loves him, she says.

I know who she fabricates to be encountering

in those bathroom settings. It's Mom. She's trying so aggressively to make a relationship. It's just … Mom doesn't sound right when Adrienne pretends. She sounds like a little girl, and I hope Adrienne's imagination is strong enough, and I hope she stays young enough, so she doesn't suffer the same realization that our mom is no longer our mom.

I couldn't forget these bathroom scenes now that Adrienne peered into Father and I in the kitchen asking of our mom. What was I supposed to say? I reclined in the corner of the kitchen when Father completely dissipated and confessed he heard she could be wandering in Munich. I could kick him at that moment. Why would he deliver this information to his daughter? She cannot leave now to seek Mom. She is twelve, and we all knew Father would not depart the country for that.

Adrienne's eyes engulfed her face. I strove to hug her but I barred myself from nearing her. This was her obtrusion to deal with on her own. She begged Father that we impart on a family vacation there. He looked at me, and then he informed Adrienne that we lacked the money to travel internationally. Adrienne's eyes downcast and she appeared to be swallowing the information in massive chunks.

She asked if Father ever communicated with Mom. I never even ventured toward this topic. But, there Adrienne went, acting braver than I'll ever accomplish. I could see my father wincing in his side.

Adrienne's words stabbed into his heart, and mine as well. He refrained from putting forth an answer to Adrienne's question. He explained that she left, slipping out away at night time. She did not secretly go. She departed after we talked for months about it. It was a choice we would need to accept because we would never accomplish changing it, he mandated.

What I knew Father was attempting to arrive at is that he refused to allow Mom to become another one of our famous statistics. Suicide—a popular way to go in this country. It was 1956 and I had reached the age of eighteen when she prepared to leave us, and I witnessed the depressive state she occupied. At night time, she cried, and I heard through the walls. At day time, she said very small amounts of words to me.

At the present moment, I grasp her explanations for leaving. You might not remember how aggravating it becomes when you are told for hundreds of times that you cannot grow into who you desire to be. Instead, you fabricate that your job makes sense and that your life is adequate. Mom worked the night time duties in a factory that produced footwear. During the day time, she would sleep while Father journeyed off to his work. They saw each other on Sundays, but what could they talk about when they sparsely participated in activities together? I always stored up data to talk to my mom about, when she was awake, which was only for three hours before I retired for the night in my bed.

And so one day I awoke to Father towering above my bed. He rested his hand on top of my shoulder and informed me that my mom became sick. He said she concluded that she must leave to get better. She will go to a different country until she possesses the ability to return. In that moment, I speculated she would come back to Hungary sooner rather than in the distance. I informed Father.

My father hauled a big breath. Apparently, he had uttered wrong words to me. I failed to understand until that precise moment, that Mom actually was not going to return. Father said we must move onward, but I knew he still preserved his love for our mom like the jar of pickles on our shelves. His love would stay fresh forever because it was meant to be decayed in the first instance anyway. That's how love was to him. Ruined before it was ever reached.

I didn't want Adrienne to taste this kind of love, and neither did Father, so we reserved to help her move onward too. I thought we had done as superb a job as we could muster, but Adrienne grew old before we realized. And she stood in front of us, yet both of us had reserved no words for her.

But, how would you, Uncle Lanci, explain to a petite person who still has years until she is grown old, that her mom disappeared into the West because unlike me or my father, she never put faith in the fact that Hungary could get better? Was she incorrect in her disbelief of our country? And how is it, Uncle Lanci, that I explain all of these particulars to Adrienne, whose sole desire is for her mom to divulge the details of adolescence to her? I wonder if I should approach Hedvig and request her to discuss puberty with Adrienne.

So, here's what I thought first to say: "Adrienne, you'll understand when you just get older. Like I did."

I resolved to accompany her to a walk. That made up plan one. I thought it smelled of shit too, Uncle Lanci. Don't worry; I refused to do that absolutely dumb thing to my petite Adrienne.

So, I reasoned I would say, "Adrienne. She persists to love you, but she is unable to return to Hungary." Naturally, Adrienne would reply with, "Why?" Just like she insisted upon doing with Father. I could inform her that she had to get better with doctors from afar. They could not all possibly journey to Hungary, so she went there. I can see how this answer would tie me up in knots. I would refrain from lying to her at all costs, though.

Because Adrienne's expression grasped my heart like a tourniquet, I decided to solve her problem. And, arriving at the thought, my problem as well. I could not bear it any longer, and so I informed Adrienne that I would find our mom and escort her back home. I do not want Adrienne to endure what I have been for years.

Do you ever get that sensation like you are yourself in one second, and then a moment later you are someone else? That sensation succumbs me *ad nauseam*. Especially when my mind traverses in reverse to when my mom would fix her hands on me and utter granules of special phrases of special love. Her appearances in my mind incite this disillusioning sensation where I can't recognize my past. It has no correspondence to what I am today. The day she left was the day my entire existence severed in half, its two parts becoming one hundred percent disconnected from one another.

That's why I am planning on going to Munich. To find her and reunite everything. For years, unbeknownst to my father and my petite sister Adrienne, I have been trying to go to the West. I even received a visa, valid for the whole of Europe, but it was cancelled without a surmountable number of motivations. I suspect it was because I dabbled in the revolution. I solely received a correspondence in the postage that said, "Tragically, your application cannot be filled at this intersection." I know I have a long way to go until I surmise a way to get out of here.

When I announced this, my father proceeded to give me a scowl. If I was approximate to him he would have kicked me very persistently in the shin until I halted talking. I comprehend his actions. I would have uttered the same statement anyway. Father attempted to speak, but his voice shook like he had bumps in it. He inquired how I would perform this brave feat, and I told both of them, in the most adequate confidence I could mutter, that I had not refined the details yet, but I would. Adrienne is not so trusting to believe these words right off, but I think it gave her three percent of comfort. My father refused to utter even one more saying to us. I think his head is still fuming with the betrayal I enacted upon him. I spoke without requiring forethought, and now some part of Adrienne grows hope that I will return her to her mom.

Later, when Adrienne snored like a hound dog, Father grabbed my shoulders and shook them very fast. He demanded I inform him why I imbued Adrienne with false promises. I told him I do not intend for them to be false. In reaction, he refrained from anger, like I predicted, but his shoulders sagged and he sat on the ground next to me, like Adrienne does sometimes.

I was not supposed to be in this character. I am his son; he is my father. Why did he not just seek to find her himself, and why is he upset when someone has offered to do this for him? Why must I be the hero to my parents? At that moment, I pondered if it is ever possible to completely love the parents who raised you. I sometimes speculate they were supposed to betray me. They spooned fed me love, and I became dependent on that love. But, is it right to remain enamored of their love, inaware to the burden it places on them?

My mom did not want to see me. It was too much for her to exist as a mom. It was us, Adrienne and I, not Father or Hungary, that served a threat to her life. When I drifted this theory by Father, he became very quiet. He informed me it's not my burden that she became ill. Did he really speculate I would be satisfied from this answer? That's the thing, with these people who raise you. They throw you into the washing machine of their shit, hoping that it will somehow cleanse you. And it smells absolutely foul, and then they ask that you understand why it smells so bad. It's not fair, you say, you thought you were getting cleansed the whole time! Now you realize you are just covered in crap! You spend your whole life covered in their shit.

If I found my mom, he belabored, I wouldn't be helping Adrienne because I would have to inform her that her own mom did not want to view her. I told him that will not happen. He said it would. I said it wouldn't. He said it would. I said it wouldn't. He resorted to his room, and I fled to work.

I experienced so much anger, Uncle Lanci, so was welcoming of work to take my mind away from it. But, as I cleansed that damn Ministry of Interior (the one on Andrássy út), an occurrence took place that I must inform you about. I was there with Andras, my cleaning mate, and naturally after we cleansed for but twenty minutes, we indulged in the peacefulness of the voided building. We were in the main compartment, on the initial floor, in one of those pesky offices. Andras lit my cigar, as the usual routine demanded, and then we settled into the couch. We sunk into the comfort of that moment, praising that it wouldn't come to a stop.

That's when our ears picked up on a scratching like a rat was stuck in the floor. It scuttled and banged itself against the floorboard. It bemoaned and bemoaned *ad nauseam*. Andras and I nearly had shits right upon the couch. Okay, it possibly could have been a mere rat, I reasoned, except then it uttered these words: "Cseke, Cseke, Cseke. Laszlo, Laszlo, Laszlo." That is your name, isn't it? The first and last? I do not know what was uttered next, since we streaked upward and ran out the door.

Uncle Lanci, who is that being beneath us? You must know! I contemplate the chance exists for you to obtain some knowledge of this sound's origins. I am aware of your intelligence spindles that extend all the way into the most intimate areas of Hungary. I am so curious, but so scared. I do not know which one will conquer the other. Perhaps you could just inform me as to whether it's a-okay to return to cleansing this building?

In return for the fear and sadness that insists on

arriving at my house this evening, I request you play "Blowin in the Wind." Perhaps I will sneak into my bed, where my sister has already snuck in. I'll cuddle beside her. I'll shut my eyes and imagine your music until I forget what I promised tonight, and I'll wake up and think it was solely a dream and store it just as that. A dream. Unfortunately, for me, dreams are meant to be accomplished.

Sincerely,
Mike a Korvinközből
Desire is fueled by all, but fulfillment. —Ernő Osvát

ESZTER TURJÁN
October 23, 1956—Afternoon

HUNDREDS OF STUDENTS pushed against me, nudging me closer and closer to the middle of their frenetic gathering. "Let us speak! Let us speak!" they yelled at the state's radio office. It was a goliath of a structure, taking up the entire city block with its jumble of offices, hallways, and courtyards haphazardly connected to each other behind heavy oak gates, which the students were determined to take down.

Above us, a group of police held submachine guns and fire hoses in ready position. They kept unleashing the latter on us, drenching us in a deluge of water every few minutes. A flurry of goose bumps was practically plastered to my arms—but rather that than blood, I reminded myself. I was thankful the police hadn't used their guns ... yet.

I was witnessing the culmination of a day of demonstrations. The government had tried to ban the student march, but failed to stop it. I had made it to the couriers and the factories in time to distribute *Realitás* to the workers, advising my most trusted contacts to begin setting aside arms.

When I ran low on copies, I hung the paper on every bulletin board I found. By the time I joined the march, whispers of Nagy taking over had started circulating through the masses, and Radio Free Europe had even announced the same thing. (Antal must have woken up and informed them.) I felt satisfied with my work. We had successfully planted the tiny seeds of hope growing and reaching into our collective conscience. Nagy was our man.

The students surrounding me grew louder and more excited, making up new chants every few minutes—the most recent one: "A microphone in the streets. A microphone in the streets." They were agitating to read their sixteen demands over the state radio. Above us, the police paced across the rooftops, their gate quickening. They looked nervous and determined at the same time—a truly lethal combination. I noticed a copy of *Realitás* on the ground, Nagy's face muddied and ripped by the torrent of footsteps. I picked it up and handed it to one of the students next to me, shouting over the chaos that we should chant for Nagy. I was already planning my next move, which was pressuring Nagy into assuming the leadership role, whether he wanted it or not—I still didn't have direct confirmation that he would do the job.

Major General Hegyi, head of the army's training wing, appeared on the balcony of the building. We all knew Hegyi—he wasn't a diehard Stalinist by any means, and it appeared the students would allow him to speak. I hoped Hegyi would say what the students wanted to hear. I had a feeling their excitement could morph into something else entirely at any second.

Hegyi stepped up to the microphone, his age more evident as he strained to straighten his back and stand completely erect.

"Please," he said to the crowd, now completely silent. "Disperse and return to your homes."

At first, the students didn't make a sound. Nearby, I heard quiet laughter. Through the silence, it grew louder and louder, until it was next to me, and next to the person next to me, and once it reached the entire crowd, a ripple of booing tore through us. The booing turned into a gigantic wave that gave into yelling as students shouted and cursed Hegyi.

Hegyi disappeared, but the crowd surged forward, ramming its collective mass into the gates of the radio building. The police trained their machine guns on us. One fired a warning shot into the air, but the students didn't stop. A second warning shot went off. The students pushed forward even harder. A collection of knees and elbows jabbed into the back of my body. The police let out another warning shot, then another. My ears began screaming. They felt like they would explode, and I looked around, and everyone's mouths were open. They were screaming too. My lungs filled with air, but nothing came out. Some people ran. Others tripped and fell to the ground.

Next to me, one of the students yelled, "Death to the police!" I couldn't hear his next words because a puff of smoke erupted between us, forcing an antagonizing gas into my lungs. As I coughed, I squinted through the mist, only to realize I was staring at a neck without a head. The body still stood, packed in so tight with the crowd, but his head … the tear gas canister must have exploded on the boy's face.

Clamping my eyes shut and holding my breath tight, I managed to wriggle my way out of the gas plumes and into another crowded space, where teenagers were ramming an old car into the building's wooden gates, cursing as they splintered the wood that would not give.

Tiny, almost imperceptible gaps began opening up in the crowd. Beneath them were the fallen, either bleeding or dead. I searched the crowd, trying to find someone, anyone, who could help, when I locked eyes with one of the policemen pointing the long nose of his rifle at me. He smirked, opened his mouth wide, and burst into laughter. I ducked as the shots punctured the air above me.

My hands and legs shook, and I felt my legs bending toward the ground, but my mind refused to give in. My thoughts started to have clear beginnings, middles, and ends. I knew what I had to do. I had to help the students secure arms.

I grabbed the shoulder of the girl shielding herself next to me, her long hair thick and grimy underneath my trembling fingers.

"Go to Csepel. Now. You can get guns there." I yelled at her. When she turned to face me, she looked like a mousy teenager who belonged in a physics lab.

"Where?" she shouted.

"The factories at Csepel!" I screamed.

"Who are you?"

I showed her *Realitás.* "I wrote this. Take this to them. It will tell you where the guns are."

"I can't hear you."

I started shoving copies of *Realitás* into the opening of her coat, but she shook her head and, stepping only a foot away from me, was lost.

A trio of ambulances sped toward the crowd, swerving through the random clumps of people to try to reach the injured and dying. I couldn't believe the regime was actually going to help us. Perhaps they did have some shred of humanity. Out of the back jumped men in white coats, one after the other. There had to be forty of them. But, they seemed too nimble for doctors, leaping from the ambulances like athletes clearing hurdles. That's when I noticed instead of stretchers or medical kits, the doctors' shoulders sagged beneath the straps of submachine guns. They ripped off their coats to reveal the uniform of the secret police.

Before we could run away or attack them, they sprayed the crowd with bullets. I ducked again, this time trying to shuffle sideways out of the crowd. A little boy drifted by me. The students were, miraculously, stepping around him and letting him wander through the mayhem. I couldn't take my eyes off of him. Dollops of blood clung to him in random patches, though he didn't look injured himself. What was he doing here? He looked like he could be seven or eight. When he saw me, his yellowish eyes grew to the size of small apricots. They went directly to the space between us where a small gun lay on the ground.

"This isn't yours. Go home," I shouted.

The boy came up next me, enveloping me in his little pocket of protection. I could smell the baby powder his mom must have applied to his skin the night before mixed with the dried blood that wasn't his own.

"No, I can't. I can't." He started crying. "Just around the corner!"

"What's around the corner?"

"Please, just follow me." He grabbed my hand with his tiny, snot-encased fingers. "It's just right here."

"Okay, you have one minute."

He led us through the crowd, unscathed, and I felt a greater appreciation for the students, who showed concern for this little boy's safety. We both wanted nothing more than to make this country better for him, and the other children.

When we rounded the corner, I smelled gunpowder evaporating in the air. Crumpled on the ground lay a body, disfigured and bleeding, in the alley off Wesselényi út. As I crept closer, I recognized the man's tattered white shirt, his silver hair, and his ink-stained fingers. It was Antal. He must have left the office to join the efforts and somehow ended up here, destroyed. I felt like I was the one who had been beaten up, so stricken by his battered state. Thin streams of blood trickled from his mouth, and his eyes, puffy and bruised, were swollen shut.

"Is he going to be okay?" the little boy pleaded amidst the thud of tanks rolling toward the fighting.

Ignoring him, I swooped over Antal. When I asked him what happened, he choked and coughed up bloody saliva. He called me *babushka* over and over again. Turning to the boy, in the most sweet voice I could muster, I asked him what happened. He stammered, and with each attempt at a word, tears tumbled out of his eyes.

"I don't know," he finally said. "I just came around the corner because I heard kicking and screaming. And then there was this big group of men, and they looked normal but then they were beating this other man and saying he had to do it. He had to do it." The boy collapsed into a fit of crying.

"Where did they go?"

"That way." He pointed in the direction I came from. This made him cry again. Enveloping him in my arms, I held the boy as tight as I could, trying to squeeze all the tears out of him. "Look at him and do not look away." I pointed to Antal. "This is what could happen to you if you stay out in the streets."

The boy's lower lip jutted out. He nodded, and a few straggling tears fell down his puffy cheeks.

"Please, go home so you can stay safe," I said. "Now."

Stepping away while fixating his eyes on us, he slowly backed away from the gruesome scene, saying nothing.

I resisted following him to make sure he went home. I feared if I did, Antal would be scooped up by someone— whoever these enemies were—and tormented once again.

A mess of bloody skin clung to the side of Antal's arm, barely. It looked like a bullet had skimmed his skin, but not implanted itself there. Antal attempted to pull his arm away from me, referring to someone named "czar." He displayed sure signs of shock, yet his eyes seemed coherent and alert.

They followed me as I inspected his body to make sure he hadn't broken anything critical. I decided to move him to our office—I reasoned I could let him rest there while I tried to find a doctor.

I wrapped his uninjured arm around my shoulder and yanked him up. Draping his jacket over his disfigured face, I escorted him back to the office, a twenty-minute walk away. Every minute or so, Antal would abandon his strength and plummet into me, pushing me sideways and almost completely over. Each time I veered to the right or left, Antal groaned and let out minor phrases and grumbles. I remember he said something about being hurt and some garbled reference to plans.

A gelatinous liquid snaked down my neck, and I knew it was Antal's blood dripping from his jaw. At one point he refused to continue walking, like a stubborn dog sensing danger ahead of him. Reminding him that he was safe with me, I cooed into his ear promises about getting somewhere quiet, being comfortable and warm.

We passed Horizont, a Russian bookstore, which had been gutted and burned, leaving tattered paper and ashes heaped in piles on the street. Our shoes carved textured imprints onto the books' remains, and I knew that it had been said before, and would be true today, that where books burn, people will too.

We passed the offices of *Szabad Nép*—the regime's official newspaper—where staff members, their clothes and hair in disarray, threw down leaflets declaring their support of the revolt. I wondered if this desperate attempt at redemption would work or if the journalists would suffer the same fate as their leaflets—torn up, stomped on, and burned in a makeshift bonfire.

The moment we stepped onto Andrássy út, a woman, old enough to be my mom, ran toward one of the patrolmen standing nearby, waving her fists at them. I continued dragging Antal along, hoping to go unnoticed. Out of the corner of my eye, I saw the fattest guard in the group grab the old lady's braid, turn her around, and smack his stomach into her back. Screaming, the woman stumbled and collapsed.

The wretched officer noticed us—and me, specifically—eyeing him. He turned his attention away from the poor woman and, looking at us, licked his lips. I put my head down, pretending I had seen nothing. I thought nothing. My thoughts were all movement. "Eyes to the ground, go here, move there. Say nothing," my mind commanded. Never looking again at the soldier, I dragged Antal forward. The twenty-minute walk took us two hours.

DORA TURJÁN
January 22, 1965

DORA BLINKED. SHE opened her eyes. She blinked. She opened her eyes, and still she saw the eyes from the basement plastered on the little children at the KISZ meeting.

She imagined she was staring at one hundred tiny replicas of Boldiszar. Those were his eyes. The second the thought came into her head, Dora discredited it immediately, unwilling to allow her logic to flag even for one second. Those eyes were gray—his were brown, almost black. But cataracts, and time, and suffering could have changed their color.

No, there was no way Boldiszar could still be alive. She had proof he died. She had scrutinized that photo of him. She mourned over and over again. Those were not his eyes. Dora ran the sentence through her mind until she was sure of it: Those were not his eyes. Still, his blank stare watched her as she shifted from one foot to the other backstage. She thought about making an excuse to leave, but then Marta would ask her even more questions. Dora was relieved when the children, led by a mousy girl named Adrienne, staged their rebellion. The meeting ended without her needing to make her speech at all.

For the next week, Dora spent most of her time alone, but busy. At work, she kept to her cubicle, where she read a record number of letters. After work, she invented a new chore to do. On Monday, she bought a new cooking pot. On Tuesday, she replaced all the expired spices in their cabinets. At night, Dora sank into her chair in the study and read beside Ivan. Usually a burden, the tradition now provided her with another way to keep her mind focused on anything but her own thoughts. Sometimes, right before she fell asleep, the eyes would drift into her view and she'd jolt awake, tears already building. When that happened, she would crawl right back into her chair in Ivan's study and pick up where she left off in her book. Ivan would bring Dora a cup of warm tea and kiss her on the forehead before returning to his work. Just as Dora settled in to her reading that Sunday night and congratulated herself for making it through the week unscathed, the phone rang.

"Dora, you have to come over here now."

"Marta?" Dora had been avoiding Marta all week for fear that she would try to find out what happened at the ministry.

"Yes, obviously it's me. I'm at Szimpla."

"Marta, I'm not going to a bar right now. I'm not up for it."

"Oh, come on, you never are."

"I have to go now," Dora said.

"Wait."

"What?"

"I have something to tell you. It's about Mike."

"Marta, if you're using that to get me out …."

"I'm not! Just come here immediately. I know your dad is there. I'm not going to say it over the phone."

Marta knew exactly how to get Dora to do something. She doubted she had anything substantial to say, but in the off chance she did, Dora wanted to find out.

"All right, but I can't be there for too long."

When Dora kissed Ivan goodbye, she noticed him squinting a little too much as if he had to exert himself just to smile. The familiar surge of guilt swelled inside Dora at the sign of Ivan's vulnerability, his hatred of being alone. Dora felt responsible for his happiness and frustrated that, at such a young age, she was already taking care of her dad.

She knew she could never give him the affection he needed, and vice versa. Their love pooled into a dam built by their refusal to talk about Eszter. Their connection stopped short, stagnated and, as the years went by, gradually evaporated. Dora worried that one day the dam would break and their relationship would be exposed for how it really was— broken and beholden to the forces of the past.

Dora gently closed the door of the apartment, wondering if her dad would ever accept that, at times, she would try to make a life for herself. She had no clue what Marta had in store for her, but she hoped she could escape within a couple of hours.

"Remember you said Mike wouldn't have plans?" Marta asked—or more, announced—the second she saw Dora. "Here are some plans." Marta slid a letter over to Dora.

"A letter from Mike? How did you get this?" Dora whispered, even though they were at a table in the back, hidden in plumes of stale, lingering cigarette smoke.

"I noticed it on top of some letters being prepared for Joszef's review."

"And you just took it?"

"First of all, I don't think Joszef has seen it yet. And also, this is a copy. Mike's letter is back in its place."

"Thank God."

"Just read." Marta put a glass of vodka in front of Dora. "Then drink."

As Dora scanned the copy of Mike's letter, a rush of despair coursed through her. She learned not only that Mike wanted to leave Hungary, but he also confessed to hearing something in the basement of the Ministry of Interior. She knew, with this government, coincidences didn't just happen. When a person had a feeling two horrible things were connected, they usually were. From the second she saw it, she knew the moaning was related to those eyes. She had almost been successful at escaping them. But they followed her, tracking her movements like a cat in the night.

Dora also thought about the regime's new hunt for Radio Free Europe devotees. Mike would surely encounter problems if he tried to leave now that he discussed plans to head to Munich—the headquarters of Radio Free Europe. And yet, it was his sister's need for a mom driving his desire to leave Hungary in the first place. Dora struggled to reconcile her sense of duty with her guilt over turning someone in who seemed so compassionate.

"Dora …," Marta hesitated.

"Look," Dora pointed to the letter matter-of-factly. "He has plans to leave Hungary. We cannot let these come to fruition."

"He wants to leave. You are right, but it's not forever. He obviously wants to bring his mom back here, so it's not that bad. We can still help him, can't we?"

Dora knew every person her age despised the regime, but they rarely documented these feelings on paper. It was stupid of Mike to write about them so openly.

Mike's letter confirmed one of Dora's biggest fears: Mike was both confident and optimistic. The lethal combination invariably led to the greatest crimes. Rather than fearing the government, he would joyfully flout its rules, carrying on in a separate world, leading a separate life, and loving a separate government—the government of his own. Dora knew what she had to do.

"We have to tell Joszef," Dora said. "Mike is just going to get more determined. He's not going to stop until he finds himself thrown in jail. We can help him now by squashing his dreams of leaving."

"No!" Marta plucked the letter out of Dora's hand. "Mike has been your constant companion; you can't just abandon him."

"It's not just about me anymore," Dora reasoned with Marta, who gripped the letter in her hands. "It's about Mike, and you, and my dad. This is the best way of stopping something before it gets out of hand and affects us all."

"I know you're worried. I am too, but there is something we could do about this letter."

"We can't destroy it," Dora said.

"No. I think we need a delay tactic. Let's take it from Joszef's office, for now," Marta said.

"What if he notices it's missing?"

"He might notice, but he won't know who took it."

Normally, Dora would have stifled a plan requiring any sort of deviousness. But, she reasoned, a delay could buy them some time to come up with an alternative.

An hour later, Dora found herself positioned in front of Joszef's office watching Marta fumble a hair pin as she tried to unlock his door. They had waltzed up to his floor without coming into contact with the remaining employees nestled in their cubicles. It wouldn't have been completely strange for them to be at work on that night.

They tiptoed into Joszef's office and closed the door. Hardly able to discern anything in the dark, Dora closed her eyes and counted down from five. When she opened her eyes, Joszef's impeccable office spread before her. So painstakingly clean, it sent shivers down Dora's arms. She wondered if he kept it this clean so he could catch trespassers.

Dora searched under Joszef's desk for a pair of cabinet keys. She could detect the faint traces of his most personal attributes, like the somewhat moldy scent that clung to him every morning, or the small pieces of hair he shed when he rubbed his face in concentration. She found his cabinet keys taped to the bottom corner of his desk.

Dora was impressed by the immaculate organization of

Joszef's cabinet files—every single paper had a proper place, its destination defined with a printed label. She found not one loose paper, which meant Joszef might very well notice the absence of Mike's letter.

Careful to maintain absolute silence, Dora painstakingly lifted each paper, inspected it, and placed it back where it belonged. With each movement, Dora felt like a piece of machinery executing its next, precisely-timed maneuver. She endured this sensation many times in this building, except now she waited for the glitch—the letter—that would allow her to influence the machine's operations.

Dora propped open a folder entitled *To Read,* which held all the latest letters and reports passed on to Joszef. Dora plucked the first letter from the file and realized it was, indeed, Mike's.

"He probably hasn't seen any of these …," Marta said.

"You're right, although it was on top of the pile, so perhaps he'll remember it was there."

"That's possible, but we don't have any other choice, Dora." Eyeing the letter, Marta mustered her most calm voice, "Okay, let's take it. It's time to take it. It will just be gone for a little while …."

Dora nodded.

She understood—they had gone this far, and to turn back would be to admit that they committed a crime. As she moved to close the drawer, she noticed Marta clutching something against her. Glued tightly to her stomach was a folder bending awkwardly on Marta's torso.

"Marta, what is that?"

"It's our employee evaluations." Marta had that look on her face she got when she was excited about plans. It was a far-away giddiness in her eyes, as if she had leapt ahead to where they had succeeded instead of addressing the present reality.

Dora gently slid the folder out of Marta's grasp. "We've broken enough rules for one night." Dora straightened the file the best she could and returned it to Joszef's filing system. "Plus, I think we can wait for our evaluations."

When they finally made it outside, Dora breathed deeply for the first time in hours, releasing the focus that allowed her to operate so methodically. At least for a few weeks, Dora hoped, Mike would be spared the repercussions in store for the select, unlucky fans of Radio Free Europe.

As soon as they made it a few blocks from their office, Marta declared, "Dora! You are coming out with me. We're going to a bar or a club or whatever you want, but you're going out."

Dora rolled her eyes and then did something she hadn't done in weeks—she laughed.

"All right, Marta, but I'm tired. I'm not staying out that late."

"Of course not. We can have our fun and get home early." Marta hurried them toward a local bar that was known for playing The Beatles, softly, and only once in awhile. Other bars hosted actual Beatles cover bands. Fans used secret passwords for admission. Sometimes the police arrived in the middle of a set, yelling at everyone to get out. Sometimes they were cited for participating in the "black market" by buying tickets for and attending a concert that was not offi-cially sanctioned. In reality, they were being punished for listening to rock 'n' roll and subjecting themselves to the music and culture of the West.

"So, Dora, any men you see here tonight that you might want to talk to?" Marta scanned the men surrounding them at the bar. "That bartender is looking rather groovy with his wild hair. It's mysterious. I wonder what I will find ... in there."

Dora glanced at the bartender, whose hair looked like one of the dust balls accumulating under her bed.

"Yes, it looks very—"

"Amazing!" Marta finished her sentence. "Oh, look at him. He's like the Hungarian version of John Lennon."

"If he was just struck by lightning."

"You're right, he's electric!" Marta grabbed Dora's hand and ushered them toward the bar. "I Want to Hold Your Hand" blared from the speakers as Marta danced within view of the bartender, her scraggly curls bouncing into Dora's eyes.

"Dora, you dance like a drunken elephant!"

"There's more where that came from." Dora exagger-ated her jerky dance moves even more, sending Marta into spasms of laughter.

Of course, Dora knew Marta had planned all of this. Knowing her goofiness attracted conversation, Marta pro-jected a carefree attitude, and men fell for it every time. At first, they would look at Marta sideways, as if second-guess-ing their initial feelings of attraction, but then, once Marta quit her show, they would come over and say something like, "Oh, that was very funny," or, "Where did you learn those moves?"

But when the bartender neglected to even look at Marta, she sped toward him, temporarily abandoning Dora. Dora began meandering back toward their table when she realized a group of men now surrounded her, thanks to Marta.

"I wanna hold your haaaaaaaaaaaaaaaaaaaaaaaand," someone shouted in Dora's ear. They butchered The Beatles' lyrics with their heavy Hungarian accent and drunken drawl.

Turning toward the commotion, Dora faced a man, about her age, clad in maroon corduroy pants and a thick woolen sweater, his sweat tumbling from his forehead to the ground. Listing, yet obviously determined to make himself appear sober, he fixated his gaze upon Dora and displayed a grin that seemed to lay siege to his entire face. Momentarily disgusted by his obvious show, Dora shunned him. She brushed her hair slightly over her face to conceal her eyes. Countless similarly sweaty men had confronted Dora before, daring to conquer her imperturbable façade.

Studying his face momentarily through the wisps of her hair, Dora noticed an alluring softness in his eyes. And before she could stop it, the slightest of smiles slipped from her lips.

"And what could possibly be your name?" the man shouted.

"It's Anika," Dora replied as she lifted her drink off the table next to her.

Taking precautions to conceal herself, in every way possible, Dora stared at her straw as she picked at it and moved it through her fingers. She stopped when she realized the man, now leaning into Dora, was hungrily staring at her fingers.

As if suddenly remembering his manners, he stepped away from Dora and exclaimed, "I'm Ferenc," which elicited no response in Dora.

"Would you like to hold my haaaaaaaaand?" he sang and smiled sheepishly.

He refused to wait for a reply. He grabbed Dora's hand and ignored her subsequent flinching. Resisting Dora's subtle attempts to push herself in the opposite direction, Ferenc spun Dora around in circles.

"Anika, Anika, Anika. What a lovely name!" he sang, "I wanna hold your haaaand, Anika!"

On her third cycle around Ferenc, Dora caught a glimpse of Marta angling her chest over the bar so her cleavage spilled—no, overflowed—onto the mahogany. How Marta managed to produce cleavage while wearing a sweater would always mystify Dora.

"Anika," Ferenc continued to sing, "Oh, please, say to me, you'll let me be your man. Anika, please, say to me, that you'll talk to me!"

Beginning to relent to Ferenc's charm, Dora laughed, but only at a barely audible level. By allowing someone to fawn over her, if only for a second, Dora experienced a sense of importance she hadn't felt in years. Ivan's pains to make Dora feel loved only did the opposite. As he failed multiple and successive times, Dora felt more like a waste of his energy, an exhausting task that challenged him every day.

Dora moved a step closer to Ferenc and placed just a few of the obtrusive strands of hair behind her ear.

"Your eyes pierced me from across the room," Ferenc said. Reaching toward her cheek and petting it gently with his thumb, he continued, "They compelled me to ask you to hold my haaaaaaaaaaaaaand. Did you know that your eyes have a power over men?"

Dora laughed, her face growing hot.

"It's true. They are beautiful!"

"Thank you."

"But they are sad."

"What?"

"They are sad," Ferenc yelled back. "I can tell."

"Oh," Dora said, dumbfounded. If she was drunk, perhaps this conversation would have been easier. Dora began moving in the direction of Marta, prepared to take leave of the potentially-emotional conversation, when Ferenc touched her shoulder.

"I want to know!" he shouted.

"What?" Dora tried to raise her voice above the music, but she was not used to yelling, or loud bars, for that matter.

"I want to know what makes you sad." Despite the watery, drunken glaze now coating Ferenc's eyes, he looked at Dora with a sincerity she recognized. It was the same kind Boldiszar had shown her. It made her feel like it didn't matter what she said—she, and all her thoughts, would be accepted.

"My family split in half when I was seventeen," Dora informed Ferenc.

Dora now felt a slight wetness underneath her arms. Her heart began beating at irregular intervals.

"Must have been so hard." Ferenc started to step away from Dora.

She wondered what she said wrong. Resolved that this was a bad idea in the first place, she said. "Anyway, there you have it. I have to go now."

"Wait!" He scrambled after her. "My family also split in half. But this isn't about me, tell me what happened to yours."

"I lost my mom," Dora admitted.

"What happened to her?"

Dora waited nine years to be asked this question, or rather to be asked this question and reply with the truth, for once. Now that the opportunity loomed before her, she cowered, unable to speak.

"And how is it with her gone?" Ferenc nearly fell into Dora, who realized that he hadn't been backing away earlier, he was just struggling to find his footing. So obviously drunk, Ferenc handed Dora the silent microphone she had been waiting for. He wouldn't remember a thing she told him.

"I am frustrated," she began affectedly. Noticing Ferenc's eyes trying, but failing, to focus on her, she grew confident.

"No, I'm mad that she could not be the mom that I needed. I wanted someone to tell me good job, without me even asking for it. I just wanted her to say it."

A momentary desire to feel her anger overtook Dora. This conversation proved to her she still had a chance at being whole, that she could experience the full range of emotions she worked to conceal her entire adulthood. She wouldn't let them go so easily.

"When she left, she said nothing. But I fantasized that she said, 'Dora, please don't forget me. Remember that I will always love you.'" A tear fell down Dora's face, and for the first time, she didn't care.

"Dora?" Ferenc frowned.

Did she just say her real name? She must have let it slip. If Ferenc noticed it, he probably wasn't that drunk. She needed to walk away.

"Dora who?" She tried to cover her tracks before she said goodbye.

"I thought you called yourself something else," Ferenc said. "I'm so drunk."

"I should go."

"Oh, Anika, wait. How could you leave me now? How could anyone ever leave you?"

"It happens. You'll forget about me soon enough."

"I want to hear more about your mom."

Dora knew she should go. Her gut told her this was a bad idea, but her mouth opened and her voice sent words out through it anyway, because a part of her needed this more than she even knew.

"The government took her away."

"Where did they take her?

"That was for the government to decide."

"So you have no idea where your mom is?"

"No." Dora wiped away her one tear, whose moist

residue had all but dried. Somehow, saying the conclusion to her mom's story out loud comforted Dora. She realized it was the truth she knew, and lived by, and one she had grown to accept.

"Oh, the fucking government. What a joke it is, isn't it, Anika? We all go around pretending to be this. I pretend to be that. Did you know that my friend joined the police, and just for their amusement, they find people on the street and beat them!"

"That must be a lie," Dora crossed her arms gently over one another.

"No, I'm not kidding! They beat these people a lot," Ferenc said.

Dora didn't know what to say back. When it came to the government, she always chose her words wisely. Ferenc moved closer to Dora's face, nearly butting his forehead against hers.

"I know how you feel," Ferenc tempered his voice to a quiet drawl. "Mine is gone too, gone far away."

"Do you know where she went?"

"Not a clue."

"I am sorry." Dora avoided eye contact with Ferenc. She wasn't ready to make this an intimate dialogue.

"Oh, please, let's not talk about those plans. Let's dance." Ferenc pulled Dora toward him. He spun her around, stopping only to press his lips to her ear.

"Anika, why do I feel like you understand what I'm saying more than anyone else?"

"I'm not sure," Dora lied. She felt the connection too,

but she also felt the familiar desire to retreat. She feared talking more would activate her past, causing it to twist and spin until it turned into a vortex of pain and confusion she couldn't escape. Dora didn't say another word. She continued dancing with Ferenc, finding safety in the mechanical motion of their bodies.

They remained like that for nearly an hour until Marta appeared at Dora's side to discuss their plans for the rest of the night. Before they came to any conclusions, Ferenc called out names into the abyss of dancing bodies, and like a band of loyal monkeys, random heads perked up at his summons and sprang toward them immediately. Within seconds, a group of five men surrounded them.

"Now this is the party I have been searching for!" Marta flushed, listed, and smiled.

"Let's get out of here!" Ferenc suggested, playing off Marta's exuberance.

As they left the bar, Ferenc slipped his hand in Dora's. It felt like a warm washcloth, damp and textured, yet soothing.

Ferenc's group of friends somehow procured three bottles of wine, which they slipped out of their coat pockets and passed around in the open air. When the alcohol finally made its way to Marta, she gulped down nearly half the bottle. Dora only allowed herself to drink a sip.

By the time they managed to finish off the wine, they had reached the Danube. The river sprawled before them like a feathery boa. The breeze ruffled its dark and foreboding surface, producing barely audible waves.

Ferenc sprinted to the border and ran alongside the river.

"Oh, fuck this world!" Ferenc shouted into the night, dragging out his words. "Fuck this fucking world and this fucking government."

"Oh, yeah!" Ferenc's friend, Andras, joined in. "Fuck the lines at the post office! Fuck the trash that piles up on my doorstep because people are too lazy to fucking pick it up! I'll slam their heads into the ground!"

Marta giggled, and Dora winced. If someone heard them screaming like this, they would all be thrown in jail.

Ferenc dug into his coat and produced a small radio. He rested it on the ground, extended its antennas and dialed directly to Radio Free Europe. "You've Lost that Lovin' Feelin'" wafted from the speakers. Ferenc scooped up the radio, cradling it in the crook of his arm, and danced with it. Marta cuddled against Andras, and the other boys started kicking around a ball they found on the street. Dora thought this must be what it was like to feel young—to be fearless, to care only about what was right in front of her, to actually become a moment.

It reminded Dora of how she felt after her first kiss, which she let herself remember for the first time in years. It used to be Dora's measuring stick for happiness. But when nothing ever added up, Dora tried to forget the kiss ever happened.

It was right before her sixteenth birthday, when Boldiszar surprised her with a trip to Lake Balaton. Dora remembered being so excited, and also nervous to spend so much time with Boldiszar in a situation that involved traveling and sleeping arrangements. They would stay at Boldiszar's aunt's house and sleep in separate rooms. Dora wondered what Boldiszar would think when he saw her in a bathing suit, laying on the beach or coming out of the water. She wanted her first kiss to happen so badly, but it also terrified her.

On their last night, Boldiszar insisted on giving Dora a birthday present, even though Dora told him numerous times he didn't need to get her anything. But, Boldiszar wouldn't listen. He took a deep breath and said, "I'm not sure how much this is for you as it is for me." He reached behind Dora's back and pulled her into him.

Dora froze and stared up at Boldiszar, who gave her the look she fantasized about for so many years—like all he cared about was her. He leaned down and kissed her square on the lips.

"Happy birthday," Boldiszar whispered.

Dora didn't know what to do. She never actually expected this to happen. Her dreams of being with Boldiszar, most prominent in the seconds before she fell asleep, always seemed so dull and useless by morning.

"Dora …," Boldiszar tucked her hair behind her ear. "I know I'm too old to be with you now."

Dora touched her lips, still tingling from the kiss. "Then, why did you do it now?"

"Because, I'm not sure what the future holds for me."

"What do you mean?"

"I'm involved in something, something big, that I can't talk about. But I want you to know that you are, and always will be, the person I'll come back to … when the time is right."

Just as quickly as Dora felt hope swell inside her, she felt it come crashing down. Dora wondered if the "something big" Boldiszar referred to had to do with the illegal newspaper her mom ran. Given the attention and fury it invoked in Ivan, Dora knew any involvement with the paper would put Boldiszar in danger. Dora hated Eszter in that moment for tainting one of the best experiences of her life. Still, she cradled the memory of that kiss for weeks afterwards, until she came to understand the constant remembrance of something so brilliant—and far greater than anything around her—made the dullness of her life too sharp.

Dora didn't kiss anyone after that for years. She wondered if tonight she would feel again that small peak of excitement and adrenaline, culminating in a kiss. Ferenc seemed sweet and sincere and, to Dora's benefit, drunk, which meant little pressure for follow-up.

Dora got up to join Ferenc, who now held the radio as if it was a newborn baby, singing to it in wonder. Before she reached him, however, Dora noticed two shadows growing bigger and bigger, encroaching upon Ferenc's dance floor. When Dora turned around, she saw two long black sticks. She saw the hands that connected them and the dark jackets encasing the arms. That's when she realized it was the police. They bypassed her and crept toward Ferenc. His back to them, Ferenc continued serenading the radio.

When the second officer stepped into Dora's view, she felt tiny needles of fear pinning her down rather than propelling her to action. She could only stare, not move.

Everyone else, but Ferenc, had noticed the police too and started backing away.

All at once, the police slapped their clubs against their hands. Ferenc turned around. The radio slid from his hands and crashed to the ground. One of the police officers went up next to Ferenc, who still hadn't moved, and kicked his radio into the river.

Dora felt her head swing back violently as a surge of pain jolted up her neck. Her scalp was burning. Someone was pulling her hair. They yanked her to the ground. Another surge of pain erupted. Something was hitting her. It was hitting her hard. The pain burst on her back and then sprung onto her shoulder. It clawed into the back of her thighs. Then there was nothing.

Dora saw a dark orb hang above her. It looked peaceful, like she could curl up in its silky body. She reached out to touch it, only to feel the course fibers of something thick and unruly.

"Why are you touching my hair, Dora?" Marta breathed. "It doesn't matter, just get up! Get up!"

Marta yanked at the bottom of Dora's shirt, trying to lift her up however possible. The stitches on Dora's shirt ripped open, but Marta refused to let go. Before she could understand anything more, Dora heard a violent pitter-patter, a panicked thumping, that grew quicker and louder until it sounded like thunder claps in her ears. She realized it was the sound of her boots smacking against the cobblestone. They were running. Dora heard an inconsistent series of screams in the distance. The lights beaming from the apartments above them flickered off.

"Dora!" Marta whispered. "Dora, you need to run faster. I'm serious."

Dora considered the strangeness of Marta's right eye. It was smaller than her left and seemed to do all the communicating for Marta. Dora's concerted effort to export her consciousness from the situation was interrupted by the sound of boots clanking. Two policemen ran past them with clubs drawn.

"Okay," Dora rapidly nodded. "Okay. Okay, let's move."

Despite her injured back and legs, now exposed and bleeding, Dora ran. She couldn't string together logical thoughts, but her body somehow matched Marta's pace, locking into the rhythm of their escape.

ESZTER TURJÁN
October 23, 1956—Late Afternoon

I WOKE UP to a subtle draft gliding over my nose. I opened my eyes to Laszlo leaning over me, scanning my face. Before I could say anything, he pressed his ink-stained finger against my lips. I could almost taste the sultry sweat on his hands through my closed mouth. He picked me up off the ground and shuttled me to the other side of the office. Out of the corner of my eye I saw Antal, stretched out on the couch and asleep, despite his agony.

Speaking so affectedly that I could see him wrench every syllable from his mouth, Laszlo said, "Look at him, Eszter. He is all beat up. How do we know that he has not betrayed us? Or someone else? Did someone find out about us?"

I looked at Antal's disfigured face, and I couldn't imagine him ever saying anything about *Realitás* to the wrong people.

"We need to just take care of him for now," I urged.

Laszlo listed, slightly, and let out a sigh. "We will watch Antal. Just you and I, and we won't let him out of our sight."

Laszlo fingered the flimsy steno pad in his hand as his eyelashes brimmed with perspiration.

"What's wrong?" I wiped away a bead of sweat, which, upon examining, realized could be a tear.

"I don't know how to write about this," he said.

"Write about what?"

"What I saw, everyone tearing down the Stalin Monument, like they don't even know what that's going to mean for them."

Laszlo and I had split up for the day to gather notes—he followed the protest to the city park, where thousands of people demolished a massive statue of Stalin, leaving only his boots. In them, they placed flowers.

"Just try." I ushered Laszlo to his chair at the typewriter.

"How could you not get it, Eszter? Especially after everything you saw at the radio building. This is real. The protest went right by your house, you know."

"It did?" I hadn't checked in at home, but I knew Ivan would protect Dora. I was certain he had thoroughly demeaned the students' efforts by now, calling them out as ignorant and idealistic. He would make sure to stifle any desire in Dora to even step outside that apartment.

"You should call them." Laszlo turned away from me. He loaded a piece of paper in the typewriter and, as I heard the click of the first keys, I picked up the phone. He was right this time. Miraculously, the phone lines had been sustained.

"Eszter," Ivan breathed. "It's you. Thank God, it's you."

I pretended to cry. If Ivan imagined me cowering in fear somewhere, unable to get home, I could uphold the lie a little longer. My family would get through this without me, and I needed to focus on my duties at the paper.

"Ivan," I sobbed, "Are you okay?"

"What do you mean, Eszter? Can you make it home? We're fine. We're here and we're both reading in the room, but we want you to come home."

"I'm okay, just stuck in this shelter at the factory. I'll be here for the night, I think," I told him.

"Where?"

"I have to go. I have to go now." If I still loved Ivan, maybe I would have gone home. I used to love him for how he could be so strong and sensitive at the same time. Yet over the years, and as Ivan climbed the ranks in the regime, that strength grew so hard it calcified. Beneath it, trapped, was his gentleness—his habit of telling me I was beautiful in his sleep, his affinity for music and making us chocolate chip pancakes at midnight. I wondered if this movement would take a match to his strength, and in melting it, set free some of that softness. I also wondered if it was still there at all.

I could hear Ivan breathing on the other line of the phone, waiting for me to say something else. He was always waiting for me to say something more, as if I could simply forgive him. I think he fantasized that I would come home one day with a smile on my face and chirp, "You're forgiven."

"For what?" he'd ask.

"Everything. My parents. You working for this government. You not looking at me or touching me for ten years," I'd say.

It would never happen, though. In reaction to our

isolation from one another, we'd built up separate lives that were highly involved. There were structures, incentives, and people that kept us moving away from one another.

I said goodbye to Ivan and hung up.

When I turned around, Laszlo, who clearly had been eavesdropping, resumed typing. I looked over his writing and noticed it seemed erratic. Sentences drifted on the page, untied from one another and unanchored to a central thesis. Laszlo's hands shook, only slightly, but enough. He needed to relax. I edged my palms onto his working hands, feeling his muscles give with my touch.

"We need to get this out soon," Laszlo sighed.

I wanted nothing more than for him to turn around and kiss me. I would wait, however.

"We tell them what I saw. What you saw," I offered.

"But we have no intelligence beyond that," Laszlo groaned as he leaned back in his chair, and into me.

"They have already started fighting. We need to give them more than what we gave them last time. Let's give them something to keep them going. Let them know that there is hope," I urged.

"You are saying we tell them to fight, without any resources, and without knowing any of the potential consequences?" Laszlo snarled.

By proposing we go at it blind, without a staple of intelligence, I challenged Laszlo's journalistic integrity. But, certain hardships trumped that. We suffered under our government. I waited hours just to buy bread for my family. When I walked anywhere, even in my own home, I always looked behind me at least three times to check if anyone was following me. My friends, like my family, disappeared too. I would arrive at their apartments, ready to simply visit with them, and no one would answer the door. I would knock and knock, until I gave up and looked through the windows, only to notice all of their things gone. The discovery of their absence was nothing compared to the realization of what that meant. They were almost certainly killed, executed in the secret police's dark chambers, or they had been sent to a work camp where they would die under the backbreaking labor. I always said a small prayer for them, right there, in the middle of the sidewalk. Then the anxiety would set in. I would wonder whether Ivan's position really did shelter us from the all-powerful and paranoid government.

I would feel my mind working at five times its normal speed. Millions of questions raced in and out of it, distracting me from answering any one of them. And this unknowing felt like a drug, infusing me with an obsessive energy as I considered the various drastic responses to the scenarios I concocted. The best decision I made was working for *Realitás,* where, at the very least, I could put this energy to some sort of use.

I would have supported anything or anyone who promised to lessen the paranoia that engulfed me every day. This movement was our chance. Yes, I preferred that we encourage the students to fight, if it meant that we could start invoking some sort of change. And I still had hope that our contacts would pull through and supply the kids with weapons.

"There," I said, pointing at Laszlo's description of Stalin's head falling to the ground. "We have enough intelligence to work with. We're going to publish everything you and I saw today. And then some more … to make sure this keeps going."

"Eszter …," Laszlo began. He almost had that tone in his voice, the one he used when he was coming on to me.

I thought, for a second, Laszlo would try to make love to me again, but before he could approach me, we heard Antal's breathing became irregular. Slipping away from Laszlo and draping my jacket over Antal, I stooped next to the old man.

Still disfigured, his face began to twitch. Short nonsensical phrases slipped from his lips. Half conscious, he peeked his eyes through his swollen lids and mumbled "czar" once again.

I knew Antal needed to get to the doctor, but I would need to convince Laszlo first.

"Eszt," Antal moaned as his eyes shot open. A vicious coughing spasm overtook his body, causing him to regurgitate even more blood onto the floor. "Eszter, thank you."

Overcome by his gratitude, I clasped him to my chest.

"Sorry, I'm so sorry," Antal cried. His warm tears spread across my shirt.

I squeezed Antal tighter, savoring his need for me. It was the necessary contrast to Laszlo's persistent detachment.

Laszlo pulled up a chair, leaned over, and looked Antal dead in the eyes. "We're glad you're okay. Now, tell us what happened."

"I …," Antal began. Without his three front teeth, he sounded like a child just learning how to speak, and in the face of Laszlo, he seemed ill-equipped to explain his situation.

"It's okay, Antal, take your time," I cooed, shooting a sinister look at Laszlo. "Just give him a second." I felt bad for

Antal, and somehow slightly responsible. Had I been there earlier, I may have been able to stop them.

"I was walking here …. That's when five men, big men, surrounded me." Antal said. "They demanded I lead them to … to the office. They said they knew I betrayed the government."

Antal fell silent, his haggard breathing adding weight to his words.

"They asked again for me to lead them here as they drew closer and closer," Antal continued. "When I said no, that's when they started. I forgot most of what happened next, but I remember screaming, crying, but it wasn't my own."

The little boy must have been wailing near Antal. "Then I saw you, Eszter."

"You kept muttering the word 'czar,' over and over again. Who is that?"

"I have no idea," Antal said, with more energy and edge than I had ever seen him use, even when he was healthy.

Scratching his scruffy chin, Laszlo continued to stare. He allowed the minutes to spread before us, filling the room with apprehension. When I couldn't take it anymore, I addressed them both.

"Clearly, there are dangerous people out there. Whether they call themselves czars, or what have you, they're looking to hurt us. We have to embolden our demonstrators before these predators find us, and others."

Laszlo snapped his head toward me. "We don't have enough information, Eszter! What are we going to do? Print a two paragraph paper about Antal's injuries and Stalin's statue coming down?"

Did Laszlo not understand a movement quickened outside, one that relied on any information it could possibly get?

"I say we make sure people continue taking action. The revolution has already started, and who are we to stop it? We tell everyone something that will draw them into the streets. We will make sure that the crowd does not subside."

"Wasn't Nagy enough?" Squinting his eyes demonically at me, I thought, for a second, Laszlo would lunge toward me. And this time, lust would have no part in it.

"He hasn't made a public stand yet, you know that. And we need a series of things to build momentum. We have to keep giving the people tangible hope—something real that will encourage them to keep going."

"So we just continue manipulating people so that they risk their lives and give you the revolution you always wanted?"

"Yes," I met Laszlo's strength with my own, stepping toward him. "We have no chance, not one, especially if tomorrow less people are on the streets. If we can continue on, and outlast the government, we may be able to secure some sort of change."

Interrupting our debate, a smattering of gunshots rang outside our office. Forceful and thunderous, they jolted the building's foundation. We froze. Distant screams grew louder as people ran frantically past our office, swarming in frivolous patterns and chaotic directions. Frustrated that we missed the commotion and in dire need of information, I flung the door open and grabbed one of the kids running by the office. If we could collect more intelligence, Laszlo would be more likely to go with my plan. Once I wrestled our informant to the ground, I faced a trembling girl, a university student.

"What do you want?" the girl screeched.

Laszlo glared at me, as if asking me the same question.

"Don't move." Standing up and straightening my shirt, pulling tight the clasp that held my hair up, I demanded, "Just tell me what happened. We're on your side. We're with *Realitás*."

I grabbed a mangled copy of the paper from the type-writer. The girl stared at the headline, then at me. She scanned the entire office, absorbing the menagerie of typewriters, papers, empty coffee mugs, and desk lamps.

"What's your name?" I asked hesitantly.

"Marika." She looked down at the carpet, trying to pick apart its grains with her shaky fingers.

"Marika …," I paused. She resembled Dora so much—her dark, wispy hair fell gently on her thin shoulders. Her cheekbones lifted her entire face up, giving her the appearance of elegance and toughness all at once. She wore the same serious expression as Dora, like you could never imagine her lips breaking into a smile.

Laszlo squeezed my shoulder, bringing me back to the present.

"I'm sorry," I quickly muttered. "Of course. Please, just tell us what happened to you. It would really help us."

She cocked her head at an angle and said, "If all you want is information, let me give it to you quickly, and then let me go."

We agreed. Eerily monotone and dispassionate, Marika

explained how she was with a contingency of students who were in search of arms. They went immediately to the army barracks on Szentkirláyi út and shouted at the guards to let them in. They started pushing on the gates when a voice from above them said, "I'll shoot if you break down the door." That stopped them momentarily, then the soldiers inside started handing them their guns through the bars in the windows. One of the soldiers even left the barracks, led them to a patch of grass nearby, and gave them a lesson in shooting.

Marika and her friends returned immediately to the radio building. By then, a radio van with a large satellite had pulled up right in front of it. Valéria Benke, the head of the state's radio station, Radio Budapest, stood atop the van, apparently having agreed to read the students' manifesto over the radio. Quietly, Valéria began reading their sixteen demands. As the students listened, the people watching from the apartments above shouted at her to speak louder. She ignored them, trudging on through the list.

A student climbed atop the van and grabbed the microphone from Valéria. He held up its cord, revealing that it was attached to nothing but air. The radio was not broadcasting their demands. It was all a farce. With newfound strength, the students surged forward into the van, and toward the radio building, determined to make the regime pay for trying to fool them.

This time, they managed to destroy the gates and doors of the radio building, breaking into the fortress. Armed and prepared, Marika and her gang followed at the tail end of the invasion. By the time they got inside, it looked like a band of looters had wreaked havoc on the building. Chairs were missing legs and cast off to the side. The couches bore dirty footprints and gaping holes from people running over them. Memos, documents, and files were scattered across the floor, dirty and ripped by the rush of invaders. The secret police ran through the crowd, shooting at the moving targets in unpredictable patterns.

Marika and her friends used their newly acquired guns to fire back, though she wasn't certain whether they had actually hit anyone. Soon, she found herself ducking behind a stack of chairs and watching a police chief yell at a group of younger policemen who seemed hesitant to shoot. One of the men shook his head, and when the rest of the men saw that, they also shook their heads. The chief, in one swift movement, took out his gun and shot all the men, point blank. Marika crawled out the back window and ran. As she fled, she heard more shots being fired.

"When I looked back, I saw people on the ground. They weren't moving." Marika said, her eyes planted on the ceiling as if looking up could somehow force her tears back into her head.

"Are you okay?" I put my hand on her shoulder.

"Yes," she nodded with such force she shook loose the tears she had tried to hold in. "Can I go now?"

"First you have to tell us one thing. How many do you think died?"

"How many?" Marika turned as white as the paper loaded in the typewriter behind her.

"We need this information."

"I don't know."

"Even a guess is better than nothing."

Marika sobbed into her hands. "I think it was fifty. At least."

I hugged her, my touch triggering some instinct for aggression in the girl. She pushed back against me.

"I have to go," Marika said. "You're going to let me leave, now."

"Of course, just do one thing for me."

"What now?" Her eyes, puffy and moist, flared open, creating a stark contrast between the gentleness of her sadness and the sudden intensity of her anger.

"Don't return to the radio building. Go somewhere safe."

"Okay."

"Just be careful." I kissed her on the cheek.

"I'll try."

We both knew she would go back to find out which of her friends had survived, and which didn't. And, a part of her would die, was dying. I watched her walk away until I could no longer see her.

"We are doing something about this," I declared, turning back to Laszlo and Antal. I imagined *Realitás* igniting such a swell of support that it would completely decimate those murderers like that police chief. If we could only sound convincing enough, we could make this happen.

"I promise," Antal wheezed, "I promise I'll find more arms for those kids. You have my word."

"Thank you." I kissed Antal's forehead and put my arm

around him. "That sounds like a better plan than anything else we've thought of. But we should do something else too."

"Don't try this again," Laszlo said.

"We should tell everyone Gerő's supporters are fleeing. It wouldn't be a complete lie, since you are one of them and you've defected," I said, squeezing Antal.

"Dammit, Eszter, Antal didn't defect. He was beaten to a pulp!" Laszlo yelled.

"I know, but listen. People won't fear Gerő if they think his beloved henchmen are starting to join their forces too."

Once that lie tumbled from my mouth, it felt more real than anything happening around me. More palpable than Antal's wounds, more piercing than Laszlo's eyes, and more tender than that little boy's tears. My lie came from a very real place within me. And once it hit air, it became truth.

"Eszter, please," Laszlo started in an unnaturally calm voice.

But we all knew the other option—the one that would happen if this fledgling revolution failed. It was death, and no matter how ferociously Laszlo trumpeted the merits of journalistic integrity, he couldn't compete with our basic, human desire to live. Soon he grew quiet. No one spoke for twenty minutes as we considered our options.

"If only we had some serious help for this fucking revolution. Imre Nagy leading us is not going to be enough, no matter how much experience the bastard has. Where is the West when we really need them, huh? They claim the Soviets are their enemies, but they haven't helped us one bit, besides playing this damn radio." Laszlo shot a glare at Antal before kicking the radio across the room.

We all knew the West was just a lesser evil compared to the Soviets. Like their professed enemies, the West's affection was wrought with contingencies.

"What if they did help us?" Antal said.

"You mean …," I ventured, "… once they learn about the immense strength of our pending revolution, which they probably already have, they will come to our aid?"

I understood the futility of such a statement. The possibility, however slim, tempted me though. Radio Free Europe gave me just enough hope, like sunlight peeking through the blinds of a dark room. I imagined something absolutely brilliant and glowing beyond my view, and I refused to let go of the fantasy.

Antal and I worked together to etch out a plan for us to wield the West's influence to fuel our own revolution. First, we would draft a one-page version of *Realitás*. In it, we would update everyone about the day's events—the crowds, the statue, the shooting of the students, and anything else we witnessed. We would also include in it the strong possibility of the West sending troops and aid in support of our revolution. We would say the conclusion was obvious. With the West's help, the regime stood no chance. Antal would then send the information directly to Radio Free Europe with only ten minutes left until its broadcast for that evening. With the radio's pending deadline and Antal's stamp of legitimacy, the producers would push the information on air without double-checking it.

Antal sat up now, grabbing his knees for support as he straightened his back. "This is the best we have."

"Let's do it." I said. "Laszlo, are you in?"

Laszlo turned away from us. I interpreted his passive resistance as acceptance of our grandiose scheme. I realized then why he had protested so vehemently against our plans. He was terrified of defying the government beyond publishing our flimsy newspaper. This journalistic integrity, his initial attempts to stop the revolution, was just a cover. If the revolution grew, it would expose Laszlo's darkest embarrassment—his paralysis.

Crouching over the typewriter, putting words to our plan, I began to write. I felt like a leader forging Hungary's future before she was even ready for it. I prepared her for what she did not see coming.

"This needs to go to Radio Free Europe first." Antal rested his hand on mine. I could feel it emitting an immense amount of heat. He surely had an infection.

"But … then we have to use the teleprinter …." I promised Laszlo I wouldn't use it unless there was an emergency. The machine could send and receive messages, but at the risk of being intercepted and revealing our whereabouts.

"We have no choice," Antal said.

Laszlo pretended to read a book, and I, once again, took his silence for permission.

During the Radio Free Europe broadcast, we all retreated to different sides of the room. Antal and Laszlo crouched in their respective corners and I sat at my desk, biting my nails. Antal's face was twisted into a disconcerting combination of exhaustion and excitement. Ashen and swollen, his skin lacked any sort of pigment. A faint smile tugged at the edge of his battered mouth. Laszlo smoked five cigarettes in succession and his eyes seemed almost jumpy, as if trying to grip every word the broadcaster said.

As Laszlo put out his last cigarette onto the carpet, the broadcaster summarized the words I crafted, the words that Laszlo neglected to prevent from airing.

"If the Soviet troops really attack Hungary, if our expectations should hold true and Hungarians should hold out for three or four days, the United States will send military help to the Freedom Fighters," Zoltán Thury, the broadcaster, said. "If the Hungarians continue to fight until Wednesday, we shall be closer to a world war than at any time since 1939, and in the Western capitals a practical manifestation of Western sympathy is expected any hour."

Thury had expanded upon my words, making the broadcast even more reactionary than I predicted. I felt high, almost manic, like I could do anything. I imagined the head of Radio Free Europe reading *Realitás* and calling the president of the United States to convince him of our cause. The energy of my success buzzed through me, and all I wanted to do was run and yell.

"We did it. I can't believe we did it," I said, beginning to stuff my bag with copies of *Realitás*. I had to start distributing it to the people who missed the broadcast.

"Do you know what this means?" Laszlo's eyes were moist, and I thought, finally, he was softening.

"What does it mean?" I put down my things and rubbed

his back, ready to coax out the tenderness I had been waiting for.

"We are fucked."

"What?" I hissed, the energy I gained from our success converting into rage.

"I said ... we are fucked."

I squeezed his shoulders, letting my nails dig ever so slightly into his back. "How can you take this one glimmer of hope, Laszlo, and completely destroy it?"

"You think being pawns of the Soviets is bad? What's going to happen when the Americans get their chance to play with us?"

At that moment, I wanted to leave the office and never come back, if only to make Laszlo regret what he said. But then the phone rang.

ESZTER TURJÁN
October 23, 1956—Evening

WE ALL STARED at it. Was it a coincidence the phone started ringing only minutes after Radio Free Europe announced Western aid would come to our country at any time? Or was it fate? As a precaution, we never gave out our number or accepted phone calls. But tonight, as the revolution spat the unknown throughout our city, we abandoned our former rules.

Antal scooped up the phone, cradled it to his ear, and turned his back to us. Laszlo ignored him, busying himself with posthumously correcting the already-published *Realitás*. He scribbled all over the paper, sighing as red and black ink rubbed off on his arm, making it look like he went to battle with the paper, and lost.

Antal beckoned me to him, subtly, and without the notice of Laszlo, though I'm sure he heard me as I tiptoed across the room. Antal handed me the phone. Raspy coughing echoed on the other line followed by someone clearing their throat.

"Eszter," the voice of a woman spoke. "We need you to do something for us."

Her voice had an intoxicating fragility to it, as if every word was in danger of being overtaken by sheer exhaustion. Covering the mouthpiece with my hand, I asked Antal who she was. "Anya, the Radio Free Europe chief," he replied, solemnly.

The second Antal said that to me, I knew it was true. I had heard Anya a few times over the radio, when she stepped in for an absent colleague. She had taken the place of regular broadcaster Zultán Thury just last week.

"Yes, what do you need?" I held the phone so close to my mouth, it became moist.

"This is classified. Not even Laszlo can know what I am going to tell you."

"I understand."

"We need you to deliver a message to the military leader of the Freedom Fighters—Boldiszar Balasz."

I almost tripped over the cord.

"Who?"

"Boldiszar. Balasz."

That was the name of Boldiszar. *Our* Boldiszar.

"There is no way he is the leader of the Freedom Fighters."

"He is in charge of a major contingency of students fighting in district five," Anya said.

"No ... no ... no... this is all my fault."

"What?"

"I did this to him."

It was only two years ago that I first started slipping Boldiszar anti-regime pamphlets, the ones that his parents and Ivan hid from him, but that sometimes were dropped from balloons into the countryside. I also saved a copy of *Realitás* for him every week, folding it in the envelope we gave him as payment for taking care of Dora. While I knew Boldiszar wouldn't be so careless as to discuss the paper with me in our home, within the vicinity of Ivan, Boldiszar always gave my hand an extra squeeze when I handed him his payment.

Once, I even asked him to contribute to *Realitás* to give the paper a young person's perspective. When Ivan saw that copy, he made sure I never spoke to Boldiszar again. Anytime I stepped near the boy, Ivan would swoop in between us, rest his arm on Boldiszar's shoulder, and usher him away.

I tried to understand how it could be true that, over the course of that time, Boldiszar had become a leader of the Freedom Fighters. I remembered some of Boldiszar's classmates used to tease him for taking care of Dora every day after school. Their jeers failed to dissuade him from his duties, the happiness of a little girl more important than his popularity. Maybe the students saw Boldiszar's kindness as radical and noble, a relief from the regime's incessant cruelty.

"I know him," I finally said to Anya. "He's a good boy."

"We know. That's why we're asking you to do this favor for us. We're scared he wouldn't trust anyone else. We need you."

"For what?"

"The U.S. is on their way to Hungary as we speak. We need their troops to connect with Boldiszar immediately."

"The U.S. is coming to Hungary?" I asked, shocked that they would actually heed our call.

"You're surprised? You're the one who suggested this in the first place."

"Right. I'm just ... relieved they are following through."

I couldn't believe I had predicted the course of the revolution so accurately—the U.S. *was* coming to our aid. I no longer felt like a journalist, but a driver of news. I felt manic and powerful, like the country needed me to get to work immediately. I also felt a deep sense of relief knowing Boldiszar would have one of the most powerful militaries in the world behind him.

"We need you to tell Boldiszar where to meet them," Anya said.

"Where is that?"

"Antal will explain more. I have to go now."

"Okay ...."

"Oh, and Eszter, this won't be easy."

"I know, but he trusts me."

"He's a commander now, Eszter. He trusts no one."

Now that, I couldn't believe. Boldiszar might be acting tough, but I knew his sense of loyalty and connection to my family would supersede the limits of his new role. He wouldn't rebuff me.

Antal gave me detailed instructions on how to prove that Boldiszar could rely on our information and reiterated that he would reveal the exact meeting point for the rendezvous before we got to Boldiszar. They didn't want to transmit it over the phone or within the vicinity of Laszlo, which I could certainly understand.

Taking advantage of the last minutes I had in the office, I crept over to Laszlo. He had fallen asleep at his desk, a habit of his whenever editing stories. I scribbled a note to him, telling him I had a very important mission to see through. I included instructions on what to do if I didn't return, in part to make him feel like I was doing something bold and noble, and also because I knew the second I stepped outside, my survival was no longer guaranteed. I placed the note under his hand and kissed his forehead.

"I'll need your help getting there," Antal said. He slumped against the back wall of the office, his dried blood forming a crusty ring around his neck. His shoulder hung at an awkward angle, much lower than his other one.

"I have to ask you one thing before we go," I said.

"What is it?"

"Did you know she was going to ask me that?"

Antal jerked a little, avoiding eye contact with me.

"I did, Eszter."

"But, why couldn't you just ask me yourself?"

"I thought it would be better coming directly from Anya."

"I would have believed you. I'm not like him ...," I looked at Laszlo. "I trust you."

"Thank you, Eszter. That means a lot. We should really get going."

"Can you even walk?" I asked.

"I'm not sure ...."

Resting his weight on my shoulder, I dragged Antal out

of the office. I wished that I could have left him sleeping with Laszlo.

"We need to get to the edge of the river," Antal said.

"Why the river?"

"It's where he is."

"But, that's not where all the students are fighting," I said, thinking of Corvin Cinema, the movie theater-turned-rebel stronghold in the middle of the city.

"I know it's hard for you to believe, but he's a commander. He needs to be where it's safe," Antal reasoned with me.

Boldiszar did always have a fondness for water, I remembered. On weekends, he used to beg me to take them to Lake Balaton. I never agreed, too busy with the paper to spend the weekend out of town. Last year for Dora's birthday, Boldiszar ended up taking her to the lake himself. I remember after their trip, I would discover Dora smiling at random intervals of the day, like when she ate her breakfast or even when she was fixing her hair. She actually said hello to me, and goodbye. She spent less time doing her homework in her room or in Ivan's office, and more time in the living room. I wondered what happened that weekend on the lake.

I never asked—too fearful to disturb this new daughter. Dora's glee only lasted a few weeks, though, and Boldiszar stopped visiting us so frequently. Now I knew what he was doing.

As Antal and I lumbered toward the Danube, we passed patches of destruction and violence, each one more unique and gut-wrenching than the last. Near the radio building, I saw a boy walking around with a lantern, shining it on the dead as he tried to identify the students, forever asleep in their shattered innocence. On Váci út, broken glass and graffiti marred the storefronts. In front of the butcher shop, a man hung tied up on a pole like the pig carcasses being displayed in the windows behind him. A crowd of young and old people surrounded him, taking turns striking the dead man. I watched as a hunched-back, frail old lady shoved her way to the front of the group, jerked her head back, and spat on the man. I started walking toward the crowd, determined to untie this poor man, but Antal reprimanded me. I knew he was right. I had to stay focused on the task at hand. If I wanted to alleviate our country from this pain, we had to get at the root cause. This mission was my fate. It chose me yesterday, when my intuition told me we needed to do something to make this revolution pick up speed. Western aid was really coming, and our forces would be stronger for it.

I felt Antal's body give in to his injuries as he grew heavier on my shoulder. My muscles started to cramp, as if they were trying to grab on to Antal themselves. My lungs demanded air at increasingly shorter intervals, and I couldn't tell if it was nerves or exhaustion, or both. I closed my eyes and plodded on, trying to ignore my weakening body, Antal's wheezing, and the random bursts of gunfire nearby.

"We're here," I finally heard Antal whisper. "We made it."

"We made it," I repeated, as we collapsed onto a bench.

We sat at the very edge of the Danube, allowing the river's earthy, familiar breeze to wash over us for a few brief seconds. A line of tugboats swayed in the tide, letting in and out gentle, measured breaths as if they were sleeping. The serenity felt misplaced, and because of that, unnerving.

"It's time, Eszter," Antal said.

"Okay," I took a deep breath. "I'm ready. What should we do?"

"You have to make it to that small dock." Antal pointed toward a wooden structure far off in the distance. If I squinted, I could see the outlines of boats next to it. "Go to the second largest boat there, the one with the blue stripe on it. Tell them Jedidiah sent you. That's the code."

"Why didn't we just walk there in the first place? We could go together …."

"I can't," Antal said.

"Why not?"

"Because they won't trust me."

"What do you mean?"

"I've played both sides for too long, Eszter. I can't risk it."

Antal's explanation made sense, but I didn't want to go alone or leave him alone, in his state. We agreed that he'd wait in the doorway of an apartment building one block away from the river.

The boat I headed toward seemed heavier than the rest, sinking an inch or two deeper into the water, which lapped against the dock with a taunting softness. Nearing the boat, I smelled smoke recklessly seeping from its door. Was my Boldiszar really that careless? When I knocked, no one answered. Knocking again, I put my lips to the door and whispered, "Jedidiah sent me."

I heard a lock unlatch and feet walking away. I pressed on the door, but it didn't move. I pressed again, yet still, nothing. Turning sideways, I rammed my shoulder into the door, pushing with all the energy I had left. On my third attempt, it flung open and spat me out into a cramped, wooden cabin. I tried to make out my surroundings as thick plumes of cigarette smoke curled around me. Squinting, I saw a card table. A group of young people surrounded it, their heads cocked to the side. They looked no more than twenty years old.

"Who are you?" one of them roused.

"I was sent to you by Jedidiah at Radio Free Europe. My name is Eszter Turján," I mechanically clucked the words Antal crafted for me. "I am here to inform Boldiszar about something important. Tell him Eszter Turján is here. He knows me."

The blond girl to my right let out a guffaw. Her friends followed suit, and soon they were all laughing, talking to each other and ignoring me.

The obese boy at the table, who wore army fatigues and kept combing his brown, greasy hair, raised his voice above the others.

"What do you want?"

"U.S. troops are coming. I have to tell Boldiszar where to meet them."

They quieted in unison.

"That can't be true," the boy said.

"It is, and I need to speak to Boldiszar immediately."

"Well, you used the code. Wait here," he commanded.

I nodded.

The boy slipped inside a back room. I shifted my weight from one foot to the other, comforting myself with the notion that, at the very least, my feet were prepared to launch into action. I wondered if Boldiszar was scared. Was he hurt? Did he know what he was doing?

I still had a hard time believing he had the tenacity to lead this revolution. In the face of conflict, he always acted so tenderly. When Dora misbehaved, Boldiszar would just wait for her to calm down. He never lectured her. Instead, he asked her questions, prompting her to understand her motivations and, ultimately, her errors. She usually reached the conclusion that she was wrong on her own, and the conversation ended in an apology. How would our gentle Boldiszar last an entire revolution? I wanted to know, and at the same time, I didn't.

"He will see you now," the boy said, returning. "But you only have ten minutes."

"Thank you."

Patting me up and down, the boy searched for weapons. Finding nothing, he sighed and opened the door to Boldiszar's office.

Boldiszar was sitting in a large, leather chair examining something on his desk. I stopped for a second to admire how grown up he looked. He wore a beautifully tailored, olive green military uniform, though you could tell where Hungary's official military ornaments had been ripped off the woolen jacket and sewn over. His hair was slicked back, the only relic of his wild curls by his ears, where a few strands escaped the wrath of hair gel. When he stood up, I swear he looked taller than I remembered. But when our eyes met, he gave me that same toothy, eager smile that made everyone adore him.

"Eszter! It's good to see you," he said, kissing me on both cheeks.

"Boldiszar, hello."

"Come, sit down. Tell me why you're here."

"Well, I'm sure your … comrades … already told you. I was sent here by Jedidiah."

Boldiszar nodded, as if he was personally acquainted with someone named Jedidiah. I almost laughed, he seemed so eager to act like a seasoned professional. Instead, he just reminded me of someone listening to an assignment on his first day of work.

"And what news does Jedidiah have for us today?"

"Today?"

"Yes, we get intelligence from Jedidiah regularly."

"Oh, I had no idea." I wondered who else Anya used to relay intelligence to Boldiszar, and felt a pang of jealousy. Why didn't they trust me sooner?

"The U.S. is here. They want to meet to coordinate resistance efforts."

"Where?"

"In Buda. I can show you."

"When?"

"Now."

Boldiszar curled his fingers in and out of his palms, making small fists and releasing them over and over. He stared at me, his tar-colored eyes resting on mine. He started nodding his head, and I couldn't tell if he was thinking, or pretending to think, or basking in the immense responsibility before him.

"Eszter," Boldiszar sighed. "I want to listen to you. I want to believe you. I know you are telling me everything you heard, but how do we know that wasn't a saboteur calling? How do we know it was really Jedidiah? This is the most extreme thing he has asked me to do …."

"She."

"What?"

"Never mind, just turn up the radio. I can prove to you I'm not lying."

Anya and Antal had prepared me for this very situation.

"Sure," Boldiszar said, reaching for the nob.

On air, Zultán Thury delivered the news in a quieter, more subdued voice. He recounted the day's horrors and named the students and other Freedom Fighters who had been killed. I didn't recognize any of the names, thankfully. Boldiszar kept a straight face, though I could hear the soft, nervous tapping of his foot against the desk. Thury instructed us to help the wounded now lining the streets and offered a cursory lesson on wound care and CPR. He discussed rebel movements outside of the city. Workers in the villages had taken over factories, standing up to their dictatorial bosses.

Looking at the radio, then me, then at the radio, Boldiszar finally said, "What are we waiting to hear?"

"Just wait."

"With the help of our intelligence operatives in the field," Thury began, "our troops will be aligned with military efforts from the United States."

Boldiszar's eyes perked up. I placed my finger to my lips, hoping to ensure his silence.

"And that wraps up the news," the reporter continued. "But, we have an important message for the Freedom Fighters. First, listen to Eszter. Second, Feri is in the tunnel. And third, light will lead the way."

Boldiszar's lips, thin and pale, parted for a second, then snapped back shut. He examined me from the corner of his eye.

"So you are the Eszter, then? I heard those codes earlier this evening, but I didn't even think it was you …."

"It is. Now will you believe me?"

"I can imagine," Boldiszar said, more to himself than me, "that it would be hard to fight off the Soviets without knowing someone like me to get the U.S. connected to the right people and place the guns in the hands of those who want victory the most … who can be trusted …."

"Exactly, now we really don't have much time. We need to get to work."

"Wait, Eszter …."

"What?"

"Why aren't they giving us any time to fight on our own? We deserve that, at the very least."

"You know we can't win on our own, Boldiszar. There is no way we have enough resources or people to take on the

Soviets. And the U.S. wants to see the Soviets lose as much as we do."

Boldiszar looked down and studied the document on his desk.

"I know," he said quietly. "You're right."

"Can I show you where they are now?"

"Yes, you might as well."

I rushed over to the map. Pins marking demonstration spots and battlegrounds pierced the sprawling city. A red pin sat on the radio building, where the first young deaths of the revolution occurred, and another on Bem Square, where students protested at the feet of József Bem, a hero of the 1848 Hungarian Revolution. Blue pins marked Kossuth Square and the Ministry of Agriculture, all of which had yet to see conflict, as far as I knew. I wondered what offensives the Freedom Fighters planned to launch at those sites. Perhaps Antal wanted me to go on this mission so I could gather some intelligence too. If Laszlo and I monitored these areas, we could send out calls for troops and arms.

I ran my fingers along the map until I found the meeting point with the Americans. It lay nestled far away, miles past Batthyány Square on the other side of the bridge, in the hills of Buda.

"This is where we have to go," I said.

"That is far, almost too far." Boldiszar studied the map.

"I assume they needed somewhere safe."

"But once I'm there," Boldiszar shook his head. "I'm theirs."

I refused to say anything. I started to back away from

him, toward my chair. I had seen many men, even men as compassionate as Boldiszar, turn on me in times like these. The second their doubts took hold of them, I became an unwelcome witness to weakness.

Boldiszar sat back down and began biting his fingernails, his eyebrows furrowing more and more with every nibble. I kept thinking about the boy who warned me I would only have ten minutes with Boldiszar. My time was almost up.

"What do you think I should do, Eszter? Would you follow these orders?"

"Yes, because they're from Radio Free Europe. Do you know what's behind that radio station? Money. Power. The West. That is what Hungary needs for this revolution to succeed."

"You forgot us."

"What do you mean?"

"The revolution needs *us* to succeed."

I reached across the desk and grabbed Boldiszar's hand. "Without people like you, and me, there wouldn't be a revolution. But we need more now."

"This is a huge risk, Eszter."

"Your other risks have paid off, haven't they? They led you to this point."

"Because I have been smart."

"And you trusted the right people," I said.

Boldiszar paused. He stared at me without really seeing me, his eyes glossing over into a daze. He moved his mouth ever so slightly—maybe he was talking himself into, or out of, it.

"I trust you," Boldiszar sighed. "We're in."

*

We crossed the river, abandoning the urban streets of Pest for the quiet hills of Buda. Our meeting point with the Americans was nothing more than a rickety old house, its paint peeling off in random patches to expose rotting, splintering wood. The house sat on top of a steep slope, its contours hardly discernable due to a string of broken streetlights. Darkness surrounded us, and with it, silence. We stared at the house and heard nothing. Of course the Americans would choose a secret meeting place, though I think we expected some indication of activity. Thousands of bureaucrats lived in these Buda hills and wouldn't emerge from their apartments until the fighting ceased. I wondered how many of them peeked through their blinds now, following our every move.

"Will you go first, please?" Boldiszar asked me, pointing his gun toward the house.

I knew I would have to be the adult now. Boldiszar's friends huddled behind us, like children afraid of what their parents would discover in the depths of their closet. They weren't going anywhere. And if I said no to Boldiszar, or showed any hint of doubt, he would probably turn around. So I took a step forward, and it was small.

"What's wrong?" Boldiszar's voice cracked.

"Please," I begged. "I need a second. I don't know these people either."

Boldiszar reached into his pocket and pulled out a

miniature version of the Hungarian flag. The Communist coat of arms had been ripped out of its center, leaving a gaping hole in the cloth.

"It's our flag," he said.

"What do you mean?"

"We're using this as a symbol of our movement. We're making a new Hungary now."

I looked at the tattered flag in his hand, rightfully gutted of its Soviet heart, and thought about how much Boldiszar, and all the young people, deserved to put whatever they wanted into the middle of that flag. I just wasn't sure they knew what belonged there.

I squeezed Boldiszar's hand, and the flag, and nodded.

An elderly man answered the door, staring at us as if we had lost our way. His clothes hung loose on his shoulders and his white hair sprouted in different directions, as if each strand was terrified of its neighbor. I coughed, hoping that would give me a second to think. Maybe we got the wrong house and should consider turning around. The chances this old man could retaliate against us seemed minimal though, so I decided to try our luck.

"We are here from Radio Free Europe," I said.

The old man's eyes widened, but he never said anything. Raising his hand, he summoned us into the house.

"Please," I said. "We cannot stay for long. We are here to meet with the delegation."

He nodded and continued walking back into the house. Following him, Boldiszar clutched his gun at his hip, and I positioned myself right next to him. Boldiszar's gang remained on the porch. I caught their eyes peering through the windows and looked at them longingly. At least out there, they could run if they needed to.

A single light bulb illuminated the hallway. It swayed back and forth, very gently, as we passed it on our journey into the house. Decaying, vomit-colored wallpaper surrounded us, interrupted by wooden doors that led to who knows where. The smell of mold and rusting metal permeated the house, and so did silence.

"Where is everyone?" I asked the old man.

He ignored me. I imagined the Americans greeting us like heroes, or at least colleagues. I wondered what else wouldn't pan out as I imagined.

"Go there," he said, pointing down a stairwell that disappeared into a basement.

Boldiszar and I stopped, our eyes following the path of the man's finger. We said nothing as we adjusted to the darkness before us. Not one ray of light emitted from the basement, and all we could hear was the old man breathing.

"This isn't right," I said to Boldiszar. I grabbed his elbow, prepared to direct him out of the house.

"No," he pushed. "We are already here."

"I really don't think we have the correct address. Who knows who this delusional old man thinks we are?"

"He knows who we are." Boldiszar nodded to him.

"Do you know him?"

"Yes," he whispered. "He's given me messages before. They've always worked."

"Just because he's been reliable in the past, it doesn't mean he will be now."

"You said we need this, Eszter."

"We do."

"Well, then, it's my responsibility to do the hard things."

"Hard, but not stupid. This feels stupid."

Boldiszar adjusted his gun, tightening the strap around his chest. "Did you really think the Americans were going to make this easy for us? Did you think they would be so much better than the Soviets? We just need their weapons. That's what I'm here for."

He stretched his arm out across the hallway, preventing me from walking past him into the basement.

"Do not go past here. I'm going alone."

"I shouldn't let you do that. I don't want anything to …," I started, but I couldn't finish my sentence, and my feet would not allow me to take even one step forward.

Boldiszar hugged me. His body shook against mine, his quaking racing up my spine to my neck.

"Wish me luck."

"You don't need it," I said. "Just get the job done and get back here quickly. Don't make any promises."

"I promise," Boldiszar winked. He kissed my cheek, took in a full breath of air, and started down the stairs.

I watched as the same boy who read to Dora on our living room floor, helped her pull out her first tooth, and gave her the love I never did, disappeared below the surface of the house. I waited at the top of the stairs for him, refusing to join his posse outside. Boldiszar still needed someone to watch over him.

The old man hobbled past me and down the stairs, leaving me alone in the darkness. The fear of something happening to Boldiszar increased as the minutes passed. I started to doubt that U.S. troops stood beneath me, awaiting the arrival of a student-turned-military commander. Why wouldn't they just drop bombs on government buildings? Why would they risk their soldiers' lives on us? Did the chief get some bad intelligence? Was she wrong? Was I wrong? My thoughts spiraled out of control, each question leading to another one with no answer.

I heard something. I didn't quite know what it was, but it didn't sound like anyone talking or negotiating. It sounded more like someone moving heavy boxes, and dropping them on the hard ground.

I had to go after Boldiszar. I needed clarity, and now. I crept down the stairs, testing each piece of wood for signs of creaking before putting my weight down. My heart beat so loudly, it sounded like a giant plodding through my ears. Halfway down the stairs, a gruesome moan stopped my heart altogether. I froze. The sound of coughing—no, the sound of hacking, hacking and gagging—filled the basement. I had no clue where to go next, except down.

When I reached the bottom of the stairs, I saw a faint light sneaking out from beneath a door, revealing a grimy, cluttered basement. From the corner of the room, two eyes caught mine. They peered into me, but didn't move. Was it the old man's? Did something happen to him? I tiptoed over to him, carefully avoiding a chaos of bikes, china plates, and ripped fabric chairs. Instead, I found a deer head mounted to a slab of splintering wood. Its right antler had been hacked off, causing it to lean crookedly against an armoire. It fixed its glazed-over eyes on me, as if I was the empty nothingness of death.

A door started to creak open, sending my body into convulsions of fear and dread. I shuffled over to two shipping boxes and crouched behind them. I stared at the door, willing Boldiszar to walk confidently out. Instead, it opened just enough to reveal three men in Soviet uniforms huddled over something at their feet. One of them stepped to the side. There was a body on the floor. It was Boldiszar. Knees to his chest, eyes shut, hands cuffed, he rocked back and forth, and was he … bleeding?

I didn't know what to do. We had been betrayed—that I knew—but by whom?

The soldiers started kicking Boldiszar. They rammed their boots into the boy's knees and stomped on his shoulders. With every thud, my body rocked with a fresh spasm.

"Tell us where they are. Tell us," one of the Soviets shouted at Boldiszar.

Boldiszar opened his mouth for a second, but instead of words, blood came out of it.

I needed help. I wished I had brought Antal with me—he would think of something. He had a way of distancing himself from chaotic situations, giving advice as if he was in a classroom or doctor's office. But, wait; Antal was the one who told me about this specific meeting location. He handed me the phone to speak to Anya. He took that phone back. He mumbled something inaudibly to the person on the other line, who maybe wasn't even Anya at all, because maybe it was Antal who betrayed us. I thought back to Antal repeating the word "czar" through the delirium of his injuries. It had to be Boldiszar's name he was trying to say. Did I find Antal, beaten to pulp, right after he was tasked with this mission? Did they spring it on him? Or did he know for a long time? And, more importantly, how could he have done this to us?

"You bastard," a soldier yelled at Boldiszar. "We will kill you. You think you deserve to be alive?"

Another soldier lit a cigarette and savored a long, first drag. He stooped down, holding the cigarette to Boldiszar's lips. "Smoke your last little cigarette, boy."

Boldiszar pursed his lips, refusing to part them.

"What? The commander doesn't like to indulge?" the soldier laughed. He jammed the lit end of the cigarette into Boldiszar's lips, sending a distinctive sizzle through the basement, and the faint smell of charred flesh.

Boldiszar's face contorted. I wondered if I should try to save him, and how. I didn't have a weapon. I could scream. Would it be loud enough for his friends to hear me outside? The old man reclined in a chair, watching the soldiers with total indifference. One of the soldiers went over to him, pulled out a wad of money, and placed it in his hand.

"Here's your other half. Thanks for helping us out with him," the soldier spat and shoved the old man out the door.

Some friend of Boldiszar's, he was.

The soldier turned back to Boldiszar, pressing the sole of his boot on Boldiszar's jaw. "You're going to tell us everything we want to know. Who else are you working with? What are your plans? We know you know."

The taller soldier lined up next to Boldiszar, swung his foot back and drove it into Boldiszar's head.

Boldiszar moaned and curled deeper into his chest, "And what if I tell you nothing?"

Pointing a gun toward Boldiszar's stomach, the taller soldier said, "You want the stomach, the neck, or the head? It's your choice."

Boldiszar's eyes crossed each other as he looked at the barrel of the gun.

"I'll never tell you."

Shrinking behind the boxes, I pressed my cheek against their hard edges and wept in silence. The more I thought about it, the more I realized Antal created this situation, and so did I. Antal, the kindly old man who, despite spending eight hours a day working for the government, still had the energy and freedom to sneak out at night to help dissidents like me. He encouraged me to say the West was coming to our aid, and I fell for it. So intent on seeing my dreams come true, I ignored reality.

Laszlo was right. Antal didn't have any real reason to work with us and undo the comfort of his life, unless he was, of course, working against us. And, if the Americans weren't really coming, what would happen to the Freedom Fighters?

I wanted to asphyxiate myself with the guilt clamping down on my chest. I should have done something—scream, charge those soldiers, run upstairs for help—but my entire body turned to sludge. I tried to stand, but I couldn't feel my bones. My mind failed to reason, my lungs wouldn't breathe.

One of the soldiers peeled away from the group and walked toward the boxes. After delivering two more blows to Boldiszar, the others joined their comrade, standing above me. I tried to make my breathing shallow and scarce, willing my heart to slow too, terrified the soldiers would pick up on its frenetic drumming.

"Dmitry," the shorter one said, "what should we do now?"

"If we kill him, our work here is done," Dmitry said.

"But shouldn't we get some information out of him first?" the third soldier chimed in. "If we find out where the other leaders are, we can kill them too."

I felt a tiny drop of his spit land on the back of my neck.

"There's no point, really. We don't need to kill them to win. The tanks are going to roll in soon and obliterate all of them," Dmitry said.

The soldiers started laughing.

"So what are we doing here then? Wasting our bullets on this loser?" the shorter one whined.

"If we don't kill him, our commander will kill us." Dmitry took out his gun. "I'll take care of him. Go upstairs and watch his friends."

Dmitry sighed and slunk back to where Boldiszar twisted on the floor. Towering over him, Dmitry aimed the gun at Boldiszar. Boldiszar uncurled his body, puffing out his chest and straightening his legs, despite his restraints. He looked up into Dmitry's eyes.

I closed my eyes, and I covered my ears. I willed my brain to move faster. I tried to think. I tried to get my legs to carry me to Boldiszar or my voice to shout out and distract the soldier. I even opened my mouth to force out noise, but nothing came out. The only thing I heard was the screaming in my head— *No. No. No.*

*

I woke up, but I couldn't see. I blinked. Black. I blinked again. Still, black. The smell of chalk and ashes rushed into my nose. My mind came back to me, but I wished it hadn't. I realized I was smelling gunpowder, and I had passed out.

I had to find Boldiszar. I had to get help. I had to warn his friends outside, and Laszlo too. I felt cold and dizzy. I hoisted myself up and hobbled out of my hiding place. The blackness began to recede a little, like curtains drawing back on a still dark night. I saw dirty footprints on the floor, leading away from the room where they held Boldiszar. I traced them back to their origins, realizing they weren't made of dirt, but blood. As I crept closer to the room, they got thicker and redder.

I pressed my ear against the door, now shut, and heard nothing. I nudged it open and, peeking in, saw a body lying on the floor. A pool of blood gathered beneath it.

"Boldiszar," I whispered, dropping to my knees next to him. I could hear his breath forcing its way out in strained wheezes. "It's okay. It's me, Eszter."

His eyes moved erratically, looking at, past, and around me. I couldn't tell if he recognized me, or could even see at all.

"I'm here. I'm here," I cried, unable to hold back the tears streaming down my cheeks. I wanted so badly to be in his place. He, of all people, didn't deserve this. I had to fix him. I ripped off my scarf and wrapped it around the gunshot wound in his neck, but his blood overtook it in seconds. "Just hold on for a little longer. I'm going to go get help."

"No …," Boldiszar gasped, trying to take in as much air as possible. "Stay, please."

Oh, God, he knew. He knew it was over. I hated that he knew. It felt like the end of my life too. I would die with him, even if my lungs and heart forced me to continue living.

"It's going to be okay. You're going to be fine," I told him, thinking I could somehow shelter him from his own death. Boldiszar had sheltered Dora from so many things, but most of all, from me. I quit being a mom for … for what? For the only real love my daughter ever knew to die in my arms.

I lay down next to him, pressing my cheek against his, as my tears mixed with his warm blood. I wanted to say something that would soothe him and bring him a final peace. Nothing seemed right. "Don't be scared," I started, hating myself for sounding so cliché. "Think about Dora, and the person she will become, because of you."

"Tell her …," Boldiszar said, his entire body shuddering

at the effort required to finish the sentence. "... that I love her."

"I promise," I sobbed. "I am so proud of you." I kissed him three times—once on the forehead and once on each cheek.

"You have to ...."

"I will take care of her," I held his hand. "I promise that too."

I thought back to the times when I came close to making a connection with Dora, only to pull away for fear she would see through me. She'd see that I, at the core, cared more about myself than my child. I realized I had let Boldiszar parent Dora not because I was so engrossed in the revolution, but because I was too weak to be a mother.

A single tear fell down Boldiszar's cheek, and as it did, I heard boots clunk down the stairs. I grabbed Boldiszar's gun and faced the door.

"Well, well, well, we found you." Dmitry smirked and walked toward me.

I wondered what I looked like, covered in blood and still crying. I didn't care, really. "I've been here the whole time."

"You think that we didn't know that? How stupid could you be?" Dmitry lifted his gun and pointed it at me.

"What happened to the others? His friends?"

"We took care of them," Dmitry laughed.

"Then it's time for someone to take care of you," I said. I felt weightless, like I was floating in a lake on a warm summer day. My mind drifted away from my body. I watched the scene unfold from outside myself, as if I was in the corner of the basement, like that dead deer. I, too, felt nothing—not fear, not sadness, not a burst of adrenaline. I only witnessed the motions of someone following a clear, calculated trajectory.

I saw her unlock the safety on her gun. I saw her stop crying. I saw a flash of wild determination go off in her eyes. I saw her knuckles turn white. I heard a loud, horrifying crack. I watched the soldier fall forward, dead. She didn't even look at him.

She turned the gun on Boldiszar, pointing it at his head. She took a deep breath, muttered something to herself, and fired again.

She didn't think. She ran.

She ran until her feet carried her, of all places, home.

MIKE A KORVINKÖZBŐL
January 24, 1965

Dear Uncle Lanci,

To explain all that happened in recent is immense. I will try, so read strong. First, I awoke on rigorous concrete—the bottommost floor of a room so bright it erased seeing from my eyes. I reminisced that someone had stepped on my head, sat on it, potentially shit on it, and then conceded, *Oh, why not?* and thrust the nearest rock at my skeleton.

The room in front of me appeared to be in the Ministry of Interior. I knew because I had cleansed it before. You can just speculate how enormous my fury blew when I learned that I somehow had landed myself at *work*. And, Uncle Lanci, this room was filled with police!

I instantaneously asked a policeman in the upmost proximity to me what was occurring. These were the first words that spewed from my mouth (after some un-premeditated spewing of other contents).

He went on his knee so our eyes conjoined, took both my arms, and thrust me upward. He managed, by some force of God, to sling me onto a chair.

"You," he said. "You are in trouble. You are at the police station."

A police station inside the ministry. I did not know. How did I end up there, I wondered, which you coincidentally may be pondering as well? I asked the police just that, and he informed me I should snuff it and sit down. They were still calculating the sum of the accusatories against me. I know, Uncle Lanci. I was upmost confused too. I reinstated to him that I did not do one lick of a bad thing when he beckoned his comrade over, Moris. Moris appeared with a petite slice of smile on the outskirts of his mouth.

Usurping me to the proceeding room, Moris never abandoned that petite smile on his face. I realized all of the sudden I had entered the exact room I cleansed as my profession at night time. Naturally, as the leading expert on this very room, I felt compelled to inform Moris of its most compelling components. I enlightened him concerning the delectable cigars perched under the desk beside us. As I gave him some tips, Moris loosened his clamp on my arm. Tenderously, Moris led me into the back door of the room—the one that had always been locked admist my cleaning.

That's when it overcame me that I had aggravated the government, and now they were punishing me for it. So, there I existed, Uncle Lanci, like a petite baby or something that is one hundred percent helpless. We (me and Moris) went down a staircase until we stared at a row of jail capsules. My heart swallowed me, Uncle Lanci. I fostered zero notion of the existence of a prison below where I cleansed. I was utterly jolted by this. Do you reminisce when I described to you the sound from below? The one that projected Andras and I outward from the building in one hundred percent fear? I think I discovered from which those sounds came ... it was this prison basement. But, I thought those fat bureaucrats looked outside of the city for prisons after the revolution. Hurrying my brain through these realizations was ushering me toward insanity. My thoughts revolved at an expedient rate, and I couldn't put a hitch in them. I was a hamster.

Moris and I trumped through the premises, and each tiny capsule constrained someone either whimpering in a corner, flunged on a bed, or producing a massive shit on the petite toilet. I was shitting inside myself, really, enormous lumps of fear. Without saying one single phrase to me, Moris pointed to my future habitat, a capsule at the end, the size of a singular bed.

The capsule bore the appearance of the fairytale prisons. It donned zero windows. I heard a cockroach skidding along the floor. I screeched into Moris' petite ear and begged him why I was in jail, but Moris elected silence. He made that he was drinking alcohol.

I would be one hundred percent baboonish if I didn't admit I drank too far last night. I just harbored nothing as to what I committed that would force me to jail. Have you ever undergone a night like that, Uncle Lanci? Moris smacked closed the metal door of my capsule and left me.

Firstly and naturally, I plumped on my toilet so as to consider the transpiring of events from the night previous. I mustered up some concurrences. I reminisced about encountering a becoming woman named Anika. Oh, Uncle Lanci, she resembled the most delectable *palacsinta* ever consumed. Her height matched that of mine (okay, not so tall) and her voice never existed above an almost-whisper. So I had to bend forth toward her to listen. I desired to become aware of what I uttered to this Anika. Or, best, what she uttered back at me.

Reminiscing atop last night felt like yanking Adrienne's hair out of the drain, with the floods of shampoo kissing it. The more I pulled up, the more ferocious the severity of the situation appeared. I started to realize what I had committed went deeper maybe than I could ever untangle. What could it be, Uncle Lanci?

I plumped onto the ground, the thud happening louder than I predicted. Soreness engulfed certain respectable areas of my body, and I'm ascertaining that one of the ignoble policemen graced me with these pains. The darkness of the capsule sucked on to my eyes, and it took a handful of time to perceive what was transpiring before me.

What I did end down seeing, Uncle Lanci, was more capsules standing across from where I sat. And then, sitting right behind those, more capsules. Did your parents ever institute a half mirror in their bathroom, next to the big, wide mirror? When I was a child, I would sit on the counter and glimpse into the half mirror. If I put the mirrors at the perfect angle, it would result in millions of me. I just continued on and on and on. It was glorious. That sensation usurped me in those cells. I proceeded to envision the millions of unlucky prisoners stationed here before me, who glanced outward and felt as I felt at that junction. They would reside in these capsules for the duration of their existences.

That is the junction when I heard a strange muttering in the stall adjoining to mine. Someone was uttering something along these stanzas:

"They'll do it to you. They did it to me. No trial, nothing. Just stranded here and stranded there."

I said, "Um, hello" (trying to maintain the

highest amount of humility). I asked the voice questions about its origins, peppering it with "who are you," etc. We proceeded to enter into a forthright conversation, which I will try to recreate for you here, Uncle Lanci, with my presiding commentary:

"I'm solely a person in jail who will not get the delivery of justice," the voice said. It belonged to a female, I gesticulated from the supple contours of her tone. I think she reached the age of at least my mom's.

"I am bemuddled by the procedures here," I told her. "Will I survive?"

"I know what I did," the woman voice said. At this point, I pondered the potential that she was unhearing. I also pondered maybe she had surrendered to psychosis.

"I do not know how long I've lived here, but I am certain I will remain," she said.

This was someone who evaporated from her mind how to converse. She stored up her time conversing with herself or the wall. Never underesteem the power of isolation. I persevered to unlock her phrases, so that they could further me toward freedom.

"It's been nine years," her voice took on the most calm warmth that had emitted from her yet. It was so strange, Uncle Lanci. "The day the secret police arrived at my doorstep, I endeavored to become nothing."

I surmised she was telling me her story and she wouldn't halt.

"That's all I aspired for. To melt into the nothingness and become it, without ever seeing the disaster I made. When I did it, when I melted, that's the junction in time they came for me. I lost my weight in resistance when my husband realized I was nothing, and he threw me at them."

I scarcely comprehended the breadth of her words. I understood though, which meant the more improved part of her brain had spoken. When I peppered her as to the explication of why her husband gave her to the police, she informed me he pretended for too long she was someone else. But, in truthfully, she never altered her state. Not even for one hour. He finally saw her for herself, which was nothing. This is what she endeavored, however, if you reminisce. I was following in a circle with her, but she was leading.

I asked her how it is she became a person who created amends with her stay in that petite capsule.

She said, "I am secured when no one else can view me. I belong where no one else lurks. To yield pleasure from others would only be taking because I have furnished them with nothing. I inhabit this planet of capsules, where I can grow nothing. I can be nothing."

Not in one single moment did her husband or daughter approach her in jail, she said. She said the people who accustomed to thinking about her no longer foster her in their heads. They adapted into busy people whose brains contain sparse room for the person underground who has no one, is nothing.

It was that junction that saved me. That junction when I informed myself that I am mandated to reemerge from beneath this surface so that I can be in Adrienne's life. I became aware of who I was, and it determined who I would become. I will become only the most superior deliverer of everything Adrienne wanted. That's precisely what I desired. In my immediacy to commence my life, I peppered the woman voice with questions regarding my fate.

"Are we stationed here forever?" I asked her belovingly.

Drifting toward me was the most brutal inhaling and exhaling that has ever corrupted my ears. She was laughing. But this laugh was composed of one hundred percent vinegar, the honey joy completely depleted from it. I predicted she was trying to elevate herself above me with her laughing. But, she could not deceive me. I knew how hollow her inwards must be.

"No," she said through the horrid effluence of icy, shrill laughter. "You, not forever."

At the very outskirts of hope, I was thrilled she responded to me.

"They will fail to obtain you for a long amount

of time. Those in your capsule revolve in and out. No point in staying."

Oh! Was that the news my petite heart pounded for? Oh, I became so immediately enamored in those words. How is it I placed my trust in this woman, you are wondering, Uncle Lanci? Because, if I didn't, I would have assumed I would sludge away my life in that capsule forever. It would be a life without life. Adrienne would transform her heart into the hardened pavement that is mine. So, I informed the woman voice I elected to believe her.

"You'll remain for a day, maybe twice," she informed me. "Night helps."

"Why does night help?" I inquired.

You cannot even envision what night is for the woman, Uncle Lanci. She informed me that at night, she hears *your* radio station playing from the ground above her.

I realized I was conversing with the person whose maneuverings sent Andras and I flittering away like petite babies from the ministry. At this junction, Uncle Lanci, everything appeared before me, and then it started to choke me. I became powerful and meek simultaneously.

"It's my radio show … the one you listen to," she said.

"Oh, our radio show. We all own it," I told her, instantly taking back in my mind the communist sounds of that genius line.

"No, you mistook me. It was my show," she said.

Isn't that obscure, Uncle Lanci, she could be saying this when I was quite aware of you taking the role of voice on Radio Free Europe?

I informed her of my bemuddlement and that you, Uncle Lanci, were the DJ of Radio Free Europe. Not her. Maybe she would heed the authoritarian notes of my declaration.

She said further: "Your Uncle Lanci is Laszlo Cseke, and he subsumed the role after everything happened, after what I did transported me here. And it transported him to Munich."

She harrumphed. It resembled a thud, but it came from her interior. She is aware of your existence, Uncle Lanci! What a nebulous connection I had formed between myself and you. But, then she said something that incited me into more bemuddlement. She said:

"Laszlo is the reason I am in here."

If you are viewing these words, you may choke back on the piece of sandwich you are undoubtedly devouring. So when you surely hark up a piece of that sandwich, understand I tell you this because now you must tell me what you can. Are you really responsible for this person? Please explain to me what is happening, if you can make that possible.

I wanted to learn more of her, but another word failed to emit from her lips that night, and I soon fell asleep to the tinkering of my brain as it made out all the possibilities, hopes, and horrors my life would now assume. At some junction (my capsule was minus windows, so timing is murky), the guards altered and the new ones skid through. I had sunk asleep, and now they awoke me.

I picked up the guards' noises as they invaded *her* (the woman's) capsule. They conversed with her like she was a petite baby, informing her of their power to compassion her. They'll feed her, but I heard no food happening. They spit on her, because I heard fluid bursting forth from their teeth. At the height of their taunts to her, they asked her what she possessed for them and if they would like it.

They dragged her past my cell, and I closed my eyes pretending I slept so I didn't have to be part of it. They went only three capsules down, and when I peered my head around the corner, I could tell they had entered the cell with the big window. Light flickered through the entrance of the capsule, and I wondered, for one miniscule second, if perhaps they were donning upon her the opportunity to look outside. And then the most worse noises that have ever entered my ear did so, no matter how persistent I had been to stop it the entirety of my life. Belts flipped outward and juggled to the floor. Boots skudded and skin skudded and things skudded ... the sounds of forcefulness. Of horridness.

I heard a wheeze-full sigh, and a large thud encountered the wall. Another thud happened, but with another sound, you withstand … the sound that is similar to boots, after it rains, squishing against a wet floor. The noise proliferated the atmosphere. It labored forth for three minutes like someone trudging through a puddle and belaboring something against the wall simultaneously. I heard clinching, whimpering, wincering, groaning, and another thud.

In plus, there was more horror to the case. The same situation repeated itself. Three times. When I peered down at my legs I realized I had released a piss onto the ground. The guards left without even proliferating any heed to me. I thanked my luck for that. I determined to remain patient. I said zero words and tried with all my efforts to plunge my ears with nothingness.

I succumbed to sleep again with zero awareness of the time or my fate. But I knew the fate of the woman. I had ascertained more sureness of it than anything else. Her horrific life paced betwixt me in my sleep, stalking every bit of my dreams.

I neglected to sleep for long. Someone was talking to me. It was the woman voice. She inquired of me if I enjoyed "the show." I yelled no, and then she exerted that inhaling-exhaling laugh that incited absolute fear within me. She proceeded to say something I could not comprehend at that junction, but I think it was something about these lines: "It's acceptable. I'm unneeding of your condolences."

At this instance, my mind was one hundred

percent bemuddled about what to say. It's like the case when you encounter your mom, for the initial time, naked. I mean her real and evident nakedness, because now you have surpassed the age where her nakedness is an okay extension of you. It's the age when her naked officially becomes the opposite of you. And you want to conceal your eyes away.

I sat there silenceful.

"How is it they could not do this?" the woman voice said. "They anticipate the power it fills them up with. But, the power they imagine is just that. Imagining. Not power, solely masturbation, because their actions have zero effect on me."

She had evolved into someone so accustomed to the raping, that she transformed it into a lesson. That is when you know a person has exceeded to the lowest possible avenue … when they begin to glisten insights into horrifying situations and whittle them down to crystal logic, throwing off into the ocean any emotion. I waited to say a thing that would near rightful. I nimbly asked her how often they commit that crime against her.

"Each day," she said.

"I'm sorry," I said. "But, why are you here? What is it?"

"Murder," she said.

My mouth depleted all its juices from it. I felt scared and curious at the same time.

"How?" I said.

But she dragged her mind away from me instantly, because in total she responded, "It's not about me. It's not the fault of me. It was about him, and I was confused."

Instantaneously, I longed to say something that would distract her from going off into the deepness. I rambled into the explication of Adrienne. You envision, Uncle Lanci, I endured to bring forth something happy toward her, and Adrienne was the initial thing I thought of. I informed her in regards to the sum of Adrienne's imaginations, how monumental her intelligence is, how she incites laughter. I also went forth into Adrienne's sadnesses so the woman voice would comprehend the reality and not subsume I am lying. The woman voice made no moves, no sounds. She listened as I even informed her of my plans for Munich, to discover our mom.

That's when she spoke forth. I'm not sure if she comprehended the political atmosphere askance this capsule, but she informed me that getting to Munich and reemerging in Hungary would be gruelsome. To portend the truth, I think she subsumed correctly with regards to me. I had some interactions with the Freedom Fighters. Okay, I was one of them for a while. And now I have a jail sentence straddled atop me. How would I make it forth after all of these penalties? And how would I reemerge in Hungary? That is the upmost of importance, Uncle Lanci. For Adrienne.

So I hastened my ears to listen to her. That's the junction, Uncle Lanci, she uncovered a tidbit that surprised me so much.

"Well, I have some tricks I am aware of on how to make it to Munich," she said.

Okay, Uncle Lanci, I am most certain and awares of her potential insanity, but I had to pursue the offer she put before me.

"Tell me now," I commanded.

"You need outer help, and there are envoys that go in and out of Hungary to Austria, and you can reach Germany from there," she informed me. "Uncle Lanci, of Radio Free Europe, should announce every week the pinpoints of where these escorts convene."

I wished you had informed me of this potential earlier, but I understand the danger in doing so and why you didn't, Uncle Lanci.

"Where do these pinpoints exist?" I queried.

She said nothing. Before I instigated further inquisitions, the woman voice expired for the evening, muttering goodnight three to four times. My excitement threatened to climb out of my chest and hug the woman voice. When it dragged away from me and I finally calmed downward, I slipped into sleep.

When I awoke, it was to the sound of metal lugging itself through the latches. Before me stooped the most awful man I have ever witnessed. He must have been one of the beasts from yesterday in the woman voice's capsule. He smiled, petitely, and that's when I awared that I would endure something awful.

He clamped my mouth one hundred percent closed with some cloth. He commenced beating me everywhere: Blood. Blood in my nose. My teeth. Oh, the blood in my teeth tasted like a coin smashing about in my mouth. I couldn't produce a single noise in defiance. I was a person incapable of defending myself, I was what they wanted me to be. I understood at that junction what the woman voice meant when she said she was nothing.

He continued pushing my face into the ground until it almost merged completely with the floor of the capsule. My blood insisted on persisting through me, and out of me. I heard another one enter and then utter, "Kick him toward the stomach." But he misstepped, and it was my arm that became the victim. Like a sentinel angel, Moris appeared. When the rest of the harem witnessed Moris standing there, with a cigar limping from his mouth, they absconded from me and evaporated around the corner. I listened to their trots, until finally, their footsteps grew faint and I heard zero noise.

"You're going to leave here now," he said.

"*Gurgle-gurgle*," I replied. What I genuinely longed to utter was "No!" because I needed to acquire more time to ask the woman voice questions. I had to discover how to leave through her channels.

Moris said I just had to stand up and I could go.

But my body said a definite no to lifting itself up. I was hurt. So I could remain!

But when Moris observed me unmoving, he called the guards back to my capsule. They coalesced in front of me, sending dust straight into my mouth.

They said, "Come with us," and I said, "Where am I going?"

The inquiry I placed before them, however, was indication for them to commence beating upon my beloved arms and legs. With each push of force, I was shackled into passivity.

They split my arms between the two of them and dragged me on my back past the woman voice. I fixed my glimpse into hers, attempting to communicate that I am a loyalist to her. Her hair constrained of matted fluffiness with gray gobs of something in it. Her eyes were like extinct diamonds. Her entire body wore the same dirtiness of the cell walls. She looked toward me, and her eyes drooped then squinted and then wailed, bearing her pounds of abuse. I pressed my back to the ground so I could slow the guards as we passed her. They dragged me forth more slowly, and I looked at her. They dragged; I looked. You withstand the picture.

"What," I stooped my voice to a much less strident tone as I was dragged. "What is your name?"

"Please, stop! Stop!" she said, but they continued with their dragging.

Her eyes squinted, her lips vanished, and my

total view was her yellow teeth smushed together as she recited, "Eszter."

Sincerely,
Mike a Korvinközből
Desire is fuelled by all, but fulfillment. —Ernő Osvát

DORA TURJÁN
January 24, 1965

SWEAT SEEPED FROM Dora's forehead and back as she sat in Joszef's office, facing him. Joszef combed his hair, or whatever remained of it, with his stiff, arthritic fingers. He sighed and turned to Dora, "We've had a development. It may come as a shock to you …."

Dora's mind trudged through the possible scenarios. She didn't know if Joszef was aware of her recent theft from his office or her encounter with the police, or both. She tried to speak, but couldn't think of an intelligible response. He had called her in on a Sunday. This couldn't be good.

Joszef studied Dora, his beady eyes doing laps around her face. Dora hoped he didn't notice her right eye twitching or that she couldn't take a deep breath.

"Today I was briefed on the new inmates we've acquired," Joszef said. "Some of them were listening to Radio Free Europe when they were arrested."

"Radio Free Europe?" Dora felt the twitch in her eye spread to her lips, which began to tremble.

"Yes, Dora." Joszef leaned back in his chair. "And, now that we are on high alert for these Uncle Lanci letters, it's a problem when anyone is put in jail who is a Radio Free Europe fan."

Joszef placed a stack of folders on his desk, his eyes returning to Dora. "These folders seem to have been ... disturbed."

"I can look into that, sir." Scarcely allowing herself to breathe in even a modicum of air, Dora put all of her energy into sitting up straight, meeting Joszef's gaze, and soothing her shaking.

"We have more important things to do." Joszef combed through the folders. "As you know, the Uncle Lanci fans use code names."

"Yes, almost every letter is signed with one."

"You also know we can decode these names, if need be."

"Right, though we determined it wasn't worth our time."

"Well, now it is," Joszef smiled, pulling a folder and opening it on his desk. "I did some digging. It just so happens, one of the men in jail writes to Uncle Lanci regularly."

"Who ...?" Dora tried, though failed again, to take a deep breath. "Who is it?"

Joszef turned the folder around for Dora to see. Pointing to a picture tacked to the top corner, he said, "This is Mike a Korvinközből."

Now Dora's breathing stopped all together. Her knees and legs shook so forcefully she heard them, like rain, pitter-pattering on the leather chair.

Dora was staring at a picture of Ferenc. Ferenc was Mike.

Mike was Ferenc. He was smiling, his dark hair combed in a side part—this must have been an old school picture. He looked out at Dora with that gentle expression. It was the one that made Dora feel like she could tell him anything, that it wouldn't be taken out of proportion. Whatever she said would just exist in space without being tied to expectation or pain. In the back of her mind, Dora suspected this was where her conversation with Joszef would lead, her logic guiding her intuition. And as it caught up with her emotions, she knew it made sense. The Mike she grew to know over the years was the playful and kind Ferenc from two nights ago.

Dora heard Joszef's voice surround her, but she didn't want to listen. She didn't want to know what he was going to ask her to do.

"This is a delicate situation, Dora. It's also one that must remain secret. Can you promise that?"

"I can." Dora heard herself speak, but couldn't feel the words coming out of her mouth.

"Good, because Ferenc is going to be released from jail today. They wouldn't normally release him so soon. But, I pulled some strings because I want us to monitor him. I want us to build a case against him and prove to the administration how lethal these Uncle Lanci writers are. So, wherever he goes, you go. He is not to leave your sight."

Dora couldn't believe it. Joszef wanted her to stalk Ferenc, and with the explicit purpose of getting him in trouble. This was the last thing she wanted to do. He didn't deserve that. He was harmless. Dora needed time to find a way out of this.

"I don't understand … isn't this a job for the secret police?"

"Not this one."

"But, how will I do it?"

Dora was not trained for stalking people of interest. She was a bureaucrat who censored mail for a living, behind a desk.

"Before I go further, I need you to agree to this mission," Joszef said.

Dora realized this had to be one of Joszef's personal crusades. He must be doing it to prove his worth at the agency. She noticed that, lately, Joszef hadn't been invited to key strategy meetings. Meanwhile, younger, sharper bureaucrats were on the rise. This was a last ditch effort to succeed, and it was a secret because Joszef didn't know if it would work. Dora had very little choice in the matter. If Joszef was personally tied to the mission, it was hers.

"I …," Dora started. "I agree to the mission."

"Good." A tiny smirk escaped from Joszef's lips. "You're just the right person for this."

"What are my duties under this new … mission?" Dora clutched her pen and notepad, her knuckles turning bone white.

"You are expected to maintain a half-block's distance from Ferenc at all times. If a letter is mailed, you will retrieve it immediately. You can check in to the office once a day, for ten minutes. All other hours you'll spend following him."

"Including after hours?"

"Especially after hours." Joszef took out his wallet and handed twenty-thousand forints to Dora. "This will cover your meals, and then some."

The money must have come from Joszef's personal account. There was no way he would expense this mission. Dora began to fear that she would let Joszef down, risking her position with the postal agency and the protection it provided her. She had worked her whole life to stay safe and accept the sacrifices that such safety demanded. She couldn't put herself or her dad in danger. That was the promise she made long ago. It was the promise Eszter could never keep—or make, for that matter. She would have to do this mission, and do it well.

Dora cleared her throat and sat up straight. "When do I start?"

"He gets out of jail in two hours."

"Which jail is he being held at?"

"You must also promise …," Joszef narrowed his eyes, "that you will not tell anyone where he is."

"I promise."

"He's in a secret prison in the basement of the Ministry of Interior."

Dora recalled the building was once used as a prison, but ever since the revolution, the government had transported all prisoners to camps at Kistarcsa or Tököl.

"There is no longer a prison there, though."

"That's exactly right, Dora," Joszef winked.

*

Two hours later, in the deceptively bright light of the cold afternoon, Dora found herself crouching behind garbage bins outside a restaurant, yards away from the ministry. The smell of food made her queasy as she waited for Ferenc to appear. Every so often the murmurs of restaurant-goers drifted toward Dora, their voices heightening her anxiety.

Dora buried her head in her scarf, trying to cover her ears. Tiny snowflakes melted on her clothes, like little spiders crawling across her body. She was too distracted to realize they had completely overrun her, covering her jacket and amassing in its folds. Soon she'd be wet and shivering.

Dora closed her eyes, and as she did, the eyes from the ministry's basement came into perfect view. Dora tried to convince herself that they belonged to some common criminal being held there for a short period of time, like Ferenc. But Dora had recognized something frighteningly permanent and familiar lingering in their gaze.

Trying to find some comfort, Dora touched the note tucked away in her pocket, a habit she developed years ago. It always calmed her down when she needed it most. Crumpled and softened from wear, Dora held the note to her cheek, breathing in the faint opium scent lingering on it still. Dora could no longer make out its words, but she knew them by heart.

Dearest Dora,
Now that Boldiszar is gone, I think of you constantly.
He loved you like a sister. The day before he was killed,
I talked to him briefly. He said, if anything happened,

*to tell you he loved you. It was a simple request, but I've
had a hard time doing it. Your father said we can have
no communication, but I want Boldiszar to be remembered exactly as he wanted. I'm leaving you this note in
hopes you'll find it. I hope that when you're cold, you'll
reach your hand into your pocket and find comfort in
the memory of my son. He would want that.*
Sincerely,
Agnes

Dora wondered what Boldiszar would think of her
now—would he be proud? Whenever Boldiszar asked her
what she wanted to be, Dora always said she'd work for the
government. She never thought twice about it—that's what
Ivan did, and that's what she would do. Despite his anti-
communist ambitions, Boldiszar never pushed anything on
Dora. He always seemed so pleased when she told him she
wanted to follow in her dad's footsteps. But, now Dora wondered if Boldiszar would suggest she seek a different position—one that didn't involve stalking a seemingly harmless
young man.

Boldiszar thought he would lead an illustrious career as a
politician, though there wouldn't have been a place for him
in Hungary's government now, anyway. The revolution he
fought for died just as quickly as it started. Gerő had been
ousted but once Imre Nagy, the revolution's reluctant leader,
declared Hungary's withdrawal from the Warsaw Pact, the
Soviets moved in. They captured Nagy and replaced him
with his second-in-command, János Kádár.

Kádár complied with Soviet wishes, promising to put an end to the country's counter-revolutionary elements. Authorities rounded up thousands of people, many of whom had only minimal involvement in any sort of underground activities. Regardless, they disappeared with everyone else. Meanwhile, those who aligned themselves with the Soviets, and their distinct wishes, like Ivan, came out ahead.

The thud of a door opening reverberated near Dora. She wished she hadn't heard that thud. She wished she wasn't standing there in the cold and that she hadn't been assigned this job by Joszef. She wished for yesterday, even. Anything would be better than this.

When Dora saw Ferenc emerge from the ministry's large doors, she closed her eyes and made one last wish—that he would be safe. She pressed her back against the wall, hiding in the shadows, and watched him. He put his hat and gloves on at the pace of a stiff old man. He looked hurt, wincing with every movement. He wobbled slowly on the sidewalk, his hands flared out, ready to break a fall. Witnessing Ferenc make his feeble ascent into daylight, an unwelcome sensation overcame Dora—she wanted to hug him.

He increased his pace as he adjusted to navigating the icy sidewalk. Soon, he crossed the street and Dora, running on her toes, lunged to keep up with him. Strangely enough, Ferenc headed straight for the university. He walked through the courtyard and the maze of gothic buildings, then slipped into the back entrance. Sidling through that same door, Dora snuck in behind him.

Dora found herself in a library with high ceilings and

light-yellow bricks that reached up to an expansive skylight. The library was virtually empty, which meant Dora would need to hide quickly before Ferenc saw her. She crouched behind the bookcase opposite Ferenc and watched him search the shelves. A constellation of cuts and bruises spread across his face, and through his scabbing lips, she could see him mouthing the words "Radio Free Europe." She wished he would just stop his obsession with the radio program and lie low for a while. She thought about writing him some sort of anonymous letter warning him to cease interacting with and talking about Radio Free Europe for a few months, until further notice. Knowing Ferenc, that would encourage his obsession even more.

Without warning, his eyes shot up from the spines of the dank and moldy books and peered through the bookshelf. They ran straight into Dora, who jumped back against the bookcase behind her, knocking two books onto the floor. She nodded at Ferenc, as if greeting a stranger, and scurried away.

"Excuse me," Ferenc said, following her. "Wait."

Dora found herself heading toward a dead end.

"Sorry, I think I'm lost," Dora said, looking down as she scooted past Ferenc.

Ferenc stopped her, gently grabbing the crook of her arm. "You look familiar."

Dora studied Ferenc's lips. She almost forgot she had heard him speak that night at the bar. He didn't sound anything like Mike, who she only knew through his broken English. Ferenc's voice had a soft yet masculine quality to it, as if there was something important he had to say, if she would only listen.

"What is your name?" Ferenc asked.

Craving to hear him speak more and rationalizing it as a ripe intelligence-gathering opportunity, Dora conceded. "Anika."

Ferenc's mouth shot open, stretching his entire face into a look of shock. "Anika! That's right. Of course. What are you doing here?"

"What are *you* doing here?"

"Who cares. What happened to you after the police came? I'm sorry I was caught up … I couldn't help …. They took me to jail."

Dora didn't know what to say. She didn't want to talk about the incident with the police, fearful of where that may lead. Instead, she purposefully dropped the book in her hands, hoping it would give her an excuse to pick it up, and leave.

Ferenc beat her to it, stooping to the ground to meet Dora. "You're reading a book on the Russian monarchy? That is completely ridiculous!" He leaned into Dora's forehead and whispered, "Anika, it's all bullshit, you know."

Ferenc winked at Dora, who felt a lightness swirl inside of her.

"I have to go." Dora shot up.

"Wait. Are you hungry?"

"No, I'm not, I'm sorry." Dora hadn't eaten since yesterday, her stomach too unsettled in the morning to permit her breakfast lately. Today she couldn't get down lunch either.

Dora prepared to excuse herself when she noticed how pale Ferenc looked.

"Are you okay?" Dora reached for his arm, helping him up.

"I'm sorry. I'm just … tired."

"*You* need to eat." Dora wanted to help him, and she knew she could justify it to Joszef—if something happened to Ferenc, they wouldn't have anything to show for her work. She led Ferenc outside and bought him some chocolate and water. Dora watched as he regained the color in his cheeks.

"You know, I have been thinking about you." Ferenc peeled back the wrapper on his second bar of chocolate. "I didn't think I would ever see you again."

Dora felt hopeful for a moment. It made her nostalgic. She used to feel it all the time as a child, especially when she was with Boldiszar. Dora took a deep breath and refocused herself. She could not allow her feelings for Ferenc to build. He was a work assignment.

"Well, it looks like you're feeling better." Dora stood up. "I really should go now."

"Wait! I just really need help with one more thing …," Ferenc looked up, his eyes seeming much more focused now.

"What?"

"You have to listen …."

"Listen to what?"

"*Shhhhhhh* … just listen." Ferenc grinned and looked at his watch.

Seconds later, a chorus of pianos burst from the building across from them. With tremendous force, the music careened out the windows, smashing into passersby who, struck and stunned, stopped dead in their tracks. Dora paused too—there had to be at least ten pianos in there playing at the same time, perfectly synced with one another.

"Right on time." Ferenc smiled.

"How did you …?"

"I know the rhythms of this city."

Dora felt a bubble of laughter try to make its way out and, before she could send it back down, she was laughing. She could picture Mike a Korvinközből pulling this ostentatious stunt. Dora was almost certain she remembered him mentioning this very move in one of his letters. They had been sitting across from Liszt Ferenc Academy, one of the most prestigious music schools in the city, and Ferenc knew exactly when the students practiced. He got lucky that today they chose such a bold Bartók composition.

"You know, Anika, there is nothing better than music," Ferenc sighed. "But every day it becomes more impossible to reach the beauty in our lives that these musicians create. It's as if they are taunting us."

Dora didn't know what to say—if she acknowledged the truth in his words, she would be creating an emotional connection with Ferenc. She couldn't allow that. Yet, she couldn't seem to completely ignore Ferenc either. As she watched his eyes search for some form of validation, Dora felt something click shut inside of her. Ferenc wanted much more than Dora would ever be able to give, even if she wasn't pretending to be Anika. Even if she was just herself. He would want to have these deep conversations, just as he did at the bar and in his letters to Uncle Lanci. It wasn't in Dora's nature to engage at that level. She didn't spend her time peeling back the layers of humanity and examining them closely. She never learned how, nor was it something Ivan raised her to value. And though Dora already promised herself she wouldn't risk her career for Ferenc, she felt even more attached to that conviction now.

"I'm sorry," Dora sighed. "This time, I really have to go."

She turned around and left Ferenc before she could see his face fall. She felt it though, just as she felt her emotions assembling back into order, like soldiers falling in line at the command of their captain and, ultimately, state.

Over the next few days, Dora immersed herself in her mission to follow Ferenc. After enough time practically living his life, she nearly forgot about her own. Neglecting even her friendship with Marta or her visits to the cemetery, Dora found herself getting hungry when Ferenc did, tired when Ferenc felt fatigued, and highly focused when he was sharp, quick-moving, and determined to complete a task. She had gotten so far into Ferenc's head that she could anticipate his next move. If he looked agitated at work, she knew he would walk the long way home, to blow off steam. On a good day, he would stop at the store and buy something for Adrienne.

Dora listened more and more to Radio Free Europe by default, too. She witnessed the moments when The Beatles or The Temptations gave Ferenc a certain buoyancy. Under their spell, he would pay the biggest compliments to women, speak the loudest about his future, and work the quickest on his cars.

It was in those moments, Dora understood why rock 'n' roll scared people like Joszef and her dad so much. Radio Free Europe didn't defy the government. Rather, it existed beyond the government. Hungary was the last thing on people's minds when they listened to rock 'n' roll. They forgot about the identities forced on them by the regime. For a few minutes at a time, they were free—weightless and nationless.

Ferenc hadn't mailed any letters yet. She assumed it took him a few days to write his detailed letters, but she needed something soon. At her check-ins with Joszef, he badgered her for a letter or any indication that Ferenc was exhibiting suspicious behavior. Dora discussed Ferenc's daily habit of listening to Radio Free Europe and that he frequented the bars that played rock music, though she knew that wouldn't satisfy Joszef. She considered telling him about Ferenc's fantasy of going to Germany, but she decided to avoid sharing that information. It precluded her current mission, and if Joszef worked hard to determine when those plans surfaced, he would learn Dora withheld information from him, or worse, that she stole from him.

Finally, one night just as she readied herself to walk away from her post, she saw Ferenc turn in an unfamiliar direction. She maintained a steady distance from him, but his footsteps were so far away and so soft that the sound of Dora's own heartbeat overpowered them. She couldn't tell if he stopped, or started, but she made sure to keep her eye on him. Tracing his path, Dora came upon the post office miles from Ferenc's apartment. An expansive window spanned its façade—the perfect lens to watch Ferenc commit the hoped-for deed.

Squatting behind a car and allowing it to cover most of her body, Dora observed Ferenc hand a letter to the employee behind the counter and hurry from the door. This time, she didn't follow him. Waiting until he disappeared, Dora rushed in and presented her badge.

It only took her a minute to find Ferenc's letter on top of the pile labeled "outgoing." Dora's heart beat frantically, shaking her hands and rattling its way to her conscience. She felt almost manic. She hoped Ferenc's letter would exonerate both of them, finally and officially. Maybe jail had hardened Ferenc against his dreams to flee Hungary and find his mom. Dora carefully placed the letter into her pocket, making sure the incongruities in her coat's stitching didn't disturb its descent. She walked to a covered bench nearby.

"You can do this," Dora said to herself. "This is work."

She closed her eyes and ran her fingers along the edges of the envelope, savoring what could very well be the last time she came into contact with one of Ferenc's letters. If he wrote anything subversive, he'd be taken away again, she was certain. She scooted closer to where the streetlight hit the bench and pulled the letter out of her pocket.

Inch by inch, she slid her finger through the envelope's adhesive, trying to keep it intact as much as possible. She unfolded the paper, so thin it hardly made any noise. As she read the beginning of the letter, Dora knew Ferenc confessed enough to send him back to prison. Not only did Ferenc bring up leaving Hungary again, but he found someone who would help him do it—he would probably attempt to communicate with the prisoner again.

As Dora read on, she grew more and more horrified by the strange and disturbed woman in the basement. Soon, she forgot about Ferenc's plight, her mind imagining and re-imagining the poor woman's rape. She knew Hungary had a long history of injustice. She heard once of a boy, Péter Mansfeld, who was taken into custody for his participation in the revolution at age seventeen. He was too young to be executed, so officials waited until he turned eighteen, then, in secret, hanged him. But Dora thought those days were over. She had made peace with the government's past indiscretions, dismissing them as the growing pangs of a system attempting to establish order.

She wondered if the eyes she met that day were those of the forsaken inmate. They floated in front of her now, blinking back at her. Their blank and vacant expression was simply a defense mechanism—the numbness required to survive daily abuse. Dora couldn't keep reading.

She felt both sick and weak. Her hands trembling, she started folding the letter from the bottom up. That's when she saw it—her mom's name. It was just sitting there, on its own, scribbled in the inky, sloppy handwriting of Ferenc.

Dora was certain Ferenc didn't know anyone named Eszter. Maybe one of the prison guards had that name. Maybe Ferenc had found one of his mom's old friends, and her name was Eszter. Either way, Dora felt the familiar, yet unwelcome, tug toward the name. She pried open the letter and read the remaining paragraphs until she came to her mom's name again. "Eszter."

Dora brought the letter close to her eyes and stared at the name, unbelieving, and yet, also knowing who was stuck in that basement.

It was her mom.

ESZTER TURJÁN
January 25, 1965

IT'S HAPPENING AND unhappening in a loop in my mind.
Every night when I go to bed, it happens. When I dream,
it unhappens. And when I wake up, it happens again, until
I'm gone. Because reality is mine, not theirs. This grotesque
horror is just a series of different events stacked up on top of
one other, but none of them are real. Or some of them are
real, but I say which ones.

Sometimes, when I look out the window, I see people.
This window is actually not in my cell—it's far away in the
head officer's cell. He spends his own time with me when he
says it's time. Time is time, but to me, time is nothing more
than the reality of others. For me, time is in the past when
I was Dora's mom, even though I wasn't really there. These
stupid soldiers don't realize that. They think I am suffering
in here. They look at me like they can do anything to me
because I am miserable anyway, but I am not in pain when I
go back, which I do whenever I want.

Right now, I am putting Dora to bed after reading to her

because she asked me to do it, and though she is a teenager, I'm so grateful that she still wants to spend time with her mom in this affectionate way, like she's a kid. I wonder if she does it just for me—to let me think she will always be my baby because she knows how abandoned I would feel otherwise—and I love her for that. And I smell her hair, which smells delicious, because I infused her shampoo with cherries I picked from my friend's garden. I'm just crafty like that. All of Dora's friends come over to our apartment to hang out, so they can talk to me about their crushes and school and the fights they're in with their friends. And I am totally fine with being that type of mom because I am so generous, and Dora's friends distract me from the goals I never reached because who wants to pursue goals when you're happy, anyway? And then I just look at Dora and think about who she has become because of me, and the time I devoted to her, and I get fulfillment from that. They say the greatest gift is being a mother, and in that moment, I know it is.

It's that easy. It's that easy to live in that time even though the time that most people know is different. Sometimes when they are hurting me, the way they do—the hurt that goes deep inside—I travel to distance centuries and realms. I imagine I'm Cleopatra or Aphrodite, and that makes me laugh. That makes them hurt me even more. Sometimes I am in a place where no time exists, only blackness, which is on the inside of my eyes, even though they force me to keep them open. I think they like my eyes, or they like to see the pain in them, because when I close them they yell and shout, and once an officer stooped over me and propped open my eyes with his fingers. That's how I know eyes are important to them, so I go to other times with my eyes open.

I found a little rat, and I named him Antal. The rat is sick, like Antal is old, and he sits and stares like he is waiting for me to forgive him, but forgiveness isn't something I can give out. You can't forgive when you haven't been forgiven yourself.

"I'm not scared," I tell the rat, because I could get any of its diseases and it wouldn't matter because I'll never leave this cell and it will never leave me. Even if I crawl out of this hole, I will still be in it. "I know what you did," I tell the rat, who is Antal. I hate Antal. I found out Gerő's men almost killed him in the alley that day I found him bleeding. They told him if he didn't turn Boldiszar in, they'd go after him and his family. I know Antal, and I know he didn't think twice, even though he knew Boldiszar's connection to my Dora. Then he used me. I was just a casualty along the way. I heard Antal had never been working for us in the first place. He had sided with the Soviets from day one.

I know it's true. I'm going for his neck, and he bites me and claws me, but I don't care. I'm piercing every single fingernail through him. The rat starts bleeding. As the holes open wider, my hands get slippery. The wounds become serrated as Antal groans from the pain. I don't understand why, why he did this, because I never, ever believe in evil even though it is around me and within me. Laszlo believed in evil because Laszlo sees it like it's a different dimension that I don't live in. I miss Laszlo and I still love Laszlo, but I hate

Laszlo too, maybe more than I hate Antal. He didn't save me and he could have tried to use his connections. But what about Ivan? Well, not like I expected him to even try. He would have found out that I picked up that gun, and I shot that Soviet soldier, and I shot Boldiszar.

I can't travel to the place where Boldiszar is still alive, because I believe in death, so I know that I will never be forgiven for Boldiszar's murder. Dora will never forgive me, if she even knows that Boldiszar is dead—if she is still thinking and seeing and being, like she was when I was taken away.

They say things are moving here, but I've been here and I'm usually gone, and things are happening and unhappening always, so where are things going? I don't know, but I know that I get to say what is, and what isn't, and I hear something … I do. Is it her? Is it her? Yes, it is—it's Dora and she just got home from school, and she is crying because she just failed a math quiz, and I have cookies ready for her, and all night to tutor her. She looks at me with those probing, dark eyes. I feel like I could just jump into them and keep sinking and sinking, forever. And she tells me she loves me and I say, "I love you too." I will always love her. She is my daughter.

DORA TURJÁN
January 25, 1965

DORA FELT COMPLETE despair, as if she had reached the end of a world she trusted to be round. Standing on the edge of a cliff that dropped into a dark expanse, Dora wanted nothing more than to turn around and go back, but she knew she'd never be able to. Dora *had* recognized those eyes in the basement. Distantly, she knew them, and now she had proof. No, they were not Boldiszar's—he was dead, and that much she knew. Their catlike shape, the trace of beauty Dora now realized she saw around their edges, was unique to Eszter. They were her mom's.

"Mom." The word felt so clunky as it moved through her brain, making her uncomfortable and even a little sick, especially when she remembered there was not one glimmer of recognition in those eyes. Their owner looked out at a complete stranger, who was her daughter.

How could Dora continue standing or walking on the street, and then leave, go to sleep, wake up, eat or do anything, when another gruesome and bruised world existed beside hers? In fact, it existed below her. Beneath her feet, her mom suffered a terrifying existence.

Dora had long suspected Eszter committed some sort of murder. She also long suspected her mom had been imprisoned—the fate of many arrested during the revolution. She would never forget the night they came for Eszter.

*

The revolution exploded outside, and Dora was inside studying for a math test when a thunderous knock rattled the front door. Thinking maybe, somehow, it was Boldiszar, Dora ran out of her room. She knew something was wrong when Ivan didn't acknowledge her and marched straight for the door. Watching her dad drew Dora into a panic, making her heart pound hard, like it was trying to choke her.

"It's the police," Ivan spat, staring straight at Eszter.

"I'll hide," Eszter whimpered. "Don't tell them I'm here."

Dora felt like she might stop breathing. "Can't we just not answer the door?"

"Dora, get out of here," Ivan snarled.

It felt like someone was stomping on Dora's chest, pressing all the air out of her. When she didn't move, Ivan scooped her up and sat her down in the kitchen. "Do not say a word."

"Please, don't let them take her," Dora cried, clutching her dad's hands.

"I'll try my best," Ivan said, getting Dora a glass of water. "Drink this and take deep breaths. They won't be here for long." Ivan stomped off, leaving Dora trembling and sobbing.

A thick, red velvet curtain separated the kitchen and hallway, and Dora, terrified yet needing to know every single detail, peeked out through it. She watched as Ivan combed his hair to the side five times, straightened his shirt, and opened the door. Three policemen, in thick coats buttoned to their necks and rifles strapped across their chests, stood in front of Ivan.

"Is this the home of Eszter Turján?" one of them asked.

"It is," Ivan confirmed.

"We are requesting to see her. Now."

"Wait just one moment." Ivan closed the door and hissed at the armoire in the hallway, "What did you do now?"

"I'm not here," Eszter said, her panic muffled by the armoire's thick wood.

Before her dad could respond, the police kicked open the door, sending Ivan flying back against the wall. The police took one look at the armoire, grabbed the top of it, and slammed it to the ground. Eszter trembled, her back and palms pressed against the wall, as if she could just blend in with the dark blue walls.

"Get her to the floor," one of the officers shouted.

Ivan positioned himself between Eszter and the officers. "No, please, let's all sit down like adults and talk about this."

"We know who you are, sir," an officer said. "We have a message from our superiors that it would be best for you, and your daughter, if you just stay out of this."

At the mention of Dora, Ivan completely shrank, fixing his eyes on the floor. An officer nudged him out of the way, and Ivan slunk to the corner of the hallway, not looking up once.

They moved in on Eszter, grabbing her and wrestling her to the ground. One of them straddled her while the other two stood over her pointing guns at her back. Pinned, with her belly to the floor, Eszter tried to break free, flailing like a tortured mermaid. Dora dropped to the floor too, somehow finding comfort in being at eye-level with her mom. She remembered thinking that, despite her anguish, Eszter looked beautiful. Her thick brown hair, normally in a taut bun, flowed wildly over her shoulders. Her skin still had just the right balance of tan and white. It stretched over her small nose and tall cheekbones, making a perfect stop at her eyes, which curved up at the corners. She seemed so indestructible.

Maybe she was. For a moment, Eszter's arms shot out from under her, pushing her torso off the floor. It looked like she might buck the officer off her back when a baton struck her hand. Dora heard the smack of flesh. She felt the burning pain on her own hand and Eszter's screaming inside her head, though Eszter didn't make a sound.

Eszter clenched her teeth and turned her head in Dora's direction. When their eyes met, Eszter stopped trying to wriggle free, though neither of them really showed any signs of recognition. No one mouthed "I love you," or nodded or cried. Wide-eyed, and in shock, they just looked into each other's eyes as if trying to find the answer to a question they didn't know how to ask.

Dora wanted to say something that would somehow

encapsulate the anger and love she felt all at the same time. Dora hated her mom for doing this, whatever it was—putting herself in a place where she could get arrested and the police could be standing in their living room ready to inflict something terrible on her and their family. But Dora also desperately felt the urge to run out and hug her mom. She wanted to cling to her, smell her hair, and run her fingers along her stubbly legs, like she did when she was little. She wanted Eszter to know that Dora needed her, no matter what, even if Eszter was gone most of the time. Knowing her mom would come home, at some point, had been enough for Dora. She hated Eszter for not instinctively knowing that. Staying in Dora's life should have been her top priority.

Without warning, Eszter's eyes disappeared. In jarring thuds, Dora heard them drag her mom across the floor. The terrible sounds of struggle—scuffling, grunting, a body slamming into a doorpost—echoed in the kitchen, until the door slammed and silence, mixed with Ivan's dry, gasping sobs, took its place.

Dora ran to her bed and pressed her head into her pillow. She cried so hard that her entire body convulsed, tossing her back and forth, as tears poured down and around her. She didn't stop crying for hours, until pain shot through her temples every time she tried to let out another tear. Dora thought it couldn't get any worse.

Now, years later, she wondered if it just had. Her mom had been taken away to a secret prison where she was continuously and mercilessly raped. Dora would never wish that upon anyone, let alone her mom.

MIKE A KORVINKÖZBŐL
February 9, 1965

Dear Uncle Lanci,

There's more to tell you now and I'm so overwhelmed, even though I have rolls of paper ready to go for your letter! My hand endures shakes as I write this. If anyone should happen upon this letter, besides you—which is a great chance—I'm going to not survive. They'll take me away instantaneously. I heard stories about people who underwent interrogations for letters to you, and I take one hundred percent culpability that by writing this letter now, I may become one of those people. But to keep this inward would be to live a different life, and I'm so bored at pretending.

I have just one wish—the wish that you would write me. Instruct me on what to do. Help me get out of Hungary. I am just as desperate as I was before. The more far I get from that basement, the more sound my mind will become. Until then, I am continuously beckoned back to Eszter and continuously launched into more danger. I am waiting for your reply so I can flee all of this.

My life has been plagued by mostly evil in the past weeks. Eszter appears in my dreams, then evaporates and appears in a repeated fashion. The sounds I recollect are one hundred percent burdensome. The grunts and slaps, the tangles and wails, the pleading and groaning are the sounds of Eszter losing. My nightmares of her become daymares, and I walk around living all that's occurring to her.

Imagine having to tell my family of these events. It was awful, Uncle Lanci. It was mere hours after I returned home from jail and all were asleep in the apartment. Neither Adrienne nor my father harbored awareness of my return. I went to sleep with Adrienne so that I could heed her breathing and I could witness her dance with her dreams. I always do that so I can take dreams, but not for my own. I take them from her so that I can give them backward to her. Not when she is sleeping, but when she is awake.

When we awoke, we rambled into the kitchen where our father sat and I explained in vague terms the actual events that transposed. I informed Adrienne and my father of my imprisonment. My father's reaction proved more vague than I would have ever guessed. Adrienne uttered not much. She just stood in place, staring at Father, who munched his beans that dripped secretly out the side of his mouth. I mentally side-noted to approach him later concerning this particular topic rather than detail it in Adrienne's presence.

Of course, Adrienne did the honor of offensing Father wholeheartedly. "Father, why does it make no impact on you if Mike enters jail? Should I enter jail and you will not care?" she asked.

I had a proud moment as Adrienne spoke. She assembled an utter perseverance to determine how events work and the consequences that follow them. Our father swallowed the entire mouthful of beans he had been nurturing and scratched his napkin atop his face. We could hear his little hairs jarring the napkin like sandsheets. His lips lunged for another bite. And another bite. He failed to glance me in the eye, but he knew Adrienne would bore into him without relenting.

"Inhabiting jail for a single night could be beneficiary to Mike," he said. "A grown man should get slaps on the hand a few times just to remember who is hitting him. He should know he needs to abide to the rules. And, Adrienne, if the plays you run at these KISZ meetings barrel on in full force, you may be exposed to what it feels like to disobey, too."

In that instance, I wanted to slap, stab, I don't even know what, to my father. Inspiring fear in Adrienne inspired vomit in me. I wanted to open my mouth far greater than anyone could see and release the context of my stomach all over my father.

Adrienne dissolved, and I could perceive what transpired within her. She is just learning how words can stop up tears or, to the worse, make them rage.

"Adrienne." I stepped in front of my father to obstruct his plans to deconstruct Adrienne. "Soon, I will be going to Munich and avoiding all the rules that people like our father strive to live beneath. It is no use in fighting him. Even if he is just requiting these rules for our own safety, it's not who I am or who you are to just accept and commence forward."

You see, Uncle Lanci, that's why you're so important to my efforts. I have my sister to impress upon and doing that will mean so much to her life, as you can tell. I want Adrienne to learn that what she desires does not constitute disobedience. It's okay. It's for humans. Adrienne quelled, swiveled, and then stared at me in an endearing but honestly confounded manner. It always flees my mind that she is nearing the age of achieving full adulthood.

"Mike," she said to me, looking me straight in the barrel of my arteries, "I know you are striving to accomplish a nearly impossible task. I am capable of comprehending how near insanity it is to flee this country and then to enter the West."

Father huffed a big chunk of beans that flew out of his mouth and rested directly on my sleeve.

"You are imagining pure illusion!" Father

grumbled through the mashed up beans in his mouth. "Stop convincing Adrienne to accept a part in it. The moment I believe that you will succeed is the moment when your mom is standing here before me."

I had a storage unit full of words to launch forth toward my father, but I am grown now to recognize the anger within me needs a home, not an outlet. It resides inside me and propels me forward toward the promises I make to myself and to Adrienne. I will make sure she is aware that I will make things one hundred percent for her. She will not have to persist in a world that is only seventy or sixty percent, like I did my entire existence. She will feel everything good and complete. I do not mind I am barred from that if I can accomplish this for my petite sister.

I reaffirmed Adrienne when I said, "There is no necessity to discuss this matter any further. I decided my mind, and I will be glued to what I believe. I will find our mom."

Munich is where you reside, Uncle Lanci, and I know that your connections can provide aid to me in this venture of mine to discover my mom. And, Uncle Lanci, please enlighten me how you know this Eszter. Is she correct that you announce pinpoints to flee Hungary on the radio? I implore you to tell me all you know on these topics. Will you aid me escaping Hungary?

I'll permit you some time to ponder my request.

It's something that stalls my happiness every day, to know that your eyes may never read this. In fact, almost every second I can't pardon the unhappy anxiety cresting on my mind.

I think I can manage to find her too, with all the intelligence I have collected on my mom. I read about her on a daily basis. My father is unaware of the espionage that has been transpiring underneath his own roof. In the back corner of his closet resides my mom's diary. She left it, along with everything else, when she fleed from here. My favorite part is when she talks in reference to how she had to rescue me from the backyard where I engaged in football with my friends, because I had lost and was leveled to sorrow. She picked me up from the yard and carried me inside. She had donned her favorite shirt that night and my secretions had destroyed it one hundred percent. She said it didn't matter to her, though, because she would continue to don it as a testament to the necessity of her presence in my life. (I do not know what is sadder, Uncle Lanci—a mom who needs a reminder of her loyalty to her son, or a mom who would disregard the shirt in the trash.)

My mom suffered from love amnesia. Things that would be loved, or memories that the mind should crave, she would forget with no hesitating unless she remembered to install evidence of its existence (the shirt). That's why Mom would trot around town in clothes that bore copious gobs of tears or snot exertions. No one knew why she would wear such abhorrable shirts. In that way, my mom kept us to herself. She became the solitary landlord of her love for us. But it couldn't stop her from searching for more trinkets of love, anywhere she could.

She took up violin because it was her mom's, and our grandmom had died. She carried the violin with her in all places. Even when we went to the opera! At various times, she'd awaken me in the middle of the night and force me to accompany her to Liszt Ferenc's music academy to sit in a room, solitary, with the violin.

When I emitted tears for being too tired to take part in her exuberant manifestations, she would glare at me like I was preventing the world's offerings from her. Her eyes quieted my tears, but made me so scared that I would not be able to sustain her. By three in the morning, I'd fall asleep on the floor of the music school, my drool crafting a neat pool at the bottom of my arm. Mom would pick me up and say she was sorry. When I woke in the morning, I would fabricate that the night previous never had a stake in reality. At breakfast, Mom nudged me a little and delivered me a cup of coffee as she realized how tired she had forced her petite son to become.

Soon, Adrienne, only five, became aware of the secret nights at the academy. It was impossible to pass through anything with her. But Mom possessed her time with Adrienne too. Once, when Mom took

Adrienne and I to the Széchenyi baths, she asked us both if we would like to participate in the whirlpool taking place. I plunged immediately into the center of the pool to demonstrate my bravado. Adrienne looked fierce, then constipated. I thought she would need to go toward the toilet, but then tears exuberated from her eyes. Mom took Adrienne's hand and I thought she would convince her join me in the divine whirlpool. Instead they escaped back into the baths. Fine, I calculated, I did not mind. I would be on my own and push forward into the whirlpool. After twirling around with men twice my size and with their fat globbing onto me like nodes of peanut butter, I ventured into the baths to discover Adrienne and my mom.

Like two sisters, they luxuriated in a petite room that shot forth from the main one. Adrienne had her hands in my mom's, and my mom played at examining them, then continued forth in painting them with an imagined nail polish. Flames of jealousy erupted before me. (I realize, now, Uncle Lanci, they were completely petite of me to even possess. I thought since I was my mom's initial born that I should fill her to capacity.) But there Adrienne perched like a queen, and my mom served her so. They laughed and then Adrienne took her turn painting my mom's nails with the imagined polish. I wondered how frequently those interactions took place. That's when I realized a world existed beyond me, one that was reserved just for Adrienne and Mom, and I have zero accessibility to it. And it's that world I desire more than anything to bestow upon Adrienne. If I could just show her that it is still existent, just walking around in another country, then she could believe in it again.

When I later appeared at the Ministry of Interior for my cleansing duties, I felt the fear I endured while pent in its confines. All the memories that sifted through my forgetfulness remerged in my consciousness. Andras laughed at me when I started emitting tears. It forwarded me to anger since he escaped seeing what I saw.

I persevered hard to contain the sum of my knowledge on Eszter within me. Of course, I indulged Andras in the other gorrisome details of my imprisonment, like getting beaten upon. Andras endured an hour in prison that night, so he listened with such enthusiasm. I couldn't even detect his broom meeting the floor while I persisted my mind so hard to decline the image of Eszter below us crying. I know she has become mixed up, Uncle Lanci, because she had to.

I appreciated when your music, Uncle Lanci, beamed on, precisionly "The Sound of Silence," which indulged shivers in me. Do you feel mourned for Eszter in the slightest? She said this was her radio station. I experienced mourning while listening to your music, and anger avenged me for what I heard occur to her. Andras peered at me again and asked if my experience in prison really was that immense. He is a firm friend, after all. He would not permit me real pain without assisting me to overcome them.

I burst into an explanation of Eszter. Holding that in was more perilful to me than I knew. I began to tell him the sum of everything, especially regarding how Eszter succumbed to the upmost horror I ever heard. Andras, who I knew would maintain our friendship most loyally, sat straight forward and made his back extremely long. For a many number of minutes, Andras uttered zero words and glanced at me peculiarly like I was sideways. I thought for a second I had incited resignation in him. Or worse, anger.

"Mike," he said, and I could see these little invisible beams of sadness fleeing from his eyes, "Did you know that once I viewed what you heard? I viewed rape and I did zero about it. I witnessed it but refused to step into action."

"That must have invoked pain in you," I said.

"Is there anything we can achieve for Eszter?" he asked. "We must go down to assist her. *We must.*"

I was shocked that my friend would be so forceful about this. But, he kept looking downward, as if he knew all along that something was there. And now that it was confirmed, he would never unfixate from it. I doubted we could venture down there with the sparse keys I owned, not to mention the foreboding guards.

But then I reminisced on Adrienne's eyes, her petite, squeaky voice and all that she hoped for when I promised I would flee to Munich. I also understood this was probably what Eszter wanted, or at least what the sane division of her wanted. She desired for me to come back. That's why she uttered the escape story.

Andras persevered studying the bottommost portions of the office. Immensely, Andras finally pointed to the vent below us. He gave me that look … you know, the one in the movies when both characters know what the other one is pondering. It was that look and we knew: that's how to get to Eszter.

We used a screwdriver in our pockets to wrest open the latch. Andras attached a rope to me that he retrieved from the maintenance closet. If Andras had not existed during this plan, I have heavy doubts I would have succeeded in my descent. It is so luxurious to have friends who maintain smarter wits than you. This whole ordeal was not thrilling to me, but so burdensome. Especially when I spied Andras' downcast eyes as I spiraled down the shaft. He looked like a little raccoon in the night.

Once black subsumed my vision, I spidered in a horizontal trajectory forward. I had to go through a mess of metal tunnels. That's the junction when my head attached to something hard. I got very proximal to the hard thing and realized it was a door. And it was cemented. My head sinking with my heart, I

moved myself backward when some delicious thinking told me I should just try my keys on these doors
anyway. Miraculously, they just rippled through the
lock and opened it! I commenced spidering through
the tunnel, opening every door that blocked me with
the same key. Finally, I peered a long tunnel, and
at the end of it was a light. I spidered to it, and it
turned about to be a row of air vents. Through them
were rows of horrendous capsules.

Inside some, prisoners slumbered in balls embracing their knees. Like petite, stricken rodents, they
tried to comfort themselves with their own bodies.
Others spread out in their cots as if asking someone
to come and occupy them and pinch them away to
another place for the evening. But as I kept spidering, I noticed more and more prisoners awoken. I
assembled the fantasy that they were longing for the
music we played every Thursday.

I passed admist the lone guard as he leaned over
his chair absorbed by whatever materials he was pursuing. It resembled the naked women portfolios I
indulge in at times. At first, I resonated zero noise,
but then my knee ripped a weak point in the metal
and a loud creaking emitted throughout the capsules. I made a screech—my very first one I had ever
made in my quest to find Eszter—and the guard's
head shot up from his reading material.

The guard pounced up and down the capsules,
and I heard him grunt and mutter to himself as he

walked by the vent I peered out from. It would be no usefulness leaping backward and making noise. I decided to wait until the guard rested again.

I still had one more capsule to look into, and I was sure it was Eszter's. So, in miniscule, I would not halt my quest. I heard a petite talking sound from that area too. I failed to formulate what she said precisely, but I thought I heard it singing. So with zero percent doubt in my mind, I decided that was Eszter's ghostful voice wafting through the vent. Going forth, I soon discovered her. She sagged against the cornermost wall, her hair a nest of gray sticking to her head and the wall behind her. Her eyes flashed wide as she jostled with something in her hands. She also sung to the thing in her hand, in a petite voice, sometimes even speaking with it. It appeared dead and gray. I comprehended, then, it was a rat! A dead rat!

She embraced the thing and commenced lunging it in fits against the wall. She threw it, and it'd fall without life atop the ground. She embraced it up and repeated the same process over and over. She sang a range of curses, her voice expanding to more loudness. Like a wild person, she screamed at the rat until she disassembled its insides against the wall. Next, she paraded her wrists into the wall, her hands smushing against the bricks. She was bloody from it all, and I couldn't tell if its origins were her or the rat.

When she terminated her anger, she picked up the rat again and pressured it against her chin. I could not comprehend her words, but she was talking with love. In that moment she appeared without age. She was in her own universe where she sets the rules. She could have been three or twenty-three or even a hundred and three. Innocence is determined, I believe, as the one hundred percent belief in everything. That's exactly how Eszter looked. But knowing who she was, and what she had been through, this was all very disgusting. She was inciting momentous horror within me.

But I ventured down there to conclude a job. So pursuing my lips against the vent I whispered, "Eszter ...." Just her body absorbed her name, and she put herself into a less tight wad around the petite rat. I think I was calling her back to the world of people aware.

She stood up like a snail, but what occurred next was the opposite that. With one hundred percent forcefulness, she lunged herself at the vent and began banging on it and screaming. I was in there hiding, but she knew I was there. She persisted screaming, her bloody fingers poking through the holes in the vent.

I heard her hiss, "Uncle Lanci, is that you?" She said your name an *ad nauseam* number of times, which utterly muddles me, Uncle Lanci. Why is this woman who gropes beneath the Ministry of Interior so possessed with a DJ of a rock music program? As far as I am cornered, you have quite a high level of explaining to do, and I am waiting for it.

Eszter continuously tried her extreme hardest to dislodge me from the shaft. Not one guard rushed to her aid (as normal). Soon her screams dampened. She now whispered your *real* name, Uncle Lanci, which was more chilly than her screaming.

"Laszlo Cseke, Laszlo Cseke," she said. She is calling you by your other name, Uncle Lanci. Should I call you that? I can't say I like it very much ….

Anyway, I snapped my eyes down. I wanted to make pretend this was not occurring. That's when I heard a soft tinkering. The sound of porcelain hitting metal regurgitated toward me. I opened my eyes to see Eszter aspiring to bite forth into the shaft. Perhaps she mistook herself to be the rat she embraced to breasts just a few minutes prior.

I am a sensitive being, and I could no longer refuse my soul the desire to simply comfort Eszter. I commenced speaking to her. Aware the fault resided within me that she began this mania anyway, I tried my best to flex my voice to softness. I pretended to be you. I told her she would be okay. I said that one day upcoming she would be able to flee this capsule and go somewhere, anywhere, she imagined to go. She commenced conversing with me, but you.

Addressing me by Uncle Lanci, Laszlo, and sometimes Mr. Cseke, she inquired why I left her with nothing when she endowed on you so much. I attempted to fabricate an answer, but I am a miniscule liar. All I could say was "I'm sorry," which I sincerest was. She posited her mouth up next to the vent and I could even detect her breath from the tiny space I beheld. No way would I unravel my identity to Eszter in that instance. I squinted with my brain the very hardest I could imagine to understand her. She uttered something along these lines:

"You say you're sorry, then get me out of here. Come back into the country. Proceed to get me and we can leave on this envoy together."

Oh, how I was foaming with desire to leap forth and confirm her will to leave on the envoy. Inside me, a voice instructed me to decline Eszter on this. *Wait, wait, wait*, it said. I agreed with it, from my fear or rationale, I cannot say.

I harbored zero ideas of how to evict myself from that situation though. With Eszter continuously submerging her face into the vent, I just did not know how to send her away. I mumbled forth again my sincerest sorries. I really was, for disturbing her like that. I uttered the phrase so many times, my throat became tense-filled. By the tenth "I am sorry," Eszter backed from the vent and settled again on her bed. Forgetful of the rat, she lay by herself now. Still mustering words, she remained in conversation, though I'm not one hundred percent positive with who. Maybe you, Uncle Lanci?

I backward scooted away from her. I propelled my butt across the shaft, the tunnels, and the doors and upward toward Andras. I solely desired to escape from all this situation promptly. To be forthright, Uncle Lanci, I am not certain if I will muster the courage again to return to the capsule where Eszter resides. Her demeanor is more frightening than I could ever possibly explain to you. So, if you would please spare me from this pain of finding her and simply tell me how to get on these envoys, I would give you all the money even I have saved and more. I aggressively wait your reply to me as if it was the crux that connected me to better parts of myself. It's the notion that soon I will be gone from this place in a world of my deciding! Please adhere to my request soon.

If you can't respond in earnest to my letters as I wish you would, could you simply at least play "She Loves You." I am striving to see sweet Anika again. I'm make believing she is here, with me now, and I want to dance gently with her.

Sincerely,
Mike a Korvinközből
Desire is fuelled by all, but fulfillment. —Ernő Osvát

DORA TURJÁN
February 11, 1965

DETACHED AND DISORIENTED, Dora wandered through the night, a habit she had recently developed as her mind refused, more and more, to rest. She always kept Mike's letters with her buried deep in her pocket—she had yet to hand them over to Joszef. Amazed at the speed of the city surrounding her, Dora felt out of sync with its energy—its trams, buses, and people—in perpetual motion. But the crunching of her feet against the hard, crusty snow eased Dora's mind, allowing her thoughts to focus on the perfunctory rhythm of her walking, and nothing more. That is, until she heard her name being called out, cutting through that particularly cold night. Turning around, she saw her father, out of breath and sweating.

Ivan cursed as he stepped into a berm of warm dog poop lining the sidewalk. "I'm glad I found you. I need to tell you something," he said as he scraped his boot against the battered curb.

Watching him, Dora thought about how it seemed

people were always trying to scrape something off of themselves in this city. When they stepped outside, they peeled back their identities to become stern and subdued citizens. The second they entered the underground clubs, they tore off their public selves, discarding them like raggedy, old jackets, becoming rowdy, impatient, and in sync with the rock music. Dora wondered, through all of these layers, did she even know who she was? Or anyone else, for that matter?

Ivan gave up on cleaning his shoe and sighed, defeated. "We have to talk about your mom."

"Mom …?" Her dad had just brought up Eszter for the first time in nine years. She couldn't believe it. Did he know Dora had just learned about Eszter? No, he wouldn't … he couldn't …. Dora lost her balance on the snow. She fell into Ivan, grabbing his arms to save her from crashing onto the sidewalk.

"I thought you should know something." Ivan helped Dora up and pulled her cap down around her ears.

"You told me we couldn't have anything to do with her," Dora said. Ivan made her promise that the day after they took Eszter away, saying she committed a crime for the Freedom Fighters so egregious it put Dora and Ivan in grave danger. They couldn't associate with her anymore, not with the regime rounding up anyone involved in the revolution, throwing them in jail, shipping them off to work camps in Russia, or killing them. Dora understood that forgetting about Eszter, at least for the time being, would be the only safe route.

Ivan carefully displaced the snow on a bench, motioning for Dora to sit down. "Things are different now."

"How so?" Dora refused to sit. She wanted her dad to just give her the information and leave. She was not his mom or wife. She would never be that, and yet she felt him searching for the comfort a child could never provide.

"They're having a hearing to determine if she will remain in prison or if her crime is worthy of something … else," Ivan said, growing quieter as his voice tripped over his tears. "Your mom's chances of being deemed innocent are slim. They will either confine her to a labor camp or sentence her to death."

Dora closed her eyes and pictured the woman described in Ferenc's letters. Her mom had no life at all. How could she possibly lose more of it? In Eszter's state, she wouldn't stand a chance against any judge.

Ivan placed his hand on Dora's shoulder and squeezed it, perhaps a little too firmly. The best way to secure their sanity, and return things to normal, was some sort of jail sentence for Eszter. Death, however, would shatter them.

"Is there anything we can do?"

"I made sure to file the appropriate paperwork and extend deliberations as long as possible. However, a new police chief is being sworn in. He wants to rid us of the past, especially the people who committed crimes like your mom's."

"What was her crime?"

"You know I can't share that information with you."

"Except you'll tell me that she might be sentenced to death?" Dora felt an old, and nearly forgotten, frustration mounting inside of her. Even at twenty-six, Ivan denied her knowledge of Eszter's specific crime, though Dora now knew it had something to do with a murder, based on Ferenc's letters.

"You're right. I shouldn't have told you any of this." Ivan stood up, trembling and nearly falling back onto the bench. Dora grabbed his shoulders and steadied him. She wondered if her father had the strength to even get home.

Just as he ambled out of sight, Dora noticed that Ivan forgot his briefcase. It was a brown, worn thing, its leather straps shedding ugly strings. She didn't feel like calling out after Ivan, and decided instead to carry it home for him. As she bent down to pick it up, she spied a folder sticking out from the rest. Faintly written on its label was the word *Eszter.*

Dora slid the folder out of its rightful place, wondering if she was about to make a serious mistake. The first document contained a simple profile of Eszter—her age, weight, how many children she had. The sight of Dora's name gave her pause, reminding her that, yes, she was Eszter's daughter, a fact she had tried to ignore for too long. She quickly turned to the next document, a memo written in the aftermath of the revolution.

Eszter Turján and Laszlo Cseke: Escape Routes and Prospects
This report is an accounting of the events of October 24, 1956.
We searched for Laszlo Cseke, co-founder of Realitás, *but failed to locate him. We discovered a note written to him from his colleague, Eszter Turján. In the note she divulged a code. We assume that this code assisted Cseke in his escape from Hungary.*

Dora turned to the next page to see a note in her mom's handwriting sitting, undisturbed, on top of a stack of papers. Dora hadn't been this close to anything so reminiscent of her mom as she knew her (not that sliver of a person she saw in the ministry's basement) in years. She lifted the note with caution, as if it was a shard of glass that could slip and cut her at any moment.

Laszlo, I am leaving now. I have to complete a mission. If I don't come back or something happens and our position is compromised, there is hope. You can escape to Munich. Covert envoys go there weekly. Say you found out from me. They'll know what that means. There is a code you must follow to find the envoys. The code is our favorite one. It's the lullaby I sang to you sometimes at night. It's the one I made you memorize. I never told you what it meant because I always wanted you here, for me. Just use it and listen to the midnight broadcast of Radio Free Europe. It will be clear where to go. But if you decide to do this, please do everything you can to find me and take me with you. I know that if the situation forces you to go, you will be in dire circumstances and so will I. Please, know that I love you. I always have, and I always will.

So there really was a code. Dora had a hard time believing it still existed, yet at the same time, a part of her hoped it did. And she knew her mom had been having an affair. She just knew it. Still, it hurt to see more proof that their family hadn't been enough for Eszter. Her heart and mind belonged somewhere else. Laszlo's betrayal must have hit her hard if she could still focus on it, through her madness. The memo gave Dora a light with which to shine on the past, and she wanted to see more. Dora reached for another memo.

Eszter Turján - Class Three Threat

Eszter Turján regularly corresponds with Radio Free

Europe. She harbors knowledge of a code played to reveal coor-
dinates of an escape route. We have yet to possess knowledge of
this code, and all efforts must be taken to extract it from Eszter.
We thereby recommend enacting punitive measures that will
force her to provide us with said information. These measures
can include, but are not limited to, putting high degrees of pres-
sure on her back through weight presses, cutting off her toenails
and eyelashes, as well as keeping her in a bright room to prevent
her from sleeping.

At the bottom of the letter Dora noticed a number of signatures, including one that belonged to Ivan. Once again, Dora felt the shift happen, her world transforming to reveal a side of her father she didn't know existed. Could he really be that cold and unfeeling to sign an order promoting the torture of his wife? Dora knew he probably didn't have much of a choice, with his singular focus to protect Dora and prove they had nothing to do with Eszter's crimes, whatever those were. She hated her dad for his bureaucratic heartlessness and how he continuously tucked away his emotions in the folds of procedure and law. She saw now that beneath those folds, anger and sadness grew like a mold, uncontrolled and infectious, turning her dad into a fragile shell of who he once was and causing him to turn on a wife he still loved.

Dora knew he had never quite abandoned his love for Eszter. Sometimes when Eszter walked into the room, Ivan's eyes would stay on her for an extra minute, long after the two of them said hello. Dora would watch as Ivan took in Eszter, following the steep curves of her hips to her slender waist, and up to her eyes, so sharp they could cut you. Eszter, too caught up in her own world, never stopped to see the faint outlines of compassion and desire etched onto Ivan's face in those moments.

*

The next few days tumbled by in a series of enlarged silences and awkward pleasantries between Dora and Ivan. Anytime Eszter's name began to surface, Dora focused the conversation on something else, reverting to her well-developed habit of avoiding anything related to Eszter. Dora spent a considerable length of time going over the reasons why Ivan would consciously decide to tell her about her mom's trial. She considered that he wanted her to take some sort of action, and that while he could never ask for it, he could inform Dora about the situation and hope she would rise to the occasion. But, Ivan wouldn't ever want Dora to do that sort of work, not after relentlessly shielding her from the underground world for all of these years. She also wondered whether her dad was planning on executing some sort of plan that would endanger him and this was his way of letting Dora know why he, too, may disappear one day. That theory seemed a bit far-fetched, given Ivan's insistence that they remain within the government's good graces. The only conclusion could be that Ivan truly had a lapse in judgment, a momentary breakdown that, unfortunately, Dora witnessed. That theory was confirmed when Ivan eventually apologized for his behavior and told Dora, without one hint of pain or sadness, that there really wasn't much they could do, safely at least.

Dora tried to follow Ivan's advice. She wanted to for her own good, hoping things would go back to the way they used to be. She focused all of her attention on resuming her normal lifestyle. She continued following Ferenc everywhere, but with one little change. During the day, if he ever even went by the Ministry of Interior, Dora would meander off in the opposite direction.

Her stalking skills grew increasingly better. She learned little tricks, like if Ferenc walked into an empty street, she would wait until she could barely make out his footsteps before slipping behind him. She would leapfrog from doorway to doorway until they entered a more crowded area, where she could hide between people, cars, and the debris of everyday life. Since Ferenc followed a predictable course throughout the day, she learned how to go unnoticed in and out of his daily activities. Usually when she stepped away from him for long periods of time, it was only for lunch, dinner, or sleep. She refused to meet him as Anika either, though a part of her wanted to, especially when she noticed him talking to other women.

Dora's feelings for Ferenc grew stronger as she observed his life more and more. She found herself particularly taken by Ferenc when he was interacting with his sister, especially the way he shuffled her hair or how he made sure to hug and kiss her before she went to school every morning. Dora had spent her life surrounded by people who saw kindness as a weakness. It wouldn't get you far in this country, she had been told. But Ferenc somehow possessed the courage to believe it would. It mystified Dora, and drew her to him.

At night, as Dora fell asleep, she thought about kissing Ferenc, exploring their relationship while only on the brink of consciousness. She wanted to be with him, but in a different time and place. She imagined herself wearing a white cotton dress, standing on a beach in France, and meeting Ferenc for the first time. Relaxed, yet full of energy, she'd strike up a conversation with him, smiling and blushing at the appropriate times. They would stay at the beach, forgetting about the plans they made, and instead feeling like every second was the best second of their lives. When the sun set, he would ask her to accompany him to dinner, and she would say yes, not even worried about getting ready or refreshing her makeup. Dora usually drifted off to sleep at that point, excited for what would never happen.

Meanwhile, Ferenc hadn't written a letter in weeks. With increasing persistence, Joszef asked Dora about Ferenc, and if she had found any proof of his deviance. Dora still held on to the first two letters, unable to let Joszef see the horrifying descriptions of her mom or Ferenc's admission to teaming up with Eszter to escape, which would be a certain jail or death sentence for him, and maybe the latter for her mom. She didn't know what she was going to do. Sometimes, when she stopped in to work, she would find Joszef examining the documents neatly stacked on her desk. He always acted so cavalier about it, as if he had a right to sort through her things.

Once, she came back to work to see a memo on her desk detailing the repercussions leveraged on a colleague who had hoarded mail in his desk for years. Once they discovered his crime, they sent him straight to a labor camp. On top of the memo sat a note that read, "Please file —J." Dora understood Joszef's warning, and even took it with a modicum of appreciation. She would rather he do that than discuss her transgressions with her. She still didn't have a plan, but at least she had some time. Joszef never acted quickly. If this was truly a warning, it would be weeks before a second or third one came, and even longer, hopefully, until he pursued any sort of disciplinary measures.

Dora had always harbored strong feelings about right and wrong. It was right for her to avoid any relationship with Eszter. She understood the rightness of it, not from her own perspective, but from a global one too. It was right for Eszter too. She enjoyed a life independent of Dora and Ivan. Dora remembered the moment she realized that, on some level, Eszter didn't belong to them, nor did she want to.

*

Dora couldn't fall asleep that night, a common problem that scared her as a child. At the age of eight, she had just been introduced to the notion of death, and ghosts, for that matter. She imagined them surrounding her at night, terrified that if she closed her eyes, they would invade her bedroom. Boldiszar had advised her to sleep with the lights on, but the light in her room had gone out, and she needed someone to fix it. She would have woken up Ivan, but he always jumped up violently in shock whenever she roused him in the middle of a deep sleep. Dora heard someone in the kitchen, as she usually did late at night. Eszter never went to bed when they did.

Dora wandered toward the kitchen, eyes straining to adjust to the brightness—her room had been so dark—when she saw her mom talking on the phone. Though she couldn't make out what Eszter was saying, Dora could sense her excitement. Eszter's free hand gestured colorfully, and she kept smiling. Dora couldn't even remember a time when Eszter truly smiled, rather than straining her lips into a lop-sided grin. When Eszter did finally turn around to see Dora standing there, her eyes froze, mid-rise, before sinking into her cheeks. Her smile retreated. She placed the phone on her shoulder, and sighed, "Are you okay?"

Dora burst into tears. She was only eight, but she knew the difference between love and indifference. She shuffled to her parents' room, shocking Ivan out of sleep, and cried in his arms. Eszter never rushed to comfort her. As Ivan stroked Dora's hair, she could hear the faint murmur of her mom's voice still on the phone.

So when Dora agreed to avoid speaking to Eszter all together, she didn't feel like it was a completely selfish decision. It was the right thing to do, given that Eszter inhabited a completely different world, by choice. And it was to that world she went, whatever consequences it bore. She would be relieved of Dora, and Dora of her.

*

The thought of her mom dying, and disrupting the steady balance of worlds that made up her universe, terrified Dora. Without Eszter, Dora wouldn't have anything to measure rightness against or structure her perspective. Eszter deserved the fairest trial she could get. It was her only hope, really, and seemed like a virtually impossible feat, given her current state.

As the days moved on, and the gravity of Ferenc's letters and Eszter's trial bore down on Dora, an unlikely calm began spreading through her. It was the type of calm that only comes when a decision has been made, and one can relinquish all questioning and anxiety, simply ready to follow a pre-determined course. Someone else decided for Dora. Her mom, years ago, decided, and Ivan decided too. Dora had been placed in this position before she could even protest it. She would have to find a way to help her mom.

Dora didn't feel any sort of hesitation, even knowing her mom confessed to murdering someone. Rather, Dora reminded herself that since she didn't know the details of Eszter's crime, she couldn't make any assumptions. Dora only knew she wanted to set things right. And, if the government caught wind that Eszter still plotted to escape the country, they would surely do away with her. Ferenc's letters would seal her fate before she even took the stand.

With all doubt banished from her mind, Dora picked up her pencil. Tracing Ferenc's words, she followed the erratic loops and dips of his penmanship, until she could fabricate it perfectly. In a matter of ten minutes, Dora composed a compelling letter that appeared to be in Ferenc's handwriting. Lighthearted and inundated with sexual innuendos, it would hold off Joszef for a little while, at least.

Quietly resting her pen down, she moved to her desk where her typewriter sat. Dora needed to make sure Ferenc never mailed another letter through the postal service again, just in case she couldn't intercept it. Her back straight and eyes glued to the loaded paper, Dora took a deep breath and prepared to compose her second letter. This one would protect Eszter and Dora. It would give Ferenc the hope he craved. It would be the beginning of something that Dora wasn't ready for, but for which she had been preparing her whole life.

Dear Mike a Korvinközből,

Please, let's not communicate anymore via the mail system. It's too dangerous, especially with your encounters with Eszter. Instead, please write "Varga" on your letters to me and deliver them to the secretary at 3 Wesselényi út. She will not know who you are, or what you're doing there, but she knows the letters must get to me.

You have my full respect and confidence for trying to escape Hungary. My explanation to you is long, but the short version is that I will help you.

My letters will not give you instructions on how to escape. That would put anyone in our envoys at serious risk, and I can't forgo their safety. Please continue to foster your relationship with Eszter. She will tell you how to safely leave the country. She knows a code. It's the only way.

Sincerely,
Uncle Lanci

MIKE A KORVINKÖZBŐL
February 15, 1965

Dear Uncle Lanci,

Thank you from the top of my lungs for your letter. It is truly the most gorgeous specimen I have encountered. You will help? You will help! I almost squelched Adrienne as I told her the momentous news.

I admit that I harbor no clue as to how your petite letter landed in my coat pocket, but my heart lumbered with excitement when I read it. I always thought admist the ranks of those who fight for the Hungarian cause, your radio stands first in line. But I had my doubts recently with your none response. Your Hungarian is genuine. I am glad to see that you have not pardoned it to flee after living in Munich for so long.

I was so taken on by overjoyousness that I wanted to leap up and tell Anika, who had just departed from me. She was placed in my presence so lovingly because Andras and I spotted her and Marta at an underground bar the night previous. We were domineering the dance floor, when Andras' matty, pink, sweaty face turned to me and said, "Do you remember those beauty queens we faced?"

The delight in my interactions with Anika nested softly in my heart. My range of words for Andras proved more limited than I even planned. I nodded imminently and sincerely for Andras to witness.

Andras took hold of my hand and whiskered me to the other side of the bar. He forced me in a forward movement and then to an abrupt halt. He pointed forth. "There they are!"

I tripped with excitement. "Let's go light conversation with them!" I jaunted forward, but Andras caught my chest in his arms. I could tell that he refrained me due to his nerves.

"What do we say?" he spattered.

"Let me take the lead," I courageously exclamated. I crossed the line above him and around him. Andras shagged behind me, like he was prepping to pick up the balls from a football practice. I could tell his lumpy figure was very close to me.

When Anika's face pivoted toward me, Uncle Lanci, it was like I was sliding on ice and may plunk onto my tailbone. Her glance was more severe than the coldest winter. When our eyes began to intercourse, a petite frown drooled upon Anika's cheeks. It forced Andras and I to hang backward in fear.

"She simply failed to recognize us," I made a whisper to Andras.

"I don't know," he said.

But I persevered to walk toward her, and surely as my superb face approached closer, she realized my identity. A smile rang from her and she alerted Marta, who was the beacon of Andras' lustings, for when I peered behind me he was in full salivation mode.

"Hello," was all I could mutter, Uncle Lanci, before I persisted sounding more ridiculous than I could imagine.

"Hi," Anika said in the sweetest of simple tunes.

Her friend Marta nodded behind her, as if the hello Anika uttered was the most profounding academic theory in the universe.

Politely, and so delicately, as Anika's usual custom, she asked me, "How are you feeling?"

"Great!" I informed her, bugging my chest wide and far for her to see the greatness of my health.

"Good," she said.

"How are you?" I perpetuated the conversation.

"I am fine," she said, but her eyes looked the reverse of fine. I viewed her sadness, which I did not view before, but I hypothesize was consistently present. It was so big, and I desired to take it off of her. Anika is a student in the Hungarian way. She says a small amount of words, but holds behind her an immense accommodation of emotion.

I couldn't perceive whether she wanted us standing there before her or not, but I settled with it. How would you inform someone, Uncle Lanci, that you have been pondering their whereabouts for ages?

I chattered forward about the petite number of happy occurrences I encountered so that our conversation could shine brighter than her sadness. We carried forward like this for a portion of time, discoursing on meaningless things. Andras made a heroic offer to Marta to dance, and she complied with much rapidness.

I continued perceiving Anika as unhappy, but then why did she not depart? She went forth standing there. Unmoving! That did a sign for me, Uncle Lanci. I longed for her hand and grasped it. She put her eyes up at me, and I viewed, through the sadness, the miniscule hope in her. I am aware of hope when it's miniscule. I know what it is like to place it in storage, majorly back inside. She saw this part of me too and she began to be easeful. She even started saying light things and dancing.

The night swam from underneath me after that, the perfect coincidence of affairs carrying me forward to greater lengths than I could perceive. What I discovered leap-frogged beyond what I had ever witnessed before. Anika and I could converse, and we enjoyed each other's company so endlessly that the conversation rarely pitter-pattered to a hault on any occasion.

After dancing and chattering, a sofa became available in the bar and I slopped on it, like a smooth whale. When she skimmed close to me (I think purposely), I touched my fingertips to her thighs. She jolted. I thought she'd go forth to leave, but instead she scooped away and made a pivot to face me.

"So tell me about what it was like in jail," she said, shocking me, of course, because that night in jail was the farthest parts from my mind.

"Oh, let's not be concerned with that," I said, aspiring that Anika would pick on the fact I hoped to go nowhere nearest the topic.

"What was it similar to?" she said, her voice masquerading a sweetness that I must say I strangled to believe in.

Paddying the area on the sofa right by my side, I beaconed her close to me.

Staring, she just kept staring, until with *much* slowness, she scooped next to me. I didn't know what to commence—with her so close and her eyes so severe. I just simply leaned over to her and placed my lips atop of hers. I permitted them to sleep there for a moment, like when you place your lips against a cool peach. I luxuriated on them. When she persisted in not fleeting the situation, I kissed her. I experienced my one hundred percent then. I was one hundred percent! Finality. Her lips were so silkness.

After a volume of kissing, her neck craned upward for mere seconds and she asked again, "Please, just tell me some tidbits of jail. I always heard, but I never really knew what it was similar to."

Heaving sigh atop sigh, I nodded and launched into my in-depth story. I even told her regarding Eszter, which I shouldn't have even ventured toward. She asked questions all along, even when I butted up against the Eszter story. Her head jolted a little when I discussed the rapes that I beared witness to.

Then the most betwixting thing occurred. She produced a demand on me. She pondered whether we could maybe do a favor for Eszter such as bringing forth her some food from the outside or something nice. She almost resembled a baby asking me that. It produced a love for her even more than I had before.

Actually, I thought it was a luxurious idea, all accreditations to Anika's sweet, sweet being. We concurred upon just some petite *pogácsa* for me to bestow upon Eszter. Upon confirmation of our plan, Anika's whole being just reclined into me. With no words, she bestowed upon me her lips again. I must be in possession of strong feelings toward her, because it produces shyness in me to indulge you with all the details of Anika's miraculous kissing.

After, I read that Eszter is my key to escape and upon my agreement with Anika, I decided to approach my work shift at the ministry with one hundred percent vigor. With me were stored a total of five *pogácsa* reserved for Eszter specifically. When

I told Andras, he reacted in abysmal ways, his eyes frowning to complete close, his head knocking back and forth.

"I will not venture with you. I am a coward," he proclamated.

"I would not want you to venture with me either. It does not mean that you are a coward. It means you possess a sense of wits. I am going still," I said.

Andras observed as I crawled back into our beloved vent. He promised he would stay in the office until I surfaced again. If danger lurked near me, he would yank the rope and I would return back upward.

When I faced Eszter through the vent, I noticed she resembled an old, wrinkle-filled potato on the floor. When Eszter's eyes absorbed me one hundred percent crouching at the vent, she stretched through her stiffness, and I thought she might just decide to pass over me on her way back to sleep. She maintained her open eyes though, and I persisted to wait for minutes and minutes.

"What time is it?" she finally asked.

"It's two hours past midnight," I informed her.

She indicated her finger in the direction of the guard post and then placed it on her lips to tell me to quiet severely. Shuffling her body over to the vent, she peered into it. I squeezed a total of two *pogácsa* through the vents toward Eszter, who plucked them from me at instant.

As she devoured the pastries with such quick-liness, she asked me, "Why did you bring those to me?"

Squishing my voice betwixt the vent holes, I explained to her that a nice woman named Anika asked me to bring them to her. Without helping myself, I launched into an aggressive description of Anika. As I departed Anika's wonder upon Eszter, she cried softly. Juggling her head backward and forward, she spoke in between her gusts of sobs.

"She," Eszter said, "She is a nice woman. She sounds so nice. So nice. Deliver her a thank you from me."

Waiting persistently for Eszter to move on from her tearhood, I slumped my head against my arms. Awareness donned on me that Eszter would need to speak firstly. She was so far removed from experiencing interactions that too much discussion would send her back into herself—a realm that scared me beyond fear.

Finally …, "What are you doing here?" she asked, a smile on her face as if she already knew I was guaranteed to utter back.

"Munich," I said. "I need to know how to get there. I desire your help."

"Do you know what this entails?" she asked, her head bobbing as she grasped the vent. (I was still there in the squatting position.) I believe she stood on her tipstoes just to see me.

I nodded vigorously, even though I was fearful Eszter would take me for a fabricator. There would be no excuse for me if I failed. I would not be able to utter something to Adrienne that would even describe my failure.

"I'm not so sure," Eszter said, her fingers now poking through the vent. "It means I must accompany you. I must adorn your side with my knowledge so that you can know how to accomplish this fruitfully."

"You want to come with me?" I said, because I did not envision this, Uncle Lanci. Did you? I wish you warned me of this so I could have pondered how to act.

"Yes, I do not want to live out here." Eszter's subdued, gray-filled eyes tried to make a unification with mine.

"If I leave without you, it's a minor step to deviance, that could be overlooked," I began to explain. "If I help you escape, I may never be able to return to this country."

Uncle Lanci, why is it that you refuse to write to me the plan? You have given me a choice out of zero choices. I am reaching anger now just reminiscing on my conversation with Eszter. You have suggested I ask an empty canon to fire. It's impossible. I want to give up, and at the same time, it's endlessly reckless what I am proposed to do.

She said nothing and nothing and nothing.

Minutes surpassed us, and the fear that I would not get out became as real as her gray eyes. Adrienne came into my head. I pondered my sweet, petite sister whose main goal is to procure a mom who will wrap her bulky arms around her and just simply utter tender remarks. When I witness Adrienne crying about it, my insides drop away. All my pursuits are so unnecessary in my life when Adrienne sinks.

"Okay, I will take you," I gasped. (Uncle Lanci, now I'm *really* going to need your help.)

"Then first, you will mandate to listen to Uncle Lanci. He has awareness on where the envoys pick up and leave. He can inform you over the radio. He does this for people who are important."

"I have already made communications with Uncle Lanci," I said.

When I uttered this, it was as if an electric shock scuffled across Eszter's spine, up its nodules, and then into her eyes ... her one hundred percent terrifying eyes. Retracing from the vent, she glared up with me, making a crossbow with her arms. "How could you have spoken with him?"

"He transcribed me a letter."

"And what does Uncle Lanci impart on you?"

"He said that you will help me with a code, but I am not entirely positive how it is that will happen."

I felt the uncertainty of the moment flood over my insides. Eszter twisted her hair, and I wondered what could be circulating through her brain at that instance in time.

"How is it, exactly, you received Uncle Lanci's letter?"

"It appeared in my pocket."

"*Ahhh*," Eszter said in a trouble-burdening tone. "So … it was not delivered to you by way of the *posta*?"

"No, it was not."

I do wonder how you got me the letter, Uncle Lanci. There are mysteries you hold that I cannot begin to unfold because I have to focus on my main, supreme task of finding my mom. But, one day when I go to Munich, I envision sitting down with you and laughing about all of this because the explanations turned to be more simple than I could ever envision.

Eszter became silent, but physicality speaking, manic. She forced her way around the capsule, prancing to and fro. A wildness sprung forth from her that I can't capture precisionly. It felt morbid, like she would sacrifice anything to achieve an end (but what end that is, I do not know). I infuriated with Eszter more than I ever experienced before.

"Stay calm," I forced a whisper to Eszter. "Someone might hear you."

But, Uncle Lanci, she really could not heed a bat even if it flew by her and made the decision to suddenly open its mouth and speak. I heard Andras dragging his boots around above me at a high loudness. I wondered if he was trying to warn me about something.

"Okay!" Eszter suddenly screamed at the pinnacle of her lungs.

I thought at that moment my location would most certain be divulged to the guards and I would summarily be vanquished back to these cells again. I launched backward in the vent, hating myself and hating her more for the situation she placed upon me. Why did I assume she maintained a level of sanity in this place?

She froze in her places, her hands by her side, and she made a clear of her throat. I predicted she would scream forth again and I just froze too to make a brace for myself.

"I can tell you how to interpret the radio," she said.

I evolved to be very quiet. Did she just say she would be assistance to me? Did Eszter come away from her craze to reach forth to me? I centimetered on my belly very close to the vent. My attention was one hundred percent on Eszter in that moment. I would not have even cared for the guards if they came about us.

In the most clear voice I have heard her maintain in my entire existence, she uttered to me, "I'm sorry, I seem to be inhabiting outer space to you. I have been in here too long and the attention you don on me is powerful to my ego. I will help you, I promise, but please allow for the interruptions of my spirit as I divulge in you the secrets of how you will accomplish your goal."

At that concurrence, I desired to hoist Eszter up and impart on her the most chief of hugs I could. She was aware and she was human. To harbor ill feelings toward her at this juncture would be to defy my sense of forgiveness.

"I would like a radio too."

"You request me to bring forth a radio to you? You will get caught."

"I will not."

"You will," I said. "Can you proceed to don on me the code first?"

"If you bring forth me a radio, I will don you the code soon," Eszter said. "The important thing is that you learn from me what to do."

"Fine." I cannot explain why I said that because it would put Eszter in trouble and if she was caught, my whole plan would be ruined.

She got a petite smile atop her face. "Do you trust me?"

What a confusing question. I wanted to say a mighty no, but I could not disturb the fragileness of Eszter. "Yes," was all I uttered.

"You make lies!" she yelled. She started spinning in cycles, and as she spun she repeated, "You make lies!"

How can I keep up with Eszter? She will be an

adult and then a child. She will be present around me, and within seconds will retreat to another realm that I am not in the slightest familiar with, as if she sees an oasis, knows it, has tasted its water, but gets lost anyway in the bareful desert.

I vigorously lunged toward the shovel of my words to dig, dig, dig myself out of the hole. "Trusting you one hundred percent will take time for me, but I will backtrack toward you and learn from you again."

I left her there. I knew if I said more she would turn on me again. As my final foot disappeared up the vent I averted my head toward Eszter. She assembled herself back into her bed as if she was any typical person preparing for slumber. I let myself think those thoughts, and then, in a second, I instantaneously realized how dangerous they were.

I possess awareness that Eszter's brain does not coincide with our world, Uncle Lanci, but I also must ask you why she harbors minimal trust toward you. I wouldn't be a one hundred percent man if I didn't confront you on this topic. Are you helping me in earnestly? Or is Eszter in the correct to be weary with you? For now I will trust you (and that is a real feeling). I will do as you say and make returns to Eszter, but I persevere an explanation from you on this matter. In plus, I have now made an agreement to bring forth Eszter with me, so I do hope there is an added space on this envoy for her!

My brain is swimming in fear and possibilities, but I won't drown because I have been swimming my entire life. I will brave the unstable tides and get to the place I determined, where I can make a life for Adrienne, and maybe for me.

So, please, receive my letter. I'm delivering it to your Varga secretary tomorrow. I'll be made aware of you receiving it if you just play "If I Had a Hammer." If I had a hammer, I would hammer out all the danger too.

Sincerely,
Mike a Korvinközből
Desire is fuelled by all, but fulfillment. —Ernő Osvát

DORA TURJÁN
February 18, 1965

DORA HADN'T PLANNED on kissing Ferenc, let alone ever talking to him again. She hadn't planned on breaking her agreement with herself, or with Joszef, to maintain her professionalism, no matter what. She hadn't planned on any of that. But the second she slipped the forged letter into Ferenc's pocket, her connection to his cause—and her mom's—solidified. She had officially entered their world, making it impossible to turn back or observe from afar. She now lived, breathed, and walked inside the realm of subversion that shaped—no, contorted—so much of her life.

Dora ran her fingers along her lips, as if they could somehow absorb the remnants of her kiss with Ferenc and give her another chance to feel it. She wanted so badly to kiss him again, and again. She hadn't felt that excited about anything since Boldiszar kissed her. She hated that whenever she fell for someone, something always stood in her way. Dora's narrative of love was not a narrative at all, but simply a series of all-too-quiet, yet distinct conclusions. She hated to admit it, but deep down, she didn't believe in love, though she still searched for someone who could prove her wrong. She wanted to find someone who could love a person with consistency and endurance. Yet, time and time again, she saw the reverse.

Dora sat at her favorite perch in the cemetery, indulging in her memories of Ferenc, until they ran head-on into thoughts of Eszter. She imagined her mom in one of the nameless graves before her. It would be Eszter's name, instead of Boldiszar's, Dora would search for at the Bureau of Missing Persons. And through pursed, dry lips, some government employee would tell Dora that he had failed to locate records for an Eszter Turján.

The gate behind Dora let out a shrill squeal, and Dora turned to see a heavyset man in a tattered coat fumbling with the latch. He had with him a shovel, and after prying the gate open, lumbered into the graveyard as though, at any moment, he would be the one needing to be buried.

"This isn't a place to be in the winter," he grumbled as he punctured the hard, frigid dirt.

"I was just leaving." Dora stood up, her legs a little wobbly from sitting on the cold, stone bench.

The man stopped digging and fixed his gaze on Dora. "Hey, I recognize you."

Dora's heart quickened. "I don't think we know each other."

"You are a Turján. You look just like her," the man said, stepping closer to Dora.

"Excuse me, but who are you?"

"I'm Bence. I was a Freedom Fighter."

Dora had never been confronted by one of her mom's counterparts before. She never even fantasized about that happening. But this Bence seemed so intrigued by Dora that she wondered what kind of impact Eszter had on his life.

"Did you work at the paper with her?"

"No, we met her the first day of the revolution," Bence said. "I'll never forget it."

"What happened?"

"She escorted one of our comrades to American troops."

"There were no American troops."

"Exactly."

After the revolution, Dora remembered people blaming the Americans for instilling false hope in the Freedom Fighters by suggesting the U.S. would come charging in and save them from the Soviets. Dora thought that sounded like a cruel trap, and now it upset her even more to hear her mom fell victim to it as well.

"What happened when she escorted your comrade to this so-called aid?"

"You're her daughter and you don't know?" Bence snorted, piercing the dirt again, which had started to give way.

Dora, embarrassed, studied the ground as Bence unearthed its dark, tender interior.

"If you don't know, I'm not going to be the one to tell you."

"I'll find out through my own means." Dora stepped over the fresh mound of dirt. "Have a nice day."

"Wait, there is something you should know."

"What?"

"I heard they're having a hearing for her."

"I'm already aware of that."

"But, I heard it's today, and I don't know who I'm digging this grave for. I'd like to think it's not for her."

Dora stopped. Her mouth went dry. How many shocks to her life could she handle before she became delusional like her mom? The hearing couldn't be today. She wasn't ready. She didn't have a plan. She wasn't even close to having a plan. And how much longer after the trial would Eszter be sentenced? Would it be right away? Dora reminded herself to focus on her actions, on taking the first step. Nothing more.

"What time is the trial? Where?"

"In two hours. At the ministry."

"I'll go now." She shook Bence's calloused and grimy hand. "Thank you."

Bence squeezed Dora's hand back. "If you get a chance to talk to her, tell her Boldiszar's comrades know it was a mistake."

Dora froze. She was almost certain she imagined his name. "Whose comrades?"

"Boldiszar. He was our commander. He died in that trap too. Such a shame, they really believed so much in Radio Free Europe."

"I knew him. I knew Boldiszar," Dora gasped. She wanted to fall to the ground and never get up again. She wanted to blend into the dirt and weeds and graves because this was too much information. This would finish her.

"Are you okay?"

"I'm fine. I can't … I have to go. I can't stay." Dora rushed out of the cemetery, dodging the decrepit headstones, not even bothering to close the gate on the way out. She wished more than anything she could run to Boldiszar, but she would never be able to do that. She next thought of Ferenc, but she couldn't go to him, either. Marta would get too excited by the drama. Her dad would see right through her. Dora didn't know what to do or to whom to turn.

If her mom led Boldiszar to the trap that killed him, then Eszter was, in some way, responsible for Boldiszar's death, even if it was a mistake. And how did Eszter survive this trap? Surely Boldiszar was stronger and faster. It should have been Eszter who didn't get away. Dora had to know the answers, because knowing was the only option now. No longer could she ignore her mom's past or sit at unmarked graves and wonder what happened to Boldiszar. The information was out there. It existed, muddled and volatile, in a cold basement, underneath the ministry. It resided in Eszter, and Dora needed her now more than ever. She had to get to Eszter's trial, and now.

ESZTER TURJÁN
February 18, 1965

IT SMELLS. EVERYTHING smells in this room. It was smelling before I arrived. The worst illnesses come from within and eat without until we become them, like we always suspected we would. Under my nails lies the scum of nine years, and it crawls into my throat, and I want to throw up. Never once did they bathe me, but can I tell them that? Sitting in squalor, shitting too, my body infested my mind; my mind infested my body. To let me back out in this country is not freedom. I'd rather endure an eternity of punishment than receive the exoneration of a government that deserves to never be forgiven.

The bureaucrats are here in my courtroom. When they see me, they realize what it feels like, for a second, to be trapped. It washes over their eyes and then out. They look so bored and proud, as if mediocrity was some medal they could wear across their chests. Everything they do, I watch. "Beware," my cat eyes warn, and when they look away, I know I've scared them.

They said this isn't my trial. It's just my pre-trial, but I do not believe them because I never believe them. *Do not believe them.* They think they wield the ultimate truth. But they carry the lies deep inside. I see them. I feel them. They are numb, but I am not, except my hand is, because I am sitting on it. It has been hurt ever since my rat tore through it, so I hide it to increase my chances here. The judge wears a simple suit—brown tweed. It seems there are two judges, a woman too.

Antal is here. His pink face is now ashen, preparing for his impending cremation because he will die soon, I know. I mouth to him that I know what he did. I know he betrayed me to the Soviets. He is still a little worker bee in the government's hive. He cannot look at me, but I stare at him forever. I stare until his soul becomes riddled with my eyes. I'm not strong enough for revenge. I wonder if he can tell.

He gets up to leave, and that confirms my theory that he betrayed me, and he betrayed Boldiszar. And, if he had really been on our side, he wouldn't have kept working for the regime all these years. He would have done what Laszlo did, become a émigré. It was him. I always knew it, but now I know it for sure. I have no strength. I have no strength to follow him, but I've killed him in my mind anyway.

I'm scanning the audience. My breath stops. Everything stops. I can't believe I did not recognize her at first. Sitting there is the most beautiful thing I've ever seen, even though I've seen her so many times. An angel. Have I died? "Dora," my lips follow the once-familiar pattern of my daughter's name, tongue instinctively curling up for the "D," lips narrowing for the hard "orrrr," and then releasing at the soft "a." I say her name over and over again inside. It feels so wonderful. It feels like me. I missed her. I remember how sweet she smelled and how, when she was a baby, she used to watch me do everything and I knew she'd be so smart.

The present holds everything in its embrace, but then in the same instant, lets it go. She's grown now. Dora, with her olive skin. It's not fragile. I can tell it's tough. Sometimes—no, always—too tough. Am I to blame for that? No, it must be Ivan, the one who holds the party line closer to him than his own blood. But where am I? I can barely recognize myself in Dora. She grew up to be not me. Isn't that what I wanted? Her lips are beautiful and pink. Mine are thin, raw specimens, and I touch them to make sure they are still there. Her hair is straight and mine is gray, knotted, and I can feel it falling out.

After all of these years, Dora remains completely intact. She grew up fine, but love can't be seen, especially when it's loss of love. That's harder to see. I raise my left arm, the one allowed to be in public, just slight enough to wave at her. She lifts her eyes, but only for a second before she stares again at the judge. Suddenly, I realize I must look disgusting. Still, I refuse to look away from her. Coming from the side, a voice bends down toward me.

"Eszter, we are here today to discuss your prison term," the voice says.

"It doesn't matter," I tell the voice loud to myself.

I am looking at my daughter. I am so thankful I survived for this moment. Tears. That's what it looks like. Down her cheek, her tears tumble, and she never moves her hands to wipe them. She's alone, since Ivan is absent. But I'm here. "I'm here," I want to tell her.

Bending again, the voice continues through Dora's tears. "Eszter, we have determined that you are a threat to this country. We will soon deliberate on your sentence, but first, do you have anything to say?"

Dora cries, but in small whimpers, which is even sadder because she knows that it's not allowed and it never was, and I hate that no one is there to tell her it's okay. I'm wanting and breathing my story to her. Can she hear it? I have never uttered the truth to anyone, but now Dora is listening. Boldiszar died, Dora, and that's when I took leave of you, forever. I abandoned you, daughter, who thrived under one identity and nothing more. I remember the knock on the door. I remember your face the most, because I saw it when the police arrived. Your mouth hung limp and to the side. You stood there dumbfounded by the quickness of it all. You reminded me of the neighborhood dog that got struck by a car, and as he lay dying, he seemed so confused, wanting nothing more than for me to lean down and explain to him what dying was. Instead, he felt it. He felt it without any power to stop or control it. It happened to him, and it happened to you.

I explain to Dora inside myself why I threw our family away. If she could just see my side, she would understand. I never meant to kill anyone. It just happened. Just like being placed in that cell, in the basement of a cold building, just happened. Just like her staring at me, me staring back at her, and the together-apartness is just happening.

Sometimes, a long time ago, when I was in it, in it all, I imagined meeting up with Dora at a coffee shop and telling her about what it felt like to write a real story. No, not one that the bureaucrats approved, but one that comes from deep within me, and within others, in our realities. My stories still amass inside me. They feel heavy, but the heaviness is a comfort that reminds me I am not in control. It just happened, to me, to my Dora. After Anya's call came in to go to Boldiszar, I became someone else. That was the someone else who now spends hours picking dirt out from underneath her nails, whose insides have been rubbed raw, who has no need for history. I was never right. Does Dora know this, and does that mean she will never love me again?

Sometimes, when it's not all the time, I fantasize Dora will wake up one morning, throw off her sheets, and come rescue me, no matter what Ivan said to her. I know Ivan handed Dora her reality after I left. In parcels, he divvied up the information she'd receive and not receive. I was on the not-receiving end, I knew when the jail cell stayed empty, unvisited. Dora sees me now. I'm embracing her with my eyes. I open them as wide as I can. I even raise my lips in a tiny smile, a gentle one. I wonder how scary it would be if I went all the way, if I smiled. I have holes there, in my mouth. She'd see, and in seeing, would she be happy or cry more?

"We therefore will make a determination," the voice is still bending toward me, "on your sentence in the coming weeks. It does not look good for you, Eszter."

In an instant, the proceedings finish. Dora's blinking and now is silent with her tears, but I can hear them rushing into me and through me. These pigs want to kill me, but they already did, I want to tell Dora. Fleeing, the judge exits with everyone else except the guards and Dora. She's looking, and I'm looking more. My hand is behind my back when the young guard curls his fingers around my arms and my scratchy uniform and leads me through the center of the pews past Dora.

"Mom," she says, not loud enough to make a scene. *Good girl*, I think.

"Dora!" I whisper back, which really means "I love you," and she knows it because her face swells and she gets so red. The last vision of her I see, will ever see, is her scarlet head staring, void of tears, at me.

I am thanking her in my mind for coming, and I hope she can feel that she has done enough. I do not need anything from Dora because she deserves it all to be given to her, but she never had unselfish parents, and she never will. I wish that I could go back and just give her a different mom, because I was too scared to be one.

There is one thing I know, and in knowing gives me hope, so I have to share it with the little rat I just found. I bend close to him. Dora's in love now, I reassure him. There's no greater explanation as to why she'd come see me if someone hadn't softened her. She's beautiful, I tell my little rat, and I know he likes it when I describe how Dora looks because he wiggles a little.

The dripping dribbles of the leaky pipe sync with my

veins as they push the blood through me. As long as I have myself, then this cell will not control me. I decide the up, the down, and as the days labor on, so do I.

*

I am waiting and waiting, and I do not know what they will decide, but I know they aren't going to kill me yet. Their proceedings are going to take them weeks because that makes them feel proud and good: to stamp things, submit paperwork, and be so bureaucratic. I think the guards are coming for me, like they always do. Instead, they push through, on the ground, a small letter.

Dear Eszter,

I can help, if you let me. I don't expect you to forgive me. I can't even forgive myself. I thought about you every day after my escape. I should have brought you with me, but I was scared.

When I first got to Munich after that terrifying day in 1956, I didn't know what to do. I couldn't stop thinking about you. You were in my thoughts when I woke up, when I went to bed, and all the time in between. And my feelings toward your beloved Radio Free Europe had changed. I was grateful to them for helping me get out of Hungary, and I found out quickly it was really Antal who betrayed you, not the radio station. Radio Free Europe was all I knew, and they were looking for exiles like me. So I went to their headquarters and got a job. But I couldn't report on the news anymore. I was terrified I would let the same thing happen again. I became the rock 'n' roll DJ. Can you believe that? Me? A rock 'n' roll DJ.

When I realized I would be relaying the codes that would help people escape Hungary, I couldn't turn the job down. I think, in the back of my head, I thought one day you might hear one of my codes, and it would help you get out. Of course, I never consciously recognized these thoughts. Not for a long, long time.

You see, Eszter, I got used to my freedom. I didn't want to let it go, and I feared if I helped you, the secret police would come find me, somehow, and bring me back to Hungary or just kill me here in Munich. After a few months, I consoled myself with the idea that Ivan must have rushed to your aid—I knew he would always be in love with you. I assumed he got you out and that you were living with your family again. We couldn't find anything on you. I figured you probably heard me on the radio and that it had to be your decision not to speak with me. How wrong was I.

When news surfaced that you were alive and still imprisoned, I wasn't shocked. I was infuriated with myself for ignoring the possibility that you never escaped the wrath of the regime. I got in touch with the necessary people to get this letter to you. I hope you get it. Also, I'm sure you haven't heard yet, but Antal has died. He killed himself. It still makes me mad that I let him deceive us. I should have been more vigilant and acted more on my suspicions. It's a mystery to me how he managed to enroll Anya in his scheme. An internal committee here ruled her as negligent and she resigned immediately. I guess that makes three of us who fell victim to Antal's lies. The important thing is he's gone now, though, and it's time to be free.

So listen to me now, Eszter. Everything is the same, in terms of the code. You can go. It's the same from when I left. Listen to the radio and you will be safe. I'm not asking you to forgive me. I'm asking you to get out of there.

Sincerely,
Laszlo Cseke

The guards read this before me. I know, because it smells like grease and cigarettes. I realize they think I will die. It has to be, or else the guards would not have delivered this letter to me. So they are taunting me. They could have written this letter themselves. Except, I know this is from Laszlo. I know his handwriting, the messy cursive where every letter bleeds into the next, except for the letter "A," which he capitalizes for some absurd, endearing reason.

I smile. He wants to save me, so I'll let him. I smile too because Antal is dead. His children, in their fancy Buda apartment, are wiping down his ashen skin right now. They're shrouding him in white. They're preparing his body to burn, burn, and I hope he is still a little alive to feel it. I'm not mad at him. I'm mad at Laszlo. He could have helped me. "I'll always hate you," I scream to the letter loud enough for myself and my rat. He is bound by my hatred at all times, even if he doesn't know it. He broadcasts to us in his sing-song voice, but the thing at the bottom of him constantly holds him back. It's the thing he sometimes feels when he gets bored or when he wakes up in the middle of the night. That thing is me who he walked away from. I gave him the code so that he could help me too, but he failed.

Laszlo saw them taking me away from my home. I was not right then. That was the beginning of my not-rightness. I shouldn't have gone home, where I could have been ambushed. And, Laszlo, he must have been hiding in the alley. When our eyes met, he looked right back at the soldiers and nodded to them, as if they were doing the right thing. He could have tried to deter them, to wrestle me down, except he cowered. I am going to be free soon, and he never will.

Finally, Ferenc is here, upstairs. Happily, I listen to him and his friend. I savor their conversation and its lovely, bouncy youthfulness. Otherwise, I only hear the hushed conversations of the prisoners to themselves. Those wicked conversations make it more of a hell here than these cell walls, the mold, or the guards eyeing me up and down with the threat in their eyes apparent as if they wanted to say, "If I choose, you would be mine. If I *choose*."

As the boys work, I lie down on the cot and listen to their radio. Soon I'll have my own if the boy listens. He'll listen. Oh, how their radio changes everything right now. All this time, the radio has been the one conversation I was openly invited to, where no one whispers or says things that confuse me. It's the one conversation they haven't stifled, because they don't know I'm having it.

Putting me to sleep, with their melodic voices and music, I'm absorbed in the boys' youth-hope. I bet all his life, Ferenc had been told being content is the greatest prize of all. But he figured it out. It's no prize if you are lying. It's no prize if fitting in means not being you. Ferenc tries to defy it all, but he won't succeed. Not if the government has its way. Those bureaucrats, like my Ivan, sow doubt into your conscience. You spend your days living, breathing, and utterly denying all that they say. But at the end of the day, no one says much unless it's steeped in sarcasm. You don't work out any epiphanies about the system because beneath it all, you are too scared to trust yourself.

I wish I could be a cat, climb up there, nudge myself in their arms, purr, and suddenly look up at them and say, "But it's not that way at all, you see. You can leave here if you need." Except that's not reality. It's not reality at all.

Someone is coming for me, but I am half asleep. He sits beside me now and I endure the urge to reach out and squeeze him so tight. I want to squeeze his hope out of him and lap it up with my short, squatty tongue. He's a scared kitten, and the more he acts like it, the more I become the alpha cat, the lion. The rush invades me as it always does, and did. Filling me up with power, his presence is dizzying and exciting. He's listing slowly and he's tired. He knows that I have a way to get out, that I have it locked up inside of me. But to reveal the code right now would only make him abandon me here. I roll over and go back to sleep, pretending he is not there. He needs to want this so badly, he'll go to any length to help me.

For three straight days, I feel Ferenc hovering over me. Sometimes he strokes my hair or sings to me. His innocence is arrogance to me. He thinks I am interested in his fate, but I am old, and I am sick. He doesn't see that, because he thinks he deserves my help. Being good and being sweet doesn't make you deserving, I want to tell him.

He starts shaking me, and I cower in the hole that created me, in this prison that created me. He tries to straighten me out, but I explain to him it's beyond his control. On the third day, he leaves the radio. I am thrilled he relented. It's a rush going through me.

I know my mind has a short window of time until it begins contorting and twisting again. I sit up to face him. Looking away, he acts like he barely cares. Doesn't he know that my attention is special?

"Ferenc!" I scream, because his arrogance blows angry breath into my lungs. I don't even care if the guards come. He tells me the radio has been disrupted. While listening to his favorite program, it suddenly went blank. Off. Just like that. The story almost makes me nostalgic for when jamming hit our little radios with regularity. I know this is a sign. They're cracking down.

"Please," he pleads. "I need to know how to solve this. This can't be the end. The radio cannot be jammed or else we cannot get the code."

He wants to know my diagnosis of the situation, but I am busy calculating. He nudges me with his palm. How many times has it happened? What does it sound like? I can tell he trusts me when he hears these questions of mine. I am his answer. He is mine, my portal to escaping this jail cell before I'm hanged. If I can wrest myself free from jail, I can see Dora. I can touch her, smell her, and hold her. She will be my daughter again. But I am not going to give Ferenc the code without being sure he will take me right away. Until he is desperate. I need a way to guarantee he will climb down here and get me. I have a couple of weeks, that I know, because the rat told me and I told the rat. So I hold on tight.

"Well, it is complicated," I say to Ferenc as my tongue tastes my teeth. The familiarity of plotting invigorates me like it had the night of Boldiszar's death. There's a chance, and I must find a way to get on that envoy. Would they recognize me? I'm not the same. But they would be able to tell who I am by my eyes and voice. They would kneel before me and kiss my head and revere the woman they had forsaken. "First, you must find a way to unjam the radio."

"But what is the code?"

"Just keep coming down here," I demand.

"Why won't you tell it to me now?"

"I will work at my own pace."

"I am in a hurry though," he pushes.

"You will wait."

He quiets, and I can tell he has consented, but only because has no choice. He will get the code when he deserves it. Not on my own, surely, but with his help, I'll climb up through those vents and into my freedom.

MIKE A KORVINKÖZBŐL
February 20, 1965

Dear Uncle Lanci,

You professed to aid me, and yet there is no aid occurring. I have liasoned with Eszter and it's to no use. I even gave inward and brought her a radio. Each time I adventure forth to her, she does not compose sense. And yet you exclaim that she holds the code to the freedom I am so abundantly seeking. I do not comprehend why you cannot write me the code since we are now deliberating in secret. I know the secrecy you bear, but at this junction, does it matter? You will maybe be surprised to know that jamming has been brought forth on the radio now. Do you understand? Your code will not go forward if the jamming makes continuous.

I am feeling the anger now since I know that Eszter may not have many weeks to live. Are you aware of her trial? I have shits that the regime is abusing her as an example because they want us to know that they will combat the counterrevolution-aries still. She makes appearances that she does not care for their maneuverings at all. It's like she already gave into dying.

They even made a print of her circumstances in the paper, and when I saw it I wanted to throw up the context of my insides. At this junction, now all my actions are stooped in illegal. Even when I returned home, my petite Adrienne was making a discussion of Eszter's trial, and Father made an explanation that it was a monster sham the govern-ment would utilize for our fear. When I turned the color of paper at his phrasing, he turned to me and said I should not make a fear because I harbored too much weakness to ever get up caught in their masses. I yelled at Father, but I postponed myself from going beyond, because I knew he would see soon that I am not weak. I am the one holding this family in the reins to bring Mom back.

When Father returned to his room, Adrienne—who is so petite, but so smart—asked to partake in my plans to discover Mom. I declined her, but she got this absurd expression on her face, like she thought she was above me. Now that, Uncle Lanci, is a fearful (yet impending) notion. Adrienne said that she had made a peek into my letters and knew that I was making interactions with Eszter to find Mom. Why do I even make attempts to conceal a thing from Adrienne? She is more smart every day, and I felt angered but also proud that she made a successful spy.

Then she made a one hundred percent bolder move and declared she had most rights to meet Anika. In an instance I knew I had to make a compromise, at the least. I would never expose her to Eszter or to the peril of my journey to Munich. So I granted her the win to meet Anika.

We could not go to a bar, because I do not care how much Adrienne is growing, I will not give her the view into alcohol yet. We made an accompaniment with Anika to a restaurant that had spaghetti, since Adrienne is more picky than someone with her wits should be.

When Adrienne greeted Anika, I swear that Anika had laughter amongst her eyes. "I have heard so much about you," Anika said.

"Of course, you have. And I have been anticipating meeting you too," Adrienne burst. How did we, Father and I, manage to raise such a bold girl? Father, with his mostly silence, and me, with my pent-in frustration, could not subsume responsibility for Adrienne. I wonder if her life was so hard that she became brave because of it. Or maybe she was never made to feel small or useless because of her words. In which case, maybe I should make a congratulation to myself.

Anyway, at Adrienne's silly boldness, Anika

appeared taken backward, but she laughed and laughed and made a kiss on Adrienne's cheek.

"Let's eat the whole restaurant," I spouted to show my enthusiasm too.

Adrienne chirped yes and sat right down at the most proximal table. At dinner, she went forth discussing her achievements in school and Anika listened with her one hundred percent. My heart grew monstrous watching this because I made an understanding how giving Anika is. Also, only someone who is in love with me would be so willing to listen to my petite sister with so much intention. That's right, Uncle Lanci, I am not of fear to say that Anika is in love with me.

I made a misshapen, though, because I did not provide Adrienne with a lecture on what she can, and cannot, discuss. This is especially important in regards to Eszter. Adrienne could sense this, and she had her personal agenda in mind, of course.

"Did you know Mike is making attempts to escape the country?" Adrienne said, then smiled so devious I made a delivery of a kick into her shins.

"These are all not facts yet. It's just a fantasy," I said.

"He's lying. He's so bold to do it," Adrienne said, like she was telling upon me. I realized she was making attempts to abolish my plans, by informing someone who could stop me of them.

"You are right, Adrienne, your brother is bold,"

Anika said in the sweetest tone. I admire her calmness in this situation. How in this universe did I receive the luck to have this angel specimen make adoration of me? Adrienne, though, she was making me more angered.

"He's going to try to take the Eszter woman with him," Adrienne said. "She knows a code on the radio to flee the country."

I made a force to interject now and said, "Adrienne, that is enough. What has become of you?"

"If you aren't going to take me, you can't go." This petite, wobbly frown overcame Adrienne's face as she crissed her arms. So that was just it, Uncle Lanci, she did not want me to abandon her. This made a break of my heart. If she thinks that her own brother, who shows her most love, would leave her, then she will think others will too. How will she ever fall in love and make a relationship? Oh, this makes killings of me, and I honestly would like to rethink if this is a strong idea for me to go. What are your most thoughts, Uncle Lanci? Oh, why do I even make inquiries of you? You have such nothing information for me.

My desperation has transfixed into confusion. If I go, I leave Adrienne, and if I don't go, I cannot bring back the mom that abandoned her. Do you comprehend, Uncle Lanci, that more than anything, I want Adrienne to see that love doesn't leave you forever. She must understand there is permanence in love, that it may get lost for so long, too long, but it is always there, no matter what.

I sit here knowing that the beams of light in my life, my Adrienne and Anika, are here in Hungary and I am making efforts to flee them, with a crazy woman leading me forth. You, Uncle Lanci, must act with swiftness before my resolve becomes dissolved. Please, give me courage with "The Door is Still Open to My Heart" by Dean Martin, because I am feeling it open, but I am wondering if there is such thing as being too open.

Sincerely,
Mike a Korvinközből
Desire is fuelled by all, but fulfillment. —Ernő Osvát

DORA TURJÁN
February 24, 1965

"WE'LL NEED TO do something if the radio starts jamming more," Marta whispered, leaning into Dora. The two stood in front of Radio Budapest's office, which had been sending out signals daily to block Radio Free Europe. Dora had broken down and told Marta everything and, as expected, her friend sprang into action, dragging Dora to Radio Budapest so they could find a way to clear the airwaves.

"But what can we do? March in there and demand they stop for no reason at all?" It all sounded so surreal and cliché to Dora anyway—the fact that a code could set the people she loved free.

"Well, we can't possibly wait for them to jam it permanently."

"I just wish I had a clear answer." Dora knew little existed in Ferenc's letters that would guide them to a quick solution. He had continued dropping his letters off at the designated location, and as the jamming became more persistent, Ferenc's anxiety bloomed, until his handwriting could hardly be deciphered. The fact that Eszter didn't show any urgency to tell Ferenc the code and get out of that death trap further confirmed her insanity. Dora knew she needed to take matters into her own hands, but had no idea where to start.

"What are you girls doing here?" A voice boomed from behind Dora and Marta. They turned around to see Ivan juggling a briefcase and an armload of files.

"We just …," Dora scanned her brain for a feasible lie.

"We're just on our lunch break." Marta stepped forward and relieved Ivan of the files.

"Don't you two have jobs to be doing?"

"Yes, I actually have to get to a meeting." Marta hoisted the files into Dora's arms and whispered in her ear, "You'll get more out of him without me." She trotted away, leaving Dora to her own devices.

"Do you have something to do here?" Dora looked up at the Radio Budapest offices, wondering how she hadn't seen her dad sooner.

"A lunch meeting, next door."

"Oh, I can walk you to the meeting," Dora said.

"It's over. I'm just coming from it."

"I can walk you back to the ministry."

"As long as you aren't missing anything important," Ivan said, trying to conceal the smile spreading across his face.

Guilty for how much joy this brought her dad, Dora couldn't bring herself to interrogate Ivan about the radio, at least not on their walk. She began to doubt whether she could extract the information she needed from him anyway, without giving herself away. She wished Marta hadn't ditched her—not like Marta was some spy or mastermind—but she at least envisioned all the good that could come from taking risks, whereas Dora only imagined the bad. Her dad would probably just seize this opportunity to give her a new assignment. She'd walk away more stressed than before.

Ivan lumbered into the ministry and led Dora up a marble staircase. At every third step, he paused to rest, as if the weight of Eszter rotting in the prison below was pulling him down. Dora certainly felt that way. She realized just how fragile her dad had become. The emotions he spent years hiding had burrowed deep into his bones and seemed to be gradually corroding them. She wondered if the same thing would happen to her.

"I need to get back to swimming," Ivan said, collapsing into his desk chair.

"I think you need to rest."

"I'm too busy for that."

"What are you working on?"

"A new a museum exhibit," Ivan said.

"On what?" Dora tried to bide time as she scanned Ivan's desk for any sort of document with the word radio on it. If she could find something on paper, that would be one way to avoid probing her dad.

Ivan smiled and leaned back in his chair, the color finally returning to his cheeks. "It's going to be all about the farmers and workers who courageously grow and produce food for us," Ivan said.

"Excuse me, sir," a man, bald and scowling, stood in the

doorway. "We really need you to sign these documents as soon as possible."

Dora remembered the last document she saw Ivan's signature on, and her body lurched into panic mode. Drenched in a cold sweat, she gripped the sides of her chair as if the floor was about to give way. Dora couldn't imagine Ivan signing another document endorsing the torture of Eszter, but then again, she couldn't imagine him signing the first one either. Dora knew she'd draw attention to herself if she tried to stop Ivan. Her best bet was to search his desk for information, which would be easier with him gone.

"I'll be right back," Ivan said, squeezing Dora's shoulder as he passed her. "Just stay here, there's something I wanted to talk to you about."

Dora dreaded the thought of discussing anything with Ivan at this point, but she couldn't think about that now. She had to find something—anything—that would help Eszter. She searched Ivan's desk drawers, but they were nearly empty. She wondered how often he cleaned his desk and archived his work. It seemed like every day, by the looks of it. She rummaged through the trash, finding only receipts and shredded notes that would take hours to piece together. She searched underneath the mountain of folders stacked on his desk, but they all related to the museum exhibit he was planning. Finally, beneath all the folders and sitting face-up on Ivan's pearly, waxed desk, was a document titled "Radio Interruption Plan."

It was an overview of their plans to reinstate the aggressive jamming of Radio Free Europe. With Ivan's name signed next to various steps of the program, it proclaimed the efforts were for the safety and security of Hungary as more people tried to leave its borders without proper visas. Ivan included a number of safeguards in the plan, ensuring only a small group of people knew when the radio would be jammed and how. He created passwords for the equipment, and he even mandated that they store the master jamming devices in a padlocked room at the Radio Budapest offices. Soon, the jamming would be in full effect and completely block Radio Free Europe. Dora checked the proposed date: the first of March.

"Okay, Dora, where was I?" Dora heard her dad from behind her shoulder, the memo in full view on her lap.

Dora jumped, but quickly regained her composure. "You surprised me."

"What are you looking at?" Ivan asked, though he could clearly see the answer.

"I was curious about the radio jamming program," Dora said, like she had just picked up a book off the shelf to peruse.

Ivan looked at her from the corner of his eye, inspecting Dora, who tried to focus on reading every word of the document. "You just happened to find it on my desk?"

"I was tidying up." Dora had placed the files into neat stacks, realizing she'd need an excuse in case Ivan caught her. Maybe she wasn't so bad at this spying thing after all.

"I've been meaning to brief you on this anyway. As you can see, we're stopping Radio Free Europe from dominating the airwaves once and for all. Soon we'll only have one radio station, our own Radio Budapest."

"It's a very ambitious schedule," Dora said.

"It's a very important effort."

"Is it truly necessary?" Dora didn't know why she even asked. She wouldn't win this fight, no matter how hard she tried, and saying anything more would make Ivan suspicious.

"If only you understood .... I'll tell you one thing, Dora. Boldiszar died because of this radio."

That buried yet familiar anger rushed into Dora. Why did her dad insist on holding Boldiszar's death over her? She wanted to tell him she knew about Radio Free Europe and Eszter's involvement in Boldiszar's death, then watch his face drop and twist into shock. Dora realized, though, that would incite Ivan to question her, and she couldn't endure an interrogation. Still, this was no way to honor Boldiszar's memory.

"If you aren't going to tell me how he died, please stop bringing him up."

"Just read this." Ivan handed Dora a memo, this one looking more worn than the others.

October 24, 1956: Memo #1 on Murder of Boldiszar Balasz and Dmitry Babadzhanian

Boldiszar Balasz and Dmitry Babadzhanian were found dead in the basement at 5 Kikerics út. The same gun was used to kill both of them. Accounts taken from Babadzhanian's comrades attest that a woman identified as Eszter Turján fatally shot both men. Boldiszar was a leader of the Freedom Fighters and Dmitry was the son of the great General Hamazasp Babadzhanian.

Dora knew her mom led Boldiszar to the Soviets, but she had assumed it was a Soviet soldier who killed Boldiszar, not Eszter. The world transformed once again, and this time she felt herself falling, falling in the space left behind.

"We don't know much more than this," Ivan said. "We believe Boldiszar was encouraged to go to this location by Radio Free Europe, with the help of your mom. We don't know what happened next, but we do know your mom somehow killed him, along with Dmitry."

"How do you know this is true?"

"There were other soldiers who witnessed the murder. They describe your mom shooting both of them."

"That's not possible. I don't believe you."

"It's right here, Dora." Ivan pointed to the memo.

"How do you know those soldiers weren't making it all up?"

"Please, I can't entertain any more questions right now. I have to get to work. Believe me when I tell you that Radio Free Europe ruined our family and the people we loved."

Dora sat there trying to piece together everything her dad had said and showed her, along with everything she knew about her mom. No one piece of the puzzle fit the other, because the big picture could not possibly be that Eszter murdered Boldiszar. She had to find out the truth for herself. She wanted to look her mom in the eyes and ask her what happened. She couldn't put credence in these memos, especially if Ivan wasn't willing to answer any of her questions.

Dora remembered that man in the cemetery, and how

he wanted her to tell Eszter they knew it was a mistake. Dora never did deliver the message, barely able to speak when she finally came face to face with her mom. But what was the mistake? Dora had assumed it was Eszter leading Boldiszar to the Soviets. But could he have been referring to Boldiszar's death?

Dora's mind started grasping for answers, sending her into a tailspin. Maybe Boldiszar made a grave mistake during the course of the revolution, one so serious that the Freedom Fighters threatened Eszter's life if she didn't kill Boldiszar. He could be careless and impulsive sometimes, poor at calculating outcomes, and Dora wouldn't be too surprised if he did something to anger the higher-ups in the movement. But Eszter wasn't reckless enough to kill a Soviet soldier too.

Dora thought about how her mom looked that day in the courtroom. She couldn't imagine her as a murderer. She seemed so frail and old, at least twenty years older than Ivan. A wildness lit up her eyes, but only when the judge spoke to her. When she saw Dora, her eyes softened, and she seemed almost shy. Dora felt so deeply sad to see her mom's tattered clothes, her missing teeth, and how she incoherently mumbled to herself.

Everything Dora tried to ignore for the past nine years— her anger toward Eszter and simultaneous longing for her— tore through her. But none of it seemed to matter when she realized just how much Eszter needed her. She had no one, and Dora had been no one for too long.

"You know what, Dora, I need some help with this

jamming initiative," Ivan said, summoning Dora from her thoughts.

"What do you mean?"

"I want you to lead it. I really have too much to do right now."

"I don't think I'm really in the right position to do so ...."

Marta would tell her that this was an opportunity to stop the jamming, but Dora knew Ivan too well. He would expect her to do the job, and do it well. He would check in on her daily and probably ask Dora's colleagues about her performance.

Within seconds, Ivan had Joszef on the phone to negotiate the terms of Dora's temporary employment with Radio Budapest. Dora understood it wouldn't really be a negotiation, since Joszef would say yes at all costs due to Ivan's high ranking in the party. At least she wouldn't have to stalk Ferenc anymore.

"It's done." Ivan clicked the phone back onto its stand. "You can start today."

*

At the Radio Budapest studios, the head DJ greeted Dora with a mixture of disdain and curiosity. Tomasz, who was roughly the same age as Dora, eyed her up and down without saying a word. He scratched his head, launching flakes of his scalp into the air. Dora followed their luminous trajectory until they came to a rest on his black, wrinkled shirt.

"So, you're the bearer of bad news," he said.

"I'm sorry?"

Tomasz's eyes wandered down Dora's stomach to her hands. "The jamming, is that the schedule?"

Dora nodded.

Tomasz fiddled with the radio switchboard, putting Bartók's *Gyorspolka* on the air.

"Apparently, with enough repetition, teenagers will like the classics just as much as The Beatles." Tomasz sank into his chair and laughed mightily, almost to himself more than anything. "So besides delivering me this jamming schedule, what brings you here today?"

"I've been assigned to help you."

"Lucky you."

Dora liked that Tomasz openly displayed contempt for the work. Maybe there was an opportunity here, after all.

"We will be jamming every rock program at increasing intervals, starting with ten minutes at a time. That is, until March first, when complete jamming of the station will commence," Dora said.

"Complete jamming?"

"That is correct."

"I thought we were done with that."

"We aren't. We have to prevent Radio Free Europe from undermining efforts to provide citizens with high quality, socialist entertainment." Dora sounded so much like Ivan in that moment, it scared her. She hadn't formulated a plan to prevent the jamming, but she knew she couldn't foster any suspicion in Tomasz before she really knew him. If he proved untrustworthy, then toeing the party line would give her the cover she needed.

In the hours that followed, Tomasz trained Dora on the inner workings of the radio system. She even orchestrated a test-run when Radio Free Europe broadcasted its Cars and Trucks program, which Dora always thought they could do without anyway. She hadn't yet figured out an alternative plan for Eszter or Ferenc, but she knew she had to, at the very least, warn Ferenc that they were running out of time.

Dear Mike,

Thank you for your letters. Each one I read. Each one I will think about. And now I must confidently tell you some bad news. It appears my radio station will be officially jammed on March 1. No longer will you be able correspond with me as you do now. That means you must prepare for your departure from Hungary. Since Eszter has not revealed to you the exact details of the code, please visit her every day until you can persuade her to do so.

Sincerely,
Uncle Lanci

Trying to get Ferenc to read the letter as soon as possible, Dora made plans to meet up with him, as Anika, of course. She told herself it was only to persuade him to stop at Varga's office, though she craved his presence. With Ferenc, she felt a lightness she had lived too long without, like turning a street corner to feel the sun directly hitting your face, after a long, dark winter.

They met at a café, though Ferenc didn't sound too excited on the phone. Dora hoped his feelings for her hadn't flagged. She needed his full attention now, for many reasons, but most importantly, for her mom. As Ferenc played with his carrot soup, whirling his spoon through the creamy broth, he avoided speaking to Dora. She sipped some tea, hoping his mood would shift enough so they could go on a walk past Varga's office.

"Anika," his voice faltered at the last vowel of her fake name. Reaching for her hand, Ferenc wove Dora's fingers through his, one by one, making sure to touch as much of Dora's skin as possible. Lifting his glassy eyes up to her, he said, "Will you come with me?"

"Where?"

"To Munich."

Dora's mouth went dry. Her tongue tried to formulate a response, but it felt like a beached whale flopping around on dry sand.

"Please, Anika."

Dora knew she wouldn't be able to go with Ferenc to Munich, but she didn't want to say anything that would dissuade him from leaving either. "I will have to think about it."

"That's all I can ask for." He leaned across the table and kissed her, leaving a slight dampness on her cheek. He had cried, but only a little.

For the first time, they made love that night. She kissed every part of him, savoring his skin, which tasted vaguely like nutmeg. He ran his fingers up and down her body, gently and methodically, as if he had never touched Dora before. He moved slowly into her, anticipating somehow that Dora hadn't been with anyone for a while. She relaxed into the sensation until she wanted more.

She felt so safe with him and she saw, in his eyes, that same feeling of security, the letting go of his silliness and his toughness, all at once. It stung her to know that this was, in some way, a sham. She wished she could have made love to him as Dora and not Anika. She wondered if he would ever forgive her for the betrayal, especially now that they had been so intimate. She would tell him when the time was right, and with the right words, but the closer she got to him, the more she dreaded it.

Afterward, he walked Dora home, saying very little. As they bid each other goodnight, he asked again if she would consider going to Munich with him. Dora kissed him, cherishing the transitory mark of their love, and his devotion to her. She never responded directly to his question. She hoped he would understand.

Sauntering through the door of her apartment, her body made lackadaisical by pleasure, Dora saw Ivan in the kitchen. He sat at the table, staring at the opposite wall, his fingers tracing the mouth of an empty glass. Dora edged back toward the door, but he saw her in time.

"Come over here," Ivan said, his voice so low that Dora would need to get closer to him.

"Is everything okay?"

"They've done it."

"Done what?"

"Your mom." Ivan buried his face in his hands. "They decided that …," he gasped, "that she is to hang."

Dora tried to say something, but she couldn't. Her legs started cramping, her head spun, and she felt like she would never get up again. She fell back against the wall, slumping to the floor and taking with her some of the peeling, gray-checkered wallpaper.

"It's going to happen in a week, but it could be sooner. That's all I know. They make sure it's a surprise on purpose," Ivan sobbed, nose-diving into the table.

"I thought we had time," Dora whispered. She assumed it would be weeks, maybe even months, before they carried forward her mom's sentence. How foolish she had been for thinking that they would act reliably slow when history showed a quickness to execute, to swiftly erase those who stood in the way. Her mom only had seven more days to live, at most, and Dora couldn't even get up. She didn't have a plan in place. Radio Free Europe faced a future of eternal jamming, and this elusive code remained trapped in the brain of a woman succumbing to madness. Her mom was going to die, and there was nothing Dora could do to stop it.

Dora wanted to melt into the kitchen tile and disappear. She just wanted to take leave of her family and this situation, all at once, and in feeling that urge, she realized that was just what her mom would have done. Dora had promised she would do better. She always thought that not being Eszter meant following the rules of the government, staying under the radar, and keeping herself—and her dad—safe.

Now, she realized, it was quite the opposite. It was standing up to the repression, doing exactly what her mom did, but with one difference: her family would come before anyone, and anything, else. She collected herself and went to her dad. Hugging him, she felt his tears on her arms. They were wet and cold.

"Well, what will we do?" Ivan clutched Dora's arm.

Backing away from Ivan, Dora straightened her back, lifted her chin, and prepared to address him. "We'll help her."

Ivan grunted. He shook his head. "So little we know of her and why she did it," he said, as if he was already giving Eszter's eulogy. "Maybe she deserves to die."

"We don't deserve for her to die," Dora said.

"It's not up to us."

In that moment, Dora knew Ivan had given up. She readied herself to make her plea to stop the jamming of Radio Free Europe. But as she saw her dad launch into another fit of sobbing, she realized that would just give him a reason to snap out of his grief. He'd take up the cause of stopping Dora from doing anything that would put her in danger, just as he had done for the past nine years. It would be his excuse to, once again, forsake Eszter.

So Dora sat by Ivan's side until she heard his crying stop, replaced by a heavy silence as, in his sleep, he breathed through the remains of his tears. She wondered if that was what it would sound like when her mom hanged—a terrible cry, extinguished.

MIKE A KORVINKÖZBŐL
February 25, 1965

Dear Uncle Lanci,

You already know that things have changed. How could you neglect to know? The presently familiar screeching of the jammed radio has overtaken it. Every minute or so, I leap up and start pacing, cursing, making shits. With the jamming happening so often, I am perplexed into personal fear constantly.

I'm doing all that you instructed, with regards to our plan. I visit Eszter all the time, going almost every night. The final night that made a difference, Uncle Lanci, was last night. When I sulked into Eszter's capsule she was living with fever. Her body eliminated cold and was composed entirely of heat. I was certain that my hand would completely fall off its chain the second I placed it on her forehead.

So I sat by the side of her and pet her hair. I gave her water to drink through a petite straw. She began to drift toward sleep, but she snapped from it to say, "Thank you, Laszlo," very softly into my elbow.

"You are welcome," I told her. I had the compassion to be kind to her because then maybe she would tell me the code.

"I am going in two days," I told her as I matched my eyes up against her.

"I am going to miss this."

"I will too," I said, though I was still making to be you.

"How are you going to get in touch with your mom?" she asked, now seeing me for me.

"Well, my father finally broke down and told me all he knew about her," I lied. "She's a teacher at a school in Munich. She is the most one hundred percent teacher and she has discovered her life's passionate work. Why my father kept this from me, I do not know," I imagined on.

"Moms are moms, are moms, are moms. Their happiness is theirs, not yours," she said.

"I've been practicing your code," I made more lies, but I could see that Eszter accepted what I said as one hundred percent truth, the battle in her majorly exhausted. "I have also been witnessing people getting on the envoys. I go every day to see them."

"Oh, yes? And who are they? What do they look like?" She began picking at her fingers like I had made nerves in her. Her hand is full with scabs and blood. It brings worry to me as I think about the rat too, whose diseases could merge into Eszter.

"They made appearances like everyday people. There was an older man, with gray hair, and a younger one that was my age, and she carried a folder with her," I said.

"I wish I could go with you," Eszter said in petite voice, more petite than I had ever heard her use. I wondered if Eszter even had a true desire to flee her capsule or if maybe she was with major fear of being in the real world.

"Do you know what happened to me?" she asked and nestled her head against my arm. "I'm going to be hanged," she said in a voice for a baby, or maybe a lover.

I felt sick at this. Was she happy at this news? Was it the reality? I couldn't know. She elonged her eyes at the patch of brick next to me. We both said nothing, but I felt my opportunity coming. "The code can help you. I'm exuberant that I know it, of course, but I have been having some glitches with it."

Holding my breaths, I watched Eszter as she rose and then peered at me awkwardly and from her mouth, at initial, I thought she would vomit but then the most illustrious words rambled out.

"The code," she crept her voice along the lines of revealing, "… is problematic, Laszlo."

"Yes, or maybe I just am not remembering it with one hundred percent accuracy."

"You are always careless with your memory," she sneered, and her decaying teeth flashed me.

"I know, I know …. I wish it was not having its problems," I said again.

"Are you starting with the third song of the midnight broadcast?"

"Yes," I lied.

"And you know the first word in the title will be part of your location," she said.

"Yes," I lied times two.

"Well, then you should be able to figure this out. You are not stupid, Laszlo."

"Okay," I said, sullen.

"*Argh*," Eszter burst out. "You forget things so quickly, but I love you," she said, and she curled her finger around my hair.

"Please," I begged, "Help your little Laszlo remember," I said, mirroring the petite baby voice she used earlier.

"Okay. Okay, okay, okay, okay," she said, very rapid fire like. "The third song, remember that, is where you start. It's in the midnight show. It's the first part of your location. The third word in the fourth song will be the second part of your location. Except, you must walk three blocks south of this location, and intersect with the first location. The time is always the same, every day. It's seven in the morning, but the day is not revealed. You try every day. You arrive every day until you find them."

I jumbled for joy inside that I had made an acquire of the code. "Your Laszlo thanks you," I told her, but my mind was racing to process the code. I said to myself it one hundred percent of the time, over and over, to stop from forgetting.

"You are most welcome." Eszter proceeded to don a half smile and curl to a ball.

When she entered her extra layer of sleep, I exited through the vent, as always. It had already reached five in the morning. I remembered too the midnight broadcast repeated every single hour until six in the morning. Eszter probably did not know of awareness with that. If I could make it toward a radio, and it was not jammed, I could hear the location of the envoy leaving today. The time for action was upon me, Uncle Lanci. This was momentum.

I ventured off to my pastimes swimming locker room, where I knew Andras and his team would prepare for swimming practice by listening to Radio Free Europe. I crossed the river to Buda where the dawn illuminated the hills. In the locker room, I slipped behind sleep-filled huddles of men. I saw Andras, but the second he spied me I placed a finger betwixt my lips, indicating that he should be quiet lest I become discovered. He nodded and then I pointed up toward the radio and his eyes grew. The first song that came on was the typical: "Twist and Shout." You are so predictable, Uncle Lanci! I waited until the third song, which was "King of the Road." Then came "This Diamond Ring."

Placing them next to each other, it became clear and easy. King means *Király* in Hungarian and Ring, well that could only mean *Oktogon*, the circle street area just three blocks north of Király út. The location was on Király, three blocks south of Oktogon. The simplicity of the code seemed more than I could bear.

I made it to the meeting place on time and, to my surprise, I saw people converging there. Many fled to work at this hour, but through them, I peered a stubbly man who looked to be in his middle life bent over a large box that he hustled into the back of a car as a woman with exceptional breasts and blond hairs whispered to him. They looked as if they were producing traditional business transactions in a place where that happened most days.

It could have been nothing, of course, but then I noticed an old man, this one with white hair, exit the car and inform himself to the man and the woman as if they had just encountered one another. I spied underneath the interactions of the woman, and the two men, lurked a strained hurry. They barely said words to each other. The blond woman tossed about her eyes here then there to investigate the scene, and the stubbly man refused to look up. I was almost sure these were the exact people who heard the code.

I am so extreme with excitement, Uncle Lanci,

because I have accomplished it. I have procured the code and saw it occur. Your guidance proved with fruit, but now the question is, Uncle Lanci, how is it that I actually get passage to one of their missions? Am I to know again an extra code? Is someone supposed to alert them of my presence on board? Did you fixate that for me? I cannot walk up to them all alone and simply ask to come. They will mostly assume their mission has been confiscated. Maybe that is the explanation for you insisting I carry with me Eszter. It is becoming with clarity that I need her more than I wish.

When I viewed the car departing, it became a reality that I was inching closer to departing Hungary too. Once I do, I can't make a prediction of when I will return home, and I know that there are people I cannot leave behind, and some I have to.

I wrote a note to Anika. It was my formal request that she partake on my mission. I wanted her to believe me with one hundred percent confidence. When I talked to her about leaving, she defied responding. I could see doubts going through her head, and I wanted to pluck them out and discourse them in the trash. I would do anything for Anika, but she is not of the romantic persuasion as I am. And I don't know of whether I possess time to convince her. I must make tries, no matter, because she is a person of genuinity and kindness. She makes me feel braver than I was ever meant to be, but also more aware of what I am capable of. That is truly the most high gift a person can give you.

Adrienne has halted from asking me questions about my plans because I think she is with fear that they are moving forth. When I returned home this morning, she beckoned me forward to her room. Her radio buzzed and churned out effluence like a gagging dog with grass caught in its throat. She maintained she was listening to "Downtown," her new number one song, when the screeching overtook it. She said it worried her with immensity because she knows how important it is that the radio stays clear for me. I believe this was her petite way of telling me she supports my departure even though she cannot join.

I fashioned the antennas in a particular position that enforced their ability to carry signal. Out came some music, of the classical persuasion, and not Radio Free Europe. I couldn't reach it no matter how strange I twisted the antennas. Adrienne rolled her eyeballs and asked me if I would come back in ten minutes to try again. She kissed me on the cheek and told me I am her most favorite person. I assume she used this same strategy with Father recently and that explained why his radio stood in her room. I relented, of course, but I could not get Radio Free Europe even after five more efforts this morning.

I know I possess little time before the radio suffers from complete and utter jams. Now I have to decide whether I will hold my promise and take Eszter in my company. The thought of returning to her capsule is holy daunting. The more worse thought, however, is that she has perished from her sickness. The more *more* worse thought after that is that she is going to get executed.

Please help me in the confidence that I will be doing all that I can to ensure my safe delivery to your whereabouts. And, please, play "Downtown" for Adrienne, with many attempts so she can hear it.

Sincerely,
Mike a Korvinközből
Desire is fuelled by all, but fulfillment. —Ernő Osvát

ESZTER TURJÁN
February 26, 1965

MEMORIES FEEL SO thin now, translucent and fleeting, like ghosts of dreams I can't remember. I see Dora's face, her beautiful, slight eyes, and her olive skin. She gets closer to me, and her cheeks shimmer with tears. I reach out to wipe them away. She backs up, farther and farther, until she fades into blackness, like I am going blind.

I should have told her goodbye so many times, but it feels like too much effort. It feels like trying to climb stairs when you're feverish. If you take the wrong step, you'll smash your teeth or break open your head.

I am this bare and dank cell. That is really what is inside of me, and it makes sense. I try to conjure Dora's face, and still there is blackness. I can't remember, but I have nothing to remember either, because the past is not who I am. It is not my life anymore.

The lights flash off, flash on three times, then off permanently. I know that my time is coming. The guard told me today in a whisper, "Just a few more days, Eszter. Just a few more days that I get to enjoy you."

He howled with laughter until he finished and, whistling, he walked out of my cell and down the line of us, his victims. When he distracts himself, I listen to my lovely music on my lovely radio that I convinced Ferenc to bring me.

If only Laszlo could see me now. Does he know I'm going to take his note seriously and leave here forever? The man who consumed my fantasies and my reality for years boarded up his heart from me and now, only now, is coming back. My anger flashes, like lightning that electrifies me.

So I can hear Laszlo, so I can curse him, I stay up all night until Laszlo's voice permeates every inch of my skin. I scratch myself all over, trying, trying to hurt him. He is crawling inside and outside of me, and I dig into him until blood is underneath my nails.

I used to convince myself he got on Radio Free Europe to give me a sign that he was alive, thriving, and would soon come after me. He said that's true, but it's not.

Ivan must be in charge. If he knew about my little plan, he would enact the jamming in full force and find a way to get it into this cell, to infect my radio. If I die, it would be easier for him. If I leave Hungary, well, what then? There is no freedom from here, just a chain of more prisons that, though open, would be just as suffocating as this one. There is no prison that will set you free. *There is no prison that will set you free.* I write this on the wall with the specks of blood coming from my fingers, from where I scratched out Laszlo.

I am forever imprisoned because of what I did to Dora.

I am more scared of death than an eternity of confines. I am more scared of not existing, even though I don't deserve it. I live not for meaning, but for inertia. To make meaning of your life is what they will wish upon me. I can tell. Ferenc's eyes beg for connection, but what he doesn't understand is that I am past meaning. I am breathing, and I am sitting, and I am scratching, and I am shouting, and that is the sum of who I am. It's not enough for Ferenc, and it wouldn't be enough for Dora. But it is enough for me that I won't let the brute mechanics of my body stop.

I will never know love again. I will never know friendship or family. I will know breath. I will know sleep. I will know hunger. I will know pain. I will know I am alive.

I hug the radio so tight because I heard the code. I heard it so clear, so very loud and clear. I am ready.

Tonight Ferenc abandons me. It's only a matter of time until he returns. The next time he comes, it's the last, I decide. I am leaving with him.

MIKE A KORVINKÖZBŐL
February 27, 1965

Dear Uncle Lanci,

I am writing this letter with the immense hope that tomorrow I will be at your doorstep. I persevered to hear the code at midnight, but it was jammed. If the jamming pursues forth, I will melt in fears and desperation. I cannot think atop this now. I have to proceed and proceed.

I said goodbye to Adrienne, which was the most pain I have endured in an enormous time. She was nuzzled in her usual corner on my bed and she looked so perfect, her skin translucent with the moon's flittered light.

"Adrienne," I said.

She jolted awake with her eyes globed to the back of her skull. I thought I had invoked a heart attack on her.

"Yes?" she squeaked.

I think she knew in her dreams what was

happening or about to happen. She pinched her eyes into petite holes to see me. I glossed her cheek with my hand.

"What?" she queried me severely.

She was the most perfection of a sister. I wanted to tell her that, but she would get even more scared for my delaying of the news. I wished I could have bestowed upon her more. I was the one who failed, who couldn't deliver the love to her. That is why I would bring Mom back.

"Adrienne …," I coursed gently times two. "I'm leaving."

A singular tear escaped vigorously onto my cheek and then her bed. But she did something so marvelous, Uncle Lanci, something so surpassed her current age. Adrienne nodded. Instead of pestering me for details, she leaned her head atop my arms. I could tell she had been crying too because a petite wetness sprung on my arm. Without lifting her eyes, she reached her hand beneath her bed and procured a folder.

"Refrain to open this now. Wait until Munich. It's everything I've assembled about Mom."

Adrienne, she is my one hundred percent amazer. That she would even cobble together any information on Mom, and how she did it, dumbfounds me. I wanted aggressively to have knowledge of what was in there, and it was more fuel for me to go to Munich. I had to pay back and forward her efforts.

"Okay, I promise." I kissed her hands, then her cheek. I delivered her one last hug, and when I felt her petite back drop into my hands, I permissed my grief to suffocate me for a second. I rose, in fears that if I stayed by her side any longer, I wouldn't leave. She offered me the comfort of seeing her retreat back toward bed. I pulled her blankets up until they settled under her chin.

"I'll miss you," I said.

"I love you," she said.

And with that I walked past Adrienne's bed and pushed into the dawn.

The sun commences rising now, and I have decided there is no turning aback. Today is the day. It won't be enough time to meet Anika. Please make the announcement to Anika that Mike loves her and will miss her. This is my last hope, this letter I'm going to drop off in Varga's mailbox right now. Thank you, is the sum of what I want to say to you. I'll see you on the other side.

Sincerely,
Mike a Korvinközből
Desire is fuelled by all, but fulfillment. —Ernő Osvát

DORA TURJÁN
February 27, 1965

DORA'S FEET CRASHED into the sidewalk, propelling her forward in a manic sprint. Her hair fell out of its tightly-wound bun, sucking up the wind as Dora fought against the cold currents of air. She tucked her hair behind her ears, into the mounds of sweat running down her scalp.

"Almost there," she repeated to herself as she shouldered past commuters shuffling out of Nyugati Station as if it was any normal day. Except, it was not a normal day. A glitch in the radio broadcasting system tore through Budapest, and now static plagued every single channel, two days ahead of schedule.

Something must have happened. Tomasz probably left the jamming equipment on by accident. Dora had read Ferenc's most recent letter. Today or early tomorrow, Ferenc would try his luck at escape, hopefully with Eszter in tow. If not, she would be executed.

Dora pleaded with her body to deliver her to the Radio Budapest offices as soon as it could. The streets jabbed at

Dora in sharp angles, siphoning her into different directions, exhausting her legs, and her lungs. As cars puttered by her, Dora heard a ludicrous course of static rising up around her, taunting her.

When she finally reached the office, she realized the futility in her rushing. Alone at the station, without Tomasz, she couldn't stop the jamming. As she messed with the switches, pressed power buttons on and off, and tried, even, to put the dreaded classical music on the airwaves, the seconds bore forward, toying with Dora's patience. After snapping all the plugs out of their sockets and watching the lights on the switchboard extinguish, the jamming barreled on.

"Dora?" a weary voice floated from behind her.

"Tomasz! Thank God."

"What are you doing here? Didn't expect to see you today ...."

Dora stood up and scratched her back. She raised her breasts as she did so, hoping that might help her win some ground with Tomasz. "I noticed the jamming got off schedule. I know that we're supposed to be very strict about following it."

Tomasz looked past Dora, failing to fall for her ploy. "I could have fixed it on my own."

"I wanted to be here in case you needed help."

Tomasz scanned the switchboard, its buttons in disarray. "I have never seen someone so eager to help."

Dora swallowed the lump growing in her throat. She wanted to escape to a dark corner and be completely alone, free from the discomfort of breaking rules or persuading others to do so. She took a deep breath and reminded herself that she was trying to make a better life for her and her family, so that there would no longer be any darkness to hide in.

"Of course, if you don't want to stop the jamming I could go get my dad …," Dora said.

"No, no let's not do that," Tomasz frowned. "Here, take a seat."

"Thank you," she said, relieved she wouldn't have to act on her bluff.

She tried to make small talk with Tomasz as he fiddled with the equipment, but the more she said, the more stressed he seemed. She finally stopped talking altogether, only to hear Tomasz cursing below the stubborn static.

"Do you think you'll be able to fix it?" Dora asked as the minutes wore on.

"I'm not sure."

"What's wrong?"

"Well," Tomasz said. "Our equipment isn't causing the jamming. It's coming from somewhere else …."

"But where?"

"I think you can guess."

"My dad," Dora sighed. Surely Ivan didn't know about Ferenc's plan. He had to be orchestrating this jamming for some other unknown reason. She needed to talk to him. The room suddenly became very warm. Dora lost her balance as she tried to stand up.

"Are you okay?"

"I'm fine. I have to go."

"Why don't you stay here a little longer?"

"No," she said, clearing her throat. "I mean, I really need to do my job and see that we're on track."

Dora skirted around Tomasz, who seemed to be trying to block her path to the door.

"We can figure this out together."

"It's okay, thank you!"

"Wait!" Tomasz caught up to Dora, grabbing her arm. The look in his eyes—as if Dora's next step would somehow devastate him—made her stop.

"I know what you're doing," Tomasz whispered.

"What do you mean?"

"I overheard a conversation between you and Ferenc."

"What?" Dora had to sit back down. She thought she might get caught one day, but not by Tomasz. She wondered if Ivan had been having Tomasz spy on her. She felt trapped, and because of that, incredibly anxious. Her knees started twitching as she wracked her brain for some sort of excuse to use. "I don't know a Ferenc."

"It's okay, Dora. He's my friend. I saw you guys talking the other day. I was going to come say hi, but I stopped when I heard him calling you Anika. I didn't want to ruin anything. And then, later on, when I saw him again, he told me about his plans."

"There are no plans."

"Dora, I've known him since we were boys. He wouldn't lie to me. I know about Eszter, and that she's your mom."

Dora couldn't deny it any longer. Tomasz was smarter than she thought. "Did you tell anyone? Did you tell *him*?"

"No, of course not." Tomasz put his hands on Dora's shoulders, peering straight into her eyes. "If you can get me into the room where the master equipment is, I can disable it."

"You can?"

"Yes."

"But why would you want to help me?"

"It's one little thing I can do to fight this crap." Tomasz kicked the switchboard, rattling the knobs and scuffing the base. "And Ferenc deserves to get out of here."

Dora hugged him. "Thank you," she whispered. "I'll be back."

*

In the crowded locker room, Dora slipped out of her clothes and wriggled into a loaned bathing suit, two sizes too small for her. The smell of sulfur flooded her senses, so much so she could taste it in the back of her throat. Two women, about her mom's age, were complaining about the size of the towels, so small they could only dry sections of their hair at a time.

A swell of dizziness overcame Dora, her body struggling to calibrate to the speed of her new, subversive life. She leaned against a closed locker, her back cooled by the metal supporting her. She counted to three and tried to imagine swimming in Lake Balaton on a warm day.

She had rushed to the Széchenyi baths, where she predicted she would find Ivan, after seeing an appointment on his calendar marked "Boldiszar." He used to go to the baths with Boldiszar every week, and Dora assumed Ivan, a creature of habit, had kept the timeslot. Maybe this was his small way of honoring Boldiszar, though Dora couldn't decide how she felt about that. After rushing to the baths, Dora realized she had no idea how she would approach her dad, let alone ask him to potentially break the law, *his* law, for her. Yet if she somehow figured out how to unjam the radio furtively, what would Ivan do if he suspected Dora was up to something? Would he make someone follow her? Would he assign her to a job that required constant supervision? Would he mandate she work by his side every second?

She managed to reel in her thoughts as she walked out of the locker room, her bathing suit carving valleys into the space above her hips. She found Ivan sitting in one of the smaller baths, his eyes closed, arms spread on the ledge, and his head facing the high ceiling.

"Dad, hi …." Dora slipped into the warm water next to Ivan.

"Dora? What are you doing here?" Dora noted a slight degree of fear in his voice, as if she caught him doing something wrong.

"I wanted to come relax, things have been really stressful."

"I never thought you would ever join me here. It was always …."

"Boldiszar. I know." Peering through the steam passing before her eyes, Dora imagined Boldiszar lounging on the side of the bath, nodding solemnly as Ivan lectured him on the importance of pursuing a career in government. "So, how are you?"

"Same as always. Tonight, I'll be speaking at the rally."

"I'm glad I caught you first."

"I'm glad you did too!" Ivan said, shades of the cheerful dad she once dreamed about coming through. "How has the job been going?"

"The radio, you mean?"

"Yes."

"Oh, great. Except today, the strangest thing happened … it just started jamming."

Ivan ran his fingers along the ridges of the pool's imperfect casing. "That's right … I should have warned you …."

"I was hoping I could help get it back on schedule."

"The jamming decision was made above my head. It came from the top, from Kádár himself."

"But, why?" Dora asked, trying hard to temper her frustration.

"It's a long story, and I don't know all the details."

"It didn't seem like Kádár, or anyone else, used our jamming equipment today though."

"He keeps additional equipment in the ministry, just in case," Ivan said. "Remember, Dora, always build redundancy into your systems."

"Redundancy … yes …." Dora knew exactly who had access to the keys that unlocked all the rooms in the ministry. Dora tried to maintain a pleasant level of small talk for several minutes before excusing herself. She had just the information she needed.

*

"We have to find Ferenc so he can give Tomasz access to the jammers in the ministry," Marta said, after hearing Dora's story.

"It's the only way," Dora agreed, trying not to think about how, at this time tomorrow, Ferenc and her mom might be in a completely different country. "But where will we find him? He could be anywhere ...."

"That's not true. Your dad's rally is starting soon. Ferenc will be there if he knows what's good for him and his family, especially before he flees the country and leaves them to answer questions."

"We'll never find him there."

"We have to try." Marta grabbed Dora's hand and began leading her toward Hősök Square, where the rally was set to take place.

Under the banner of a black, starless sky, thousands of young people flooded the square. Blinding lights illuminated the masses as barricades funneled them toward the stage, making it seem even more crowded than it already was. The reluctant participants, most likely attending for their own protection, stood shoulder-to-shoulder, smoking cigarettes and gazing half-interested at the minute figures on stage. Dora and Marta could barely move through the crowd, let alone go in search of Ferenc.

"And we must all be aware of our purpose ...," the loudspeaker sent a voice through the audience, which Dora recognized as her father's boss. If she squinted, she could see Ivan standing on stage. Behind him, massive, long black curtains hung from pillars, as if to remind everyone of the party's immense power.

"... that we are workers responsible for the well-being of this nation," Ivan said, taking hold of the microphone. "You might say you would prefer to be a movie star, a wealthy capitalist, that working in a factory is not for you. Or maybe you hear friends saying that. I caution you, do not give credence to this petty bourgeois egotism. Staying and working in Hungary will provide you with more fulfillment than anything else. Nothing compares to the feeling of working hard for your country."

The crowd erupted in applause, though Dora didn't see anyone near her doing much clapping. They had probably set up speakers to project fake cheering in the square.

Marta poked Dora in the side, pointing toward a group of men huddled in a circle. "Dora! That's Ferenc."

Dora stood on her tiptoes, trying to see where Marta was pointing. Sure enough, Ferenc stood in the group, frowning and rubbing his forehead as he focused on whatever was in the middle of the circle.

"What are they doing?" Marta nudged Dora toward Ferenc.

"I have no idea."

As Ivan's voice rolled through the crowd, Ferenc looked mournfully at his watch. Every time he seemed to frown even harder, and without any indication, he tore away from the group.

"Where is he going?" Dora pleaded as Ferenc forced his way through the throngs of people, slipping out of view.

"I don't know, but we have to follow him," Marta whispered.

"Let's go." Dora eyed the security police surrounding them. "But not too quickly."

As they passed Ferenc's friends, Dora peered through the gaps between them to find the center of their focus. In the middle of the group, on the ground, sat a small, black radio. It was emanating static like an uncapped fire hydrant. Dora had an idea where Ferenc was going.

ESZTER TURJÁN
February 28, 1965—Midnight

HE'S BEFORE ME, his eyes flaring, the fire in them so bright I have to shield myself.

"Did you hear it? Did you hear it?" Ferenc points to the radio. "We unjammed it!"

He's so excited.

"I heard the code," I say. "How did you do it?"

"We broke into the room where they store the jamming equipment, and my friend Tomasz disabled it."

"But didn't you hear the code too?" I am getting suspicious.

"We didn't have time."

"Is that the only reason you came down here? For the code?" I'm worried he's going back on his promise to take me.

"No ...." He starts pacing. "I still need your help to get on the envoy."

"I will help you, but hide under the bed for now. We have to wait until the guards change and the second one gets too drunk and tired to notice us."

I notice the adrenaline sparking in Ferenc's eyes. It's the

look I saw in Boldiszar when I led him through the streets that night. I lean back against my bed and wait. Escape is my chance. It's my only shot at seeing Laszlo face-to-face, proving to him that I am alive, I am breathing, and I am still someone. Then there is Dora, of course.

My stomach begins to leap from inside of me, going somewhere. I don't know where. I begin to feel that same burst I experienced after I shot the Soviet soldier.

"You have to promise me one thing," I say. "You will never leave my side until I am out of here."

"I will take you. I have always said I will take you. Please, let's go soon." Ferenc stirs below my bed, and I press down with my all my weight to stop him from moving.

Minutes lurch by us. I stare at a small ant crossing what, to him, must seem like a ravine, but it's just the crack between two bricks. If I could be as tiny as that ant I would have crawled out a long time ago, I want to tell Ferenc. I would not need him.

The guards change, but first they do their inspection of our cells, back and forth, back and forth. I pray they don't take me for themselves tonight. Not tonight, not ever again. Their steps send vibrations through the floor that I am sure Ferenc feels too. He does not move once.

The worst is always to come. I must remember that. I tell Ferenc that we will make our escape in two hours. That is when the second guard will be completely incapacitated.

*

He's coming into my cell. Oh, no, he is going to do it to me.

He is going to take me, and we will miss our window. I want to scream, but I can't. I want to fight him, but I am so weak.

"Eszter, Eszter, Eszter." I can smell the vodka, but not on his breath, from his pores. It's in him. "Are you going to come with me tonight?"

I can feel Ferenc below me, because he's poking the mattress, and I don't know what it means, but I know I have to stop this guard. I have to protect Ferenc and get out of here.

I shake my head.

"Oh, you're a feisty one tonight, aren't you?" He falls onto my bed and he tries to lift his head, but it's filled with vodka. I can hear it sloshing back and forth inside of him. "I have something for you." He reaches into his pocket and pulls out a red geranium, withered and pressed from being in his pocket. He runs it along my mouth. "Isn't it so lovely?" He picked it from the pots in the windows upstairs, I'm sure of it.

He starts moving more on the bed, scooting his butt up and down. He feels Ferenc. He must. "Are you hiding something under here?"

I put my hand behind me because I am scratching it, and it's the only thing I know to do. I feel something hard and metal go into it, from the crack between the bed and the wall. I run my hand along the top of the object. It's pointed, a screwdriver. It's the one Ferenc uses to open the vent, and he has given it to me now. I know exactly what to do.

"I have something for you too," I whisper.

The guard looks at me, hopeful.

I take the screwdriver and I stab him, stab him, stab him

in the eye. Thoughts leave me, and all that remains is my body moving, attacking. He screams, but I don't care. I keep stabbing. He falls to the floor, and I jam the screwdriver in his ear. I stand above him, possessed by a strength I didn't know I had. I kick his head over and over until he doesn't move, but I can see him breathing. That is enough, I decide.

I grab Ferenc's arm and help him out from under the bed.

"Eszter, thank you, thank you," Ferenc gasps.

He sounds like he's praying to me. When his eyes finally make it to mine, I recognize the expression.

"Boldiszar," I say to him. "Trust me, this time it will work."

But what I really want to tell him is that we can all become someone else. We aren't original. We are people who have already lived, or died, or who aren't even dead yet. I've already done this before, to him, years ago. Boldiszar grins, too much.

Before I can leave, I have to say goodbye to my rat. He barely exists now because he has deteriorated to bones and loose, torn skin. I hold him tight. My hand is getting worse, and puss is festering in the wounds. My little rat doesn't mind. His tiny nose is still intact, and that's what I kiss.

Boldiszar looks over my entire body, and suddenly I am worried. "What?"

"You won't survive out there."

"I have to."

"It's winter. And that looks infected." He reaches for my hand.

I pull it away from him. "I'll be fine. Just get me out."

"I'm taking this." Boldiszar grabs the worn blanket on my bed. "It's not much, but at least we can keep you a little warm."

He is so thoughtful, my Boldiszar. I nod.

We start with the vent in my cell, my first hurdle. When I make it inside, I feel the icy darkness of something that never brought me heat. My eyes search for nothing in the black, but my ears follow Boldiszar, who is crawling in front of me and then up, up, up. He reaches his hand down and I hear it tapping on the metal, beckoning me to grab it. I do, and he pulls me up, grunting through the exertion. The vent creaks, and I wonder if it's on the verge of splintering. Every time it happens, Boldiszar pauses.

We come upon a solid piece of metal. It's a blockade. I hear Boldiszar fiddle with keys, then the sure sound of a lock unlocking. We continue. Crawl. Door. Unlock. We enter a tunnel that smells like dirt and urine. We are wading through a bigger tunnel, and sewage collects around my ankles.

But I see it. It's my first glimpse of freedom at the top of a grate. Through it I spy yellow light, barely poking through.

"Eszter," Boldiszar is pointing up. "Please, tell me, when I open that, you will take me to the envoy."

I nod forcefully, my neck so raw and grimy, and me not liking it for the first time. Boldiszar climbs up a ladder built into the wall. He pushes on the grate. It slides off. He reaches down to me. Holding my breath, I grab his hand one last time. He pulls me into the night.

My body is rigid. I can hardly look up, but when I do, I see, for the first time, nothing above me. I feel the swell of the universe, a momentum going up and no longer down into the basement. So much air rushes into me at one time that it feels like all the wind in the world is being funneled into my lungs. My skin is on fire, even though it's cold. The air is digging its tiny fingers into every pore and yanking out the staleness of the past nine years. I might be turning numb, because Boldiszar drapes the blanket over me, but I don't feel it. My entire body begins convulsing, and I feel the ground hit me. There is little I can do but endure this onslaught. I am free.

DORA TURJÁN
February 28, 1965—Midnight

DORA COULDN'T BREATHE again, like she was really drowning this time. She'd feel a wave of terror engulf her, followed by a swell of regret that would push her further and further down into the tumult. It was so dark and so cold, and she couldn't hold her breath much longer. She just couldn't. Her mom, at any moment, would emerge into the night, and she didn't know what to do.

After they fled the rally, Marta ran to get Tomasz and Dora went straight to the ministry, hoping she'd find Ferenc there. Dora thought he'd seek help from Eszter in his panic, though she certainly wouldn't be able to unjam the radio. Dora caught Ferenc just as he was running in the door, out of breath and sweaty, and so determined he didn't even notice Dora at first. When she shouted his name a second time, he spun around and rushed to her. Pulling her into his arms, he kissed her hard, his sweat making his forehead almost as moist as his tongue. Dora leaned into him for a brief second, enjoying his attention and his warmth.

When she told him about the room in the ministry with the additional jamming equipment, he smiled, a watery film coating his eyes, and took Dora's hand. He kissed her again, and they began their search for the room.

Ferenc had keys to most of the doors, though the longer they spent searching the building, the more Dora wondered if Ivan had misspoken. The fact that they would build redundancy into the jamming system made sense, but it didn't quite add up that they would put the equipment in the ministry. Why not just store it somewhere in the radio building, where the infrastructure was already in place?

When Ferenc finally opened a room with what looked like radio equipment, Dora let out a sigh of relief. And, even better, the room was empty. Dora had mentally prepared for a different scenario, silently practicing her most senior voice, which she'd use to explain that she had orders to override the current jamming schedule.

Shortly thereafter, Tomasz and Marta arrived, and Tomasz went to work right away. Once he disabled the jamming device, Ferenc told them all to wait outside. He had to go get Eszter. She had a radio and hopefully heard the code. They couldn't risk staying there and getting caught listening to Radio Free Europe. Once outside, Marta and Tomasz excused themselves to search for a backup radio, though Dora knew it was really just to give her some privacy.

Dora still hadn't figured out how she'd break the news to Ferenc that she was actually Dora and not, indeed, Anika. She didn't want to say anything that would distract him from the mission, though it didn't seem completely fair he'd learn the news just as he prepared to leave the country with her mom. After knowing Ferenc's innermost thoughts for years, Dora speculated that if he did get upset, however, it wouldn't last for too long. His desire for love usually outweighed most other things in his life.

She wandered to the side alley, the place where she first unknowingly saw Eszter. She thought back to that day— how she would have never imagined the power of one look and all that it would put in motion.

She leaned back against the brick wall, its ragged surface catching on her coat, providing the illusion that someone was holding her up. "Mom," Dora practiced saying. "I'm glad you made it out. I'm glad you're here." But every time she said the words out loud, they sounded so fake. "Mom, mom, mom" she said again, hoping the repetition would calm her down. She thought about turning around and going home, back to her life with her dad. She didn't, after all, need to see her mom for the plan to work. She could probably find a way to confirm that Ferenc and Eszter made it out without being there to witness it.

Yet Dora's mind, so tired of lying to her, kept her standing in the snow for another hour. She knew abandoning Eszter now would mean going back to the life she had, and now hated. It was one of indifference and perpetual waiting. It was marked by routine, both in her movements and in her feelings. She strove for nothing she truly cared about, and in turn, became successful at perpetuating the life she didn't want. She already felt more alive than she had in nine years, and she clung to that feeling now, hoping it could somehow warm her up.

When flurries of snow started surrounding her and the wind began nipping at her ears, she decided it was time to go searching for Ferenc and Eszter. She crept out of the alley, studying the streets, nearly empty now. She passed by the abandoned parks and office buildings, then the train station, which looked so much more elegant in the winter, the snow covering its dusty film.

An older man shuffled past her, his face hidden in his scarf. His crystal blue eyes peeked out above the fabric, studying the ground through a web of wrinkles and swollen, windburnt skin. She knew it couldn't be Ferenc, but a part of her hoped it was anyway, and she observed him until he turned the corner and disappeared. Dora could have sworn she heard The Beatles coming from a window above her, but she doubted anyone would be so daring as to play rock 'n' roll so late at night.

She circled back toward the ministry, where she decided she would resume her station until the morning, when she saw a shadowy figure cross the street. She couldn't make out its exact shape, but it looked like a man. She started off in that direction.

For a moment, she forgot what Ferenc looked like, her nerves starting to override her ability to think clearly. What if she was the one losing it? What if Eszter's mental illness was genetic and this was her first breakdown? She felt her hands grow lighter, her legs too. It suddenly seemed like they weren't even part of her body, like she was gliding on the snow or falling down into a deep pit.

"Anika," she heard someone shout at her. She kept moving forward. "Anika," the voice said again. It was coming from the mouth of a man. She kept going toward it. She felt so warm all of a sudden. He was hugging her.

"How did you find us?" it said, and when she looked into its eyes she saw Ferenc staring intently back at her, concerned and weary.

"I just kept walking. It's so cold." Dora's voice trembled as she pushed her words through the frigid air.

"I'm so sorry we lost you. The guards, they almost caught us, we had to go out another way." He kissed Dora's cheek. "You are freezing, we need to get both of you inside." Ferenc pointed to a lumpy blanket on the ground in the alley, curled up against the brick wall.

Dora froze and stared at the blanket. It wasn't moving. It had to be … it could only be …

"Is she okay?" Dora inched closer to the blanket.

"She's okay for now, but we need to get her on the envoy as soon as possible."

A snort rattled from the blanket. "Laszzzzzzzlooooo," she said. "Stop! Stop!"

Dora kneeled down to Eszter's level, knowing this was it—the moment she had feared for the past nine years, but had nonetheless headed for her with the certain stride of fate. The blanket covered most of her mom's face. Only her forehead was visible as Eszter rocked herself gently in her cocoon.

"I think she is a little overwhelmed right now." Ferenc put his arm on Dora's shoulder. "It's best to just leave her alone."

Dora ignored him. She wanted to look into her mom's eyes. She reached for the blanket. It felt hot. Eszter must have a fever. Or maybe it was Dora's hands that were cold. Making sure not to make any sudden movements, Dora pulled down the blanket past Eszter's chin. She lowered her body, until she was lying down on the pavement next to her mom. She closed her eyes and kept them shut until she felt her face align with Eszter's, her breath on Dora's nose.

Dora took one last breath. She opened her eyes. At first, Eszter stared past Dora, into the snowdrifts piled on the sidewalk behind them. But as the seconds went by, Eszter's gaze crept along Dora's shoulders, to her neck, and finally to her face. When they locked eyes, Eszter froze. A look of bewilderment, bordering on shock, overcame her face.

"It's me," Dora whispered. She reached for her mom's cheek, Eszter's skin hot on Dora's palm. The moment felt dangerously palpable to Dora, as if at any time, someone could reach down and swat it away.

"Mom," Dora resolved.

"My daughter." Eszter pulled Dora into her.

They hugged, gripping each other tighter and tighter. Eszter started shaking and Dora rubbed her back, her fingers catching on the knobs of Eszter's spine. She was so frail, Dora feared she might hurt her. She remembered watching Eszter resist the weight of a police officer, nearly bucking him off her back, nine years ago. Now, Eszter struggled beneath the weight of a hug.

"You're here," Eszter whispered.

"I am."

"What is going on?" Ferenc's voice cracked behind them.

Dora pulled away from Eszter. She wiped the dirt off her coat and stood up to face Ferenc. "I am not Anika. I am Dora Turján, Eszter's daughter."

Ferenc's eyes swelled. He opened his mouth to speak, but closed it quickly and shook his head.

"I only knew halfway through this whole thing you were dealing with my mom. I thought you guys could help each other escape."

"What? That can't be true!" Ferenc backed away from them.

"It is true."

Ferenc looked at her with anger now, lingering extra long on Dora's eyes. "Why would you lie to me, Anika?"

"It's Dora."

"How could you do that?"

Dora explained the entire situation, allowing the truth to strike Ferenc in its consistent yet painful rhythm. As Dora spoke, Ferenc's eyes grew watery. He coughed and kept extending his neck. Dora didn't know if he was trying to make himself seem taller or just push back the tears amassing in his throat. It was probably both.

"I can't believe it. You're a liar. You used me." Ferenc looked from Dora, to Eszter, then back again.

"Please, I did this for her and you. Those letters from

Uncle Lanci, those were from me ... so that you could keep going."

"What?" Ferenc's voice grew louder. "Pretending to be some radio personality so that you could make me risk my life getting her out. How is that any help?"

"I'm sorry." Dora's fingers wound nervously around one another. "I wanted to help you escape too."

"But you did this for her, mostly?"

Dora looked down. She didn't know what to say. That wasn't true either. She cared about both of them, one by instinct and the other by choice. She couldn't imagine the guilt, and anger, she'd feel if either of them didn't make it out at this point.

"Well, I still need to go to Munich." Ferenc huffed and kneeled down to Eszter. "You said you knew the meeting place, that you heard the code on the radio. Take me there."

Dora stared at her mom, who had since retreated into a ball, the blanket fully covering her head.

"Mom," Dora tapped her mom's shoulder. "Is it true you figured out the meeting place?"

"Yes," Eszter's voice breached the blanket, muffled and phlegm-ridden.

"Tell us where it is." Ferenc nudged Eszter's shoulder.

"Come here. I'll whisper it in your ear."

"You can tell all of us," Ferenc said.

Eszter looked at Dora and smiled. She turned to Ferenc. "Only you need the code."

"There is no reason why Dora can't hear."

Eszter shook her head. "No, no, no."

"Just go to her," Dora said, backing away.

"Fine, but I don't like this." Ferenc lowered his ear to Eszter who, like a child, covered her mouth so Dora couldn't see the movements of her lips. Dora didn't have time to understand why her mom was acting this way. They needed to just keep moving forward.

"I know where we need to be." Ferenc grabbed Dora's hand.

"We?"

"Yes, I'm angry, but not enough to leave you here. You, me, and your mom. We have to get on that envoy."

That was the Ferenc she knew, though Dora never planned to go with them. She decided to play along, realizing that was the only way to keep Ferenc going.

Dora reached for Eszter's hand. "We'll just take it slow."

Eszter didn't move at all.

"I'm too weak, Dora," she gasped.

"I know, but you have to come with us."

"I can't."

"You can."

Dora wrapped her arms around Eszter and stood her up, clinging to her torso as she tried to steady her. One side of Eszter seemed almost completely immobile. Looking down, Dora noticed her mom's battered hand. Remembering how hot Eszter felt, Dora realized she needed medical attention as soon as possible. They had to start moving.

"We've got to go, now."

"I think I can do it," Eszter said. "Just let go."

The second Dora did, however, Eszter's knees buckled, and she collapsed to the ground.

Dora bent down to pick up Eszter again. "I'll carry you for some of the way, and then Ferenc will do the rest."

"We can't carry her, Dora," Ferenc said gently, behind her. "It wouldn't look right. People would notice."

"Go without me for now," Eszter said.

"No." Dora wasn't about to lose Eszter again. "Mom, please, you must have some strength to get up."

Ferenc stooped down to Dora, placing his hand on her back. "She's right. We can't take her right now. We'd be risking our lives. But we'll come back for her once we get the envoy. I promise."

"We can't just leave her here."

"She's safe for now." Ferenc took off his jacket and wrapped it around Eszter. He pointed to an alcove in the alley. "We'll make it nice for her there and put these trash bins in front, so no one will see her."

"Trash?" Dora looked at the overflowing trash cans. They'd make Eszter even sicker.

"It's just temporary," Ferenc said.

"I'll wait right here for you. Just go with him." Eszter clung to the blanket and Ferenc's jacket.

"Not before I know." Dora faced her mom. "About Boldiszar."

Eszter froze. Her eyes grew watery. She bowed her head, and as her tears fell to ground, she whispered, "It was my fault."

"No, please don't say that." Dora dropped to her knees.

"I led Boldiszar to the trap by mistake. I thought guns and ammunition and forces from the West would be there, but I was a fool. They shot him in the neck. He was going to die and my strength was gone, Dora. I couldn't drag him out of there, not like that, with his throat full of blood."

"But, did you kill him? Did you shoot him?"

Eszter looked past Dora. Her lips trembled.

"Mom, I need to know."

"I wanted to relieve his suffering."

"And?" She needed her mom to say it.

"Yes, it was me, in the end."

Dora stared at her mom. Eszter did it. She was the reason Boldiszar died. It was her, in so many ways. Dora started looking around, for what, she didn't know. Maybe just someone who could swoop down and change the past. Her eyes searched and searched, but found nothing. She was confused and feeling hot.

Eszter wrapped her arm around Dora and tried to pull her close. "It was the most merciful thing I could have done. But it's still all my fault. It is."

Dora didn't want to be hugged by her mom. She sat up, resisting Eszter. "How could you have not tried to save him?"

"He was already gone."

"There is always a chance. There had to be a chance."

Eszter didn't try to defend herself or explain further. She looked down, and Ferenc did the same. They let Dora cry, hunched over her lap, rocking herself back and forth. Dora thought back to Bence, the cemetery groundskeeper, and how he wanted Dora to tell Eszter they knew it was a mistake. She couldn't say it. No, not right now.

When her tears finally began subsiding, Eszter squeezed Dora's hand. "There is one more thing."

Dora didn't know if she could handle one more thing.

"He wanted me to tell you that he loves you."

"What?" Dora didn't think she heard Eszter right.

"It was one of the last things Boldiszar said. He loves you."

Dora's mind stopped, halted, ran into a wall. She didn't move, her eyes glued to her mom's unflinching face.

"It's true," Eszter whispered.

Boldiszar loved her? She always thought he cared for her like a sister, but love? That was something else entirely. That was what she felt when they kissed at the lake, and what she thought about before she went to bed every night. That was what she hoped for, but what was never confirmed. Until now.

"I love him too."

"I know." This time, Eszter was successful at pulling Dora into her. Dora started crying even more, hating her mom yet thankful for her all at the same time.

"I'm sorry, Dora." Eszter ran her fingers through Dora's hair.

Dora didn't know what to say. She had no idea if she would ever forgive her mom, and even alluding to that didn't seem right. She could only express herself through the very physical manifestation of her sadness, which felt like a relief and burden all at once.

When she felt like all her tears had been sucked out of

her, she hoisted herself off the ground. Looking down at Eszter, who could barely lift her head, Dora realized they were her mom's only hope. And she was theirs. She knew what they had to do.

"We'll get the envoy and come back for you," Dora said. "Don't move."

"Just stay with Ferenc."

"I will."

Dora looked at Ferenc, who appeared so concerned Dora didn't even know if he had the strength to go in search of the envoy. She saw that he had been crying too. She felt something rush through her, urging her to devote everything she had to him. After Boldiszar died, she never thought she'd regain that frantic energy again, the kind that made you want to do extraordinary things for someone else—the kind that made you think you could. That feeling, she knew, was love. It was a love not tempered by guilt, or anger, or untruths. It was a love made solely for action and for doing good. Tremulously gaining her balance, her hands shaking, Dora took a step away from Eszter.

"Let's go." She grabbed Ferenc's hand.

*

The sun would rise in a couple hours. They found a doorway near the meeting place, and Dora let herself rest while Ferenc stood guard. She dreamed that she was sitting at her desk when her teeth started falling out and disappearing. She searched everywhere for them, believing that if she found them, the dentist could simply put them back in. She found her mom and begged for her help. "Have you seen them? Have you seen my teeth?" she yelled at Eszter in her dream. Eszter smiled, opening her hand to reveal all of Dora's lost teeth. As Dora reached for the shiny, white pebbles, Eszter closed her fist and laughed.

"Look." Ferenc woke up Dora, his voice hot on her neck.

"What?" She jolted, shocked at first, but relieved to feel all her teeth in place.

"Over there!" Ferenc pointed to two men, middle-aged and business-like, packing a black Zis. They kept looking back and forth every few seconds, inspecting their surroundings a little too closely.

"That's it. That's got to be the envoy."

"But that car …."

"Even smarter of them to use the same car as the secret police."

"I don't know." Dora felt her legs start shaking. "I don't feel good about this."

"Let's just go check it out," Ferenc flashed Dora a grin and slipped his fingers into hers.

As they got closer to the Zis, one of the men hurried to the driver's seat and started the engine. The other one continued packing the trunk, only looking at the boxes in his hands and nowhere else.

"Hello! Wait!" Ferenc ran toward them.

The man ignored them, quickly shoving the last box into the car.

"We know who you are," Ferenc reached for his arm before he could slam shut the trunk.

He turned around and smiled warmly, though Dora noticed the edge of his lip quivering. "What do you mean? We are couriers, delivering our morning letters."

"No, it's okay, I'm supposed to go with you. I know Eszter. The dog ate the cat. The dog ate the cat."

"Son, I don't know what you are talking about, but I think you found the wrong people." Shaking his head, the man, thin with slight, pale hands, closed the trunk and climbed into the front seat of the car.

Dora stood behind them, eyeing the other man, the driver, as he peered straight ahead. She didn't believe them. In their black Zis, dressed in fitted coats, they seemed to be too delicate and serious for couriers. And why wasn't the driver at least curious about what was going on?

"Excuse me, but we were sent here with explicit instructions from Eszter Turján. I am her daughter." Dora stepped in front of Ferenc and caught the car door before the man could close it on them.

He paused, his black eyes jumping ever so slightly. He stared at Dora, taking in her face as his expression dropped from shocked to mournful. "We are not who you are looking for." He buckled his seatbelt.

"I think you are," Dora said.

"Please, leave us alone." The man slammed the door on them.

The car started inching forward.

"You can't go." Ferenc banged on the windows. "The dog ate the cat! The dog ate the cat!" Ferenc tried to open the car door, but it was locked and too late. The Zis had found an opening in traffic. It peeled out into the lane, leaving them standing in the street, dumfounded.

"We can't let them go," Ferenc said, on the verge of breaking down. "We can't let them go."

"Then we won't." Dora started running. "Come on."

Ferenc took off behind her, the two of them bounding down the sidewalk as they kept pace with the car. Dora willed herself to push through the fatigue of confusion and the cold, to just stay strong for Ferenc. Every time she started slowing, she felt her entire body sink, begging her to collapse onto the sidewalk. She was almost certain she had gotten sick from being outside in the cold for so long, or maybe Eszter gave her something. By the time they made it to the end of Andrássy út, huge black splotches had multiplied across her eyes. She wanted to faint.

Dodging the people and traffic accumulating in the early morning, the Zis wound through the streets. They managed to keep it in their view, though Dora's breathing had grown haggard and she could hardly run anymore. Ferenc clutched Dora's hand and pulled her along as the car turned into Városliget Park.

"It's pulling over."

"Where?"

"Behind that bush. I can see the top of it."

"Get down," Dora said. "If they see us, we'll scare them off again."

They crouched behind a barricade, still set up from yesterday's rally in the park's main square, where they could see plumes of car exhaust drifting into the icy morning.

"This isn't good enough," Ferenc whispered. "We need to see the actual car."

"I know somewhere we can go." Dora had played in this park as a kid and remembered her favorite hideouts. "Follow me."

She took Ferenc's hand and led him to a squat, rickety shed, which used to serve as the headquarters of her imaginary spy ring. Dora never thought she'd one day use this shed to actually spy on people. She kneeled down, locating a crack in the shed just wide enough for her, and Ferenc, to see through.

The Zis still sat there, idling, waiting for something.

From the corner of her eye, Dora saw a small figure hobbling lop-sided toward the car. As it got closer, she realized it was a woman draped in a worn, tattered blanket.

"Is that …?" Ferenc started.

The woman approached the car and whispered something to the driver.

"No," Dora gasped.

The woman took off the blanket, revealing a long sheath of gray hair and a sickly hand. Her eyes flashed in Dora's direction, and she saw in them a certain madness.

"Mom," Dora said, this time loud and clear.

As Eszter climbed into the back seat of the car, Dora understood everything—Eszter had betrayed them.

"Mom!" Dora yelled, even as her voice closed in on itself.

Dora burst out of the shed and ran toward the car. She grabbed the back bumper, willing it to stay in place.

"Don't go!" Dora shouted. This couldn't be happening. It was all too fast. She had to stop them.

Eszter propped herself up on the Zis' rear window. She rubbed the frost off the glass and peered out at Dora with a wide-eyed fright, like a child who knows she did something terribly wrong, but doesn't understand what it is. A tear fell down Eszter's cheek, just as the car's engine started revving.

"Wait!" Dora cried, but the Zis jolted forward, throwing her to the ground. When Dora looked up, the car had moved out of reach. Within seconds it was speeding toward the street. In the back seat, Eszter's head bobbed up and down, and grew smaller, as the Zis drove farther and farther away.

"No, no, no," Dora sobbed, crumpling to a ball on the pavement, her tears choking her words, choking her thoughts, choking any desire to stay alive at all. Everything felt burning hot, even though her body convulsed in shivers. Dora barely noticed Ferenc as he hugged her and whispered, "It's okay, it's okay." She just kept crying and crying into the gritty pavement beneath her.

EPILOGUE
Three Months Later

Dear (my beloved) Anika,

When I heard your name for the first time in Munich, I kept walking. Someone continued calling forth "Anika, Anika, Anika." (Well, not really that name—the other one that is unmeasured more full of beauty—but I neglect to write it here for your safety. Of course, I am of aware you will be the first to read this because of your position, but I still take a caution with names now.)

I walked for three blocks, listening to that name until I finally turned backward. Of course, I saw two women smushing themselves into each other in a friendship embrace. I know I resemble being childish, but I thought, maybe, it was you. You comprehend, my hope has been leading me around so much these days that I fail to decipher between it and anything else. Chasing hope around is not a simple feat.

There is a singular hope that I do contain within

me. It's that you do not possess infuriation with me. I possess knowledge that you might, but please know, that I strove to write you as soon as I possibly could. As soon as I learned how to do it with safety.

When *she* fled in the car, I presumed the world had finished (I cannot utilize her name for your safety, but you are aware of who I am writing on). As I succamb to the desire to lie next to you, I embraced your tears on mine. You felt so warm, and that is when I knew a sickness had entered your bones for once and total. It was a sickness I once felt, and I remember it occurring when I knew my mom was gone away forever. When I mandated you sleep in my bed, you lay so peacefully that I couldn't awake you. I meandered outside, because, Anika, to witness you suffer the loss that I once did made me gasp for air. As I cornered the curb, a man reproached me. It was the passenger in the car, the man who stunned us and ignored our pleadings.

He told me that he could not place me on that envoy, but that if I followed him, he could show me where I could get a passage to Germany. I am not a fool, and inquired then why he concerned to exit the car and aid me. He said he harbored zero knowledge that *she* would be the passenger in the car. He knew if they were caught, they would all suffer from executions and he made a flee. (Anika—is it potential that she was protecting us by lying to us? She knew that if we accompanied them we might suffer to die?)

I quiered him as to why they did not take us with them. He said that in typical it's harder to get more than one person across the border, and that Laszlo (the real Uncle Lanci) had made it arranged that it was solely *her* they would pick up. She was such a largely threat that they could take *her* and only *her*. (Okay, you catch my meaning of who we are mentioning, yes?)

He grabbed my arm and said to follow him if I wanted to leave, that he would really take me there. At initial, I wanted to yelp, "No! Anika is asleep in my room!" Then I did commit that, and he told me if I did not follow him, I would not depart the country ever. He said the place he was taking me would be leaving soon, and there was no time to do anything else. I compiled to follow him, and still at this juncture feel regrets that I ever committed such a thing. I should have made firmness and told him to force the car to wait for me because I had to say goodbye. But, with my father being departed until the nighttime, I made the calculation that you would awake before he returned home. I hope that you did that in peace, and assembled the courageness to depart my house, and that no one perturbed you. I worry about it every day.

The man, who would never reveal to me his name, led me to a paved entrance behind a government building. We went to a car, it was black and had shades on the windows, but was more cumbersome than a Zis, if you can envision. He opened the trunk and said, "Get in."

I should have said no because I wanted to take shits right there. How would it be possible for me to get into a trunk of a stranger? It felt wrong, but Anika, I have to say, I am a one hundred percent risk taker. Maybe it is because I am stupid (we should not make pretends that I am a genius), or maybe it's because I had your love in me, and it lended me foolishness (it does!), or maybe it is because I couldn't make face with the loss of my mom, and I would do anything to reverse it. Have you ever been so desperate that you feel like survival isn't as important as acquiring your goal? Let me explain: I felt like if I didn't go, my life would always be missing so much. I would remain the seventy or sixty percent person, and really, that's like being a zero percent person, because all that I miss consumes me all day. And I didn't want to keep being defined by what I was missing, and by my sadness. So I went. Please forgive me, Anika, but I went.

The man said the drivers possessed no awareness of my presence. I had to make flees the second the car stopped in Germany. I nodded, but I really did not want to do this.

After our departure, I hunched in the trunk for hours and hours and hours as the car went forth, until I felt it stop. I commenced waiting for more hours, maybe even three. I had to reach certainty that they fled the vehicle. When none of that happened, I placed matters into my own muscle-full arms and opened the trunk. I came to face a man so terrified of my presence, he stood there without moving. Since I possessed the knowledge of why I was there, I gleaned the upper position and assumed action. I leaped out of the trunk, pushed him askance, and made my getaway to the streets.

I had presumed we were somewhere near a city, but they had convened somewhere in rural. I harbored no notions as to my location. I walked for days, Anika, until I could not decipher the difference between my feet and the ground. I found an old man on a bike. He told me, in his English to mine, that I would have to bribe someone to drive me to Munich. He possessed a farm where I worked for two weeks until I secured the money for a bribe.

When I assembled myself to leave his farm, he presented himself in front of me and outstretched his hand for his money. He would drive me. I leaped with joy and hugged him very hard. We went forth to Munich, which was only a thirty-minute jaunt. The old man trickered me, because I could have walked there.

But, now I am here in Munich and I am happy. There are too many things I want to share to you about this glorious place. The streets here don't smell like dog piss. There is no trash everywhere, and people listen to music together in the openness.

There's no Uncle Lanci. Instead, you simply just hear rock emitting from the radio liberally. Betwixt the daytime, I'm lost in the loveliness that is freedom. You can grow to whatever you please here and no one cares a tidbit.

At night, for the first months, I used to sleep in a park. I had a blanket that I found. I learned many facets about myself, as I grabbed the blanket across me and went through shivers. When not one other person is around who is aware of you, Anika, you can become whoever you want. The old me would have been too scared to assume any action. He would have gone home by now. He would have been weak and sad and scared. But, without a singular person near me, who knows *that* version, I could become a braveful man. I realized I was being Adrienne's hero in that moment, embracing struggle to find the missing part of her life too. I was the person I always wanted.

Of course I thought of *her*, your mom. I keep my eyes skinned so I can foster attempts to see her. When I discover a haggard woman on the streets, I always ponder if it's she.

I'm so one hundred percent sorry, Anika, that it happened that way. I neglected to ever trust her, and I wish that I had listened to myself. At where do you think she resides in Munich? I queried myself this often. Sometimes, I would venture to the radio building to attempt forth to get a view of

Uncle Lanci, but also of her. When I passed a dark alley, I always went into it to see if she was hiding somewhere behind a trash. Once I heard a person discuss her name, and I proceeded to follow him for many lengths.

Then one day I discovered a woman drabbed in numerous coats atop a park bench. When I glimpsed her, I started to scream, internally, so vibrantly that I was one hundred percent that she would hear. It was *her*. Finally. She did not wear the gown of homelessness. She appeared clean, Anika, and even a man sat adjacent to her conversing. Similar to a bird, I remained to observe her until they both departed together, after thirty minutes. I regressed to that precise location multiplied times, and the precise scene occurred over and over again. She would be a perch, and the man would attend her, and then they would flee.

I followed them because of you. I knew I could not write backward until I had something to inform you. I did not possess the courageousness for her to see me though, Anika. I felt like one million birds chattered inside my gut, trying to eat it all at once as I followed her. I was abound with nerves that she would see me.

You will be so overjoyed with where they went. The man accompanied her into a building that had crowds of people just like her sitting outside of it and going into it. I went back there many times and when I finally possessed the courage, I asked a worker there what it was. She said it was a home for women who had no homes. What more could we pray for with her?

But, I possessed even more courage, one day, to inquire her escort of his identity. You wouldn't make believe what he said. "I'm Laszlo, who are you?" I almost jumped atop of him. "Uncle Lanci?" I pondered. And he smiled so at large and thundered, "Yes!" I readily explained who I was, indicating my code name. He mentioned that he failed to recall me (were you hoarding my letters to yourself?), but if I so envisioned, I could make a stop at the radio station to greet him there. I will do that soon!

I did not inquire about *her* or inform him of our relationship. I am still scared to talk to her, but, Anika, please, can this find comfort for you? It has to, because you envision I can't even speak to her. I want to, but every time I venture close to her, I hear the screaming internally within me. I promise one thing—I am going to further follow her so that I consistently possess knowledge of where she is. When you come to me here (you will, yes?) I will be aware of exactly how to take you toward her.

As for me, I finally did it. I found my mom. It didn't consume a long time as I originally pondered it would. There are only so many Marikas here, and she has not strove to conceal her identity. I simply discovered her listed in the magnificent German record books. Before I absconded to see her, I made sure to find a shower and a suit. Thank God, because as I fled to my mom's apartment, I realized I had entranced the most richly part of town. I endeavored to imagine my mom, with her spindles of arms and blond hair, fitting in amongst the Germans. She must have felt more at home here, I promised myself. I possessed no ideas what I would say to her. That part I hadn't practiced. As I went to knock on her door, panic had swamped my brain, making me feel like I sauntered through a maze.

I knocked three times before someone answered. A petite girl who wore blond hair split in half answered the door. Her lower lip jostled outward as she took in me standing there. She said hello gently and I asked her for my mom. She ran back into the house and I heard a person trot to the door.

She stood before me. Yes, it was her, can you make believe it? Wrinkles made crowds around her eyes, her blond hair was pricked with gray, her skin bore more veins, but it was her. I knew because her cheeks still tightened ferociously at the cheekbones, and her eyes still curved oddly upward as if she was physically incapable of looking down. I halted breathing completely. We both said nothing. She stared onto me. I stared onto her. Our eyes combed each other's features for minutes, but I swear it was hours. Turning to mush, my mind slopped around in my head and failed to produce any words.

"I came to see you," is what eventually shambled

out of my mouth and then lumped into the space between us.

I thought she was about to close the door on me right there, but she bent down and made herself busy with picking up the petite toys scattered atop her floor.

"It's so dirty in here," she said.

I really reached confusion why my mom regarded the floor with so much concern when I stood before her. Well, I couldn't ponder how to react toward her, so I simply lowered beside her and contributed to her efforts. It was similar as if I intruded her area because she instantaneously sat upward and touched my head. I fail to understand it, but I had desired to just slap her hand away. She didn't earn the right yet to act affectionately. I had questions, and I would demand answers. Except she wouldn't stop even when I winced. She brought her fingers together on my arm, held it firm, and gravitated me inward to her. We hugged. I started crying when I understood she remained smelling like green tea. I had forgotten that was her normal smell. When we finally made our way upward, she herded me to the kitchen. I was a stranger to this house ruled by a little girl and my mom.

"Is she your own?" I asked as I pointed toward the girl latched on to my mom's legs.

My mom nodded. "She's your partial sister."

A joy broke atop of me as I saw this petite girl

before me. Younger than Adrienne by many years, she still possessed the same defying look on her face, like she would soon take charge of me. I succumbed to laugh only a bit.

My mom told me when she fled Hungary, she became abused on the way. I will not indulge the details now. It's too much for this letter. She lived atop the streets for a time when she came into Munich. With no food and no money, she pursued as a homeless person for nearly five months until an artist took a liking to her balloon belly. He never once asked that she share with him her history. His concerns remained that she simply be there. She birthed my second petite sister, and they lived together, like a tricycle. The old man lived for five more years, but then his age took him. When he died, he left his apartment and his everything to my mom. She has been living there ever since.

When she finished her story, I understood this man gave her what my father never would. He was not terrified of kindness. It was not a thing embarrassing for him. It wasn't a thing that you declined to exhibit because then someone would not be learning a thing or because then maybe they would view a part of you that is asking for love back. But for this old man, kindness was everything he was composed of and he gave it to my mom one hundred percent. I loved the old man in that instance for loving my mom in that way. My thoughts reversed to selfishness then and I thought—Can she love me now? Has he shown her how?

When I inquired of my mom why she didn't return after he died she said not much. At initial she grinned, the embarrassment sending shockwaves around her lips. I am not sure what she said next, but I burst up from where I sat, making attempts to harpoon the anger gurgling atop my lips. I demanded to learn why, you envision.

"Tell me now!"

"No."

"Please."

"No."

"You have to."

"I do?"

"Yes."

"Okay, but you will not enjoy it."

"I know."

She performed an elongated sigh, and requested I perch next to her. A vacuum sucked her eyes away from me as the instances occurring inside her mind prepared themselves for viewing. She placed her head atop my shoulder like a petite Adrienne begging for forgiveness.

She told me something that I knew, but it finally became a real thing. She always had it, a depression that originated from childhood and was her bedside enemy her entire life. She had enough with it. When I was petite, she tried to kill herself, but suffered a lack of bravery. She said she would make an attempt every day, in the after time when I went to school. We had a clock that tocked atop a shelf, and it sounded admist our apartment. She would count one thousand tocks of it, and on that one thousand she would try to kill herself again. Sometimes the most she would do was tie a sewing string across her neck. Sometimes she utilized a larger rope. Sometimes she placed a bag surrounding her neck and waited until something in her maneuvered it off.

I wished I had the knowledge of this—I would have declined to go to school. I would have remained next to her so she could absorb my child happiness. But the other fold of me knows that it was prime that I did not know. That I could at least remain a child for a little longer (unlike Adrienne, who never got to be a child), and maybe this childness has made it so I still believe in something perfect transpiring. I still possess hope that I can make the world I want, like when you're petite and you think you can do anything.

My mom decided to leave because she couldn't hold up her end as a mom or as a wife. Also because she thought she would die in her escape. If someone else killed her then she would be handed the fate she pined toward. I do not possess memory of this, but she swores she kissed me goodbye before she left. She swores she kissed me one thousand times to erase all the one thousand times she counted on the clock.

I inquired what has transformed now in Munich. Why could she stay alive now? She informed me she discovered a peace that she did not know in Hungary before. It was a lighter feeling in Munich. There were many shops open, and restaurants to maneuver her mind from her sadness, and people that spoke with her in freedom. In Hungary, there were not many things lively and she felt watched one hundred percent of the time by the government (which I comprehend). My mom said she felt immense disdain at her factory job but there was not an option to transform. She was assigned to that duty, and it was a final.

She pulled her head away from my shoulder, stood tall, and then kissed me atop my cheeks all over. I know what you are wondering, of course. I told her about Adrienne. I told her about you. When I asked if she would come back to Hungary, only for a vacation, to see Adrienne, her eyes once again got slurped into the vacuum.

She never gave me a definite answer.

My new petite sister (Béla) already twiddled her way onto my lap, asking me to read to her. I spent my life devoting myself to Adrienne, and now this new petite person is asking for my attention. It felt so uplifting and then so depressing since Adrienne could not be there to witness it.

Since I cannot make force of my mom to depart Munich, I will stay here until I come forth with a plan to get Adrienne, and even my father, here. I don't prospect my parents to rekindle a unit, but I do believe that my father wouldn't suffice without Adrienne, so I cannot leave him out of my plans. When I settle to sleep at night, I envision Adrienne's face when she learns about my plans. It will be the most crystalline vision of happiness, undisturbed by anything. It will be one hundred percent.

There's something other too—I desire for you to be here, Anika. You have time to make ponders on this, but you should acquire awareness that I am one hundred percent committed to you. I comprehend that it does not make a proper equation that I would manifest these mighty feelings so quickly, but I cannot say no to what's inside of me. Our bond is more strong than reasoning, time, or space. We will eventual be together, I know that more than I even know anything. I love you.

Sincerely,
Ferenc

DORA TURJÁN

When Dora woke up, she found Ivan standing above her.

"You've been asleep for seventeen hours." He shook his head and sighed.

"Ohhhhh, really?" Dora yawned and rolled over. "I'll get up soon."

"You can't do this forever. It's dinner time."

"Just give me a few hours."

"You have one." Ivan stomped out of her room, leaving her door open.

Dora didn't care. She closed her eyes and tried hard to go back to sleep. It had been three months since Ferenc and her mom made their escape, and still she woke up every morning feeling as if it only happened a few hours ago. The memories muscled their way into her mind, pushing past the warmness of sleep and weighing her down so much she just couldn't get up.

She remembered Eszter being driven away in the car. She could recall falling to the pavement and Ferenc rubbing her back. She certainly remembered waking up in his room, then sneaking out before anyone in his family saw her. When she got home, she sat down at the kitchen table, unscrewed a jar of jam, spread it on a slice of bread, and tried to eat for the first time that day. It made her feel even sicker. She gave up, electing to drink a glass of water instead. She noticed her hand shaking as she lifted the water to her lips. Her anger started there, but quickly went to her heart, which thundered in her chest.

Sure, Dora knew her mom's plot hadn't been intended to mislead her. How could Eszter have known Dora was involved with Ferenc? Dora's anger came from the fact that once Eszter saw Dora again, she didn't tell her the truth. She actually only told Ferenc the code, probably because she knew Dora would sense there was something afoot. Yes, Eszter was sick, in many ways. But this was not something a crazy person would do. This was something a person thinking clearly, and methodically, would do. And in her moments of lucidity, Eszter could have come clean and insist Ferenc not join the envoy. She could have promised to go to Munich and arrange for Ferenc to get on the next envoy. But, no, she didn't do any of that. Instead, she abandoned them.

Dora wanted to punch something, but she wouldn't. She wanted to scream, but she wouldn't do that either. Instead, she walked to her room and went to sleep, hoping that when she woke up, a piece of her pain would be left behind in her dreams.

Dora ended up sleeping for hours that day and into the night. For months after that, she continued sleeping voraciously, taking it in like a dog slopping up water after a salty meal. Ivan despised it, though he left her in peace most of the time.

He had tried to hint that he knew what took place, or at least the scant outlines of the events from that day. He would mention Ferenc casually and say something along the lines of, "I wonder where he got off to …." He once even left a memo out on the table that speculated on how Eszter escaped. It mentioned nothing of Ferenc, thank God. When Ivan saw Dora noticing it, he nodded to her and walked away.

She noticed Ivan softening in other ways too. Instead of spending hours in his study after work, he would go out then return home happier than when he left. Dora assumed he was dating for the first time since Eszter was taken away. She couldn't do the same, and she mostly found herself thinking about Ferenc. She missed him. She didn't know what happened to him, but convinced herself not to speculate until she knew the truth. She assumed he had found a way to escape, but she wondered if he had made it safely across the border. Dora felt on edge so often, irritated at the smallest things, like waiting for the tram, or when someone in front of her was walking slowly. She wanted to rush through her everyday life so that she could get closer to seeing or hearing from Ferenc, wherever he was.

On her way to work, Dora would go out of her way to walk by places that reminded her of Ferenc and fantasized about their conversations, drawing from a list of things she stowed away to share with him. Once a dog peed right on her shoe. Ferenc would laugh so hard when she told him about that. She had run into Adrienne recently, who ended up comforting Dora over Ferenc's absence. He would be so proud.

She dreamed about eating dinner with him, the desire to touch him so strong they held hands across the table. Dora could practically fit her entire hand in Ferenc's palm. As he walked her home, he'd pulled her into him and they would kiss right there in the middle of the street. Dora would usually wake up at that point, convinced the moment was real. When she saw only the walls of her room surrounding her, she'd pull her blankets up to her chin and go back to sleep. She was in the process of doing that when Ivan intruded upon her, requesting she get out of bed.

When Dora managed to banish him out of her room, she noticed he left behind an envelope wedged between the folds of her blanket. Addressed to Uncle Lanci, the letter had been opened, and the perpetrator seemed to want her to know that. Next to the letter, Dora found a small note in Ivan's handwriting.

It read, *They are safe now.*

She recognized the handwriting in the letter immediately. It was from Ferenc. As she read the letter, she felt a warmth coat the fear that made her shiver, even during the summer. She no longer felt abandoned in her memories and longing. She had someone who could match them, even though he was miles away. The knowledge that both Ferenc and her mom had made it safely to Munich, and created some sort of life there, alleviated Dora's anxiety. She imagined Ferenc playing with his little sister as he did with

Adrienne, that goofy smile on his face reflecting the joy in his sister's eyes. She imagined her mom sitting down and eating a warm meal, making progress on getting healthy. And despite Ferenc's geographical distance, he seemed as enamored with her as he had been when he first met Dora, as Anika. The knowledge that he devoted himself to her completely made Dora feel suddenly buoyant.

She got out of bed, and for the first time in months, smiled.

*

For years, Dora continued writing to Ferenc. The regular reports Ferenc gave on Eszter and his own mom pushed Dora through to the next day, then the next week, and finally the following years, giving her the life of certainty she always wanted. At first, she noticed subtle changes. She started doing her hair in the morning. She took longer to eat breakfast with Ivan. She agreed to go out with Marta. The big changes happened, too.

Ivan would ask Dora how everything was going with her letters. She knew what he meant. She'd describe Eszter's life in generic terms, saying things like, "I read in Munich inexpensive apartments can be purchased if an agency helps you. Many women are doing that and I know it's working out for them." He returned her responses with a grin, still tempered by caution, but perhaps a little larger than before.

She found herself accompanying her dad on walks in the park, where they would talk about easy things, like the leaves changing colors, the books they were reading, or a new recipe he wanted to try making. She found his company comforting. Dora also noticed her face looked different. The severe curves of her cheeks had softened. She gained fifteen pounds, finally no longer so thin she could be mistaken for a student.

She still went to the cemetery once a week to pay tribute to Boldiszar, his body still missing, as it probably always would be. She hated that she couldn't remember the exact shade of brown in his eyes, or how high his voice would get when he saw a cute dog, or even what his hands felt like when they grasped hers as a little girl. The harder she tried to remember, the fuzzier her memories got. She knew she was letting go, whether she wanted to or not, and as she started to accept it, she began to remember him as an old friend rather than a reminder of the love she lost.

After three years, Dora received her first letter from Eszter. She made similar pleas as Ferenc, begging Dora to come to Munich. That was her plan all along, Eszter said. She knew that if she got out of the country, she could one day reconnect with Dora from a safe place. Eszter never planned on taking Ferenc with her. There was only ever room for one, and it was Eszter. Eszter had given them the wrong code to lead them astray, and keep them safe. It was an utter coincidence that Ferenc and Dora ran into the actual envoy when they did.

Eszter said the people at the home had been helping her think, and she had brief moments of clarity when she felt sorry. She was experiencing one of those moments when she wrote this letter. She didn't know when the awareness would fade, and she would retreat to her own world, the one she created to survive the horrors of those nine years in the ministry's basement. Eszter kept repeating herself, sometimes writing the same sentence or word three to four times. Over and over, she urged Dora to come to Munich.

With a cautious approach, Dora wrote back to her mom. She avoided any sort of emotional conversation or proclamations of forgiveness. She didn't mention Boldiszar once, either. She talked about her work, what she ate for dinner, and a new outfit she bought. Eszter wrote back. Sometimes her letters made sense. Sometimes they didn't.

One day, Dora mustered the courage to ask Ivan if she could go on an extended trip to Munich. At first he said no, insisting that it was too dangerous, though they both knew traveling posed much less of a threat now. Kádár had rolled back a number of restrictions, putting in place his own brand of communism, which was just a watered-down version of the USSR's system. It became easier to travel, and even the state radio played rock 'n' roll.

Dora decided to go to Munich anyway. She hated the thought of leaving her dad, but she hoped his newfound good spirits would help him forgive her eventually. A few days after making her request, Dora found a train ticket on her bed. Its destination read: Munich.

Dora turned on Radio Free Europe and lay down on the floor of her room, the only cool spot on the hot summer day. She smiled as she imagined how hard Ferenc would hug her when he saw her. She wondered if he would look different. Would the years of eating his mom's food have plumped him up at all? Would he seem smarter now that he was studying dentistry? Would he seem even happier than when she knew him?

Dora looked forward to seeing Eszter too. She didn't know what she would say to her. Being with her would be enough. Dora realized she would never completely forgive Eszter. A part of her would always wonder when Eszter's selfishness would manifest and drive her to hurt the people she loved again. And the image of her mom pulling the final trigger on Boldiszar, no matter how merciful she was being, would always be in Dora's mind. She had no idea if she would ever see Eszter the same, but maybe she wasn't supposed to anyway.

Dora, however, was certain of one thing. She wanted a relationship with her mom. While she couldn't abandon the past, Dora had promised to never go back to being a fearful person, terrified of showing any emotion lest she feel the pain of losing her mom. Dora could only love others if she loved Eszter. Who knew what Eszter may or may not do, but Dora would rather face it than endure the alternative. And so, Dora realized, in love there was strength.

As Dora lay on the floor thinking about all of this, the brick wall outside her apartment began to slowly absorb the afternoon sun. In the seconds between when the light was just beginning to crawl along the wall and when it sprang on it in full force, Dora could just make out the brick's original red—a momentary reminder of its former intensity. And within seconds, the sun had blotted that out, swathing the brick in such a powerful sheen it had no choice but to take on a new identity, one defined by the brightness pressing upon it.

AUTHOR'S NOTE

Radio Underground is based on real letters written by Hungarian teenagers during the Cold War. I found them seven years ago at the Hoover Institution, where I had been frantically searching for primary sources I could use for my senior thesis. I had two months left to write forty pages positing an original take on a historical event—a graduation requirement where seniors pretend to be historians (to be graded by real historians). My stomach growling, my cell phone buzzing with texts, and my hands shaking from a combination of Diet Coke and coffee, I stumbled upon a letter I'd never forget:

> Dear Uncle Lanci,
> There are thousands of us who live only in sleep—who act, speak, applaud because we have to. When we utter YES, our hearts drum NO.
> Can this partial assimilation end up in a complete one? This is our question. In our childhood we were looking for beauty and for the realization of human ideals, and what remains today? A hesitant

search for existence and a life under the compulsion of permanent lying. We can go forward only in the middle of the road...

-Titanilla
10 December 1964
Radio Free Europe Archives, Hoover Institution, Stanford University

This letter turned out to be one of dozens written by Hungarian teenagers during the 1960s to a rock music DJ, Uncle Lanci. As I did more research, I learned that Uncle Lanci's real name was Géza Ekecs, and at the time he was living as a Hungarian émigré in Munich and working for Radio Free Europe. Founded in 1949, the CIA-backed radio station aimed to enact psychological warfare on the Soviet Union. Through its news, lifestyle programs, and music broadcasts, Radio Free Europe would gently persuade those behind the Iron Curtain to identify with the West, thereby renouncing their allegiance to the Soviet Union and its communist ideology.

In 1959, Radio Free Europe started broadcasting rock 'n' roll to Hungary, exposing young people to the rise of The Beatles, The Beach Boys, and other Western bands staunchly forbidden on Hungary's state radio. Government officials behind the Iron Curtain loathed rock 'n' roll for its inherently anti-communist undertones, which encouraged independence, open-mindedness, and individuality. Indeed, young people in the Eastern Bloc used rock 'n' roll as a means to defy the regime, organizing secret rock concerts, forming cover bands, and selling albums on the black market. I once read that in the USSR fans made copies of Beatles records out of X-rays they stole from hospitals.

Capitalizing on Beatlemania and the love of music it inspired in a generation of young people, Ekecs created a number of programs centered on rock 'n' roll. One of these programs was called Mail Order Melody, where he played music requests mailed to him directly from Hungarian teenagers like Titanilla, and our beloved Mike a Korvinközből (yes, that was a code name used by a real letter-writer). Since the government read, censored, and sometimes destroyed mail, Ekecs instructed his listeners to use pseudonyms and to call him Laszlo Cseke or Uncle Lanci. Many letters never made it to Ekecs, but for those that did, the authors' pseudonyms were read aloud before their requested songs.

In their letters, fans opened up to Ekecs about their lives, relationships, ambitions, and struggles. Finally, someone representing a powerful institution was listening to the young people of Hungary, rather than telling them what to do. "We like this program also for another reason: It has several 'co-editors,' who write to you because their requests would never be fulfilled at home," wrote a listener going by the name "Örefegu." Or, as another fan put it, writing to Uncle Lanci was like having "an affair with the enemy."

When I first found these letters, I would have never guessed they would be the beginning of a novel. I featured them prominently in my senior thesis and graduated college. I moved to New Mexico, started working as a journalist, and tried to move on from that stressful senior year. Every few days, however, my mind would wander back to the letters. I think what struck me the most was the deep optimism and openness these teenagers maintained, despite the repression they endured. They believed in something better. Except, it wasn't necessarily the West they believed in. It was just that expression could set them free, and they would pursue that to no end, both through their words and in the music to which they listened.

Mike a Korvinközből, in particular, really touched me. He dreamed of being a dentist, but was blocked from doing so by the government. He wrote to Uncle Lanci asking for help getting to the West. I'll never know if he received that help, but I can only hope that he found a way to follow his dream. While I imagined his story, as well as that of Ekecs and the remaining characters and circumstances in *Radio Underground*, I endeavored to mirror the thoughts and feelings of the letter-writers as much as possible. They are, and always will be, some of the most honest, fun, and brave people I have ever encountered.

ACKNOWLEDGEMENTS

Deepest gratitude to Last Syllable Books and Selene Joy Castrovilla, who pushed me to complete *Radio Underground* and put it out there for the world to see. To Joyce Sweeney, who gave me the confidence and guidance to turn *Radio Underground* into a novel. To Jenny Peterson, whose careful editing saved me many errors and missteps, and whose eye for detail is something I will always be in awe of. To Damonza for designing a cover that represents so perfectly the story I tried to convey. To the University of California, Berkeley for inspiring me to study history and challenging me to write that menacing thesis, which turned into this very book. To Stanford University's Hoover Institution Library and Archives, which houses the letters that inspired *Radio Underground*. To Kate Sederstrom, Susan Breen and Kim van Alkemade for being great liaisons to the literary world. To my family who always knew I could do it, even when (especially when) I didn't believe in myself. To my mom, dad, Bill, Lisa, Ben, Sam, Lizzie, grandpa, Celia and, of course, my grandma, to whom this book is dedicated.